PRAISE FOR SA

T0012991

Cinder-Nanny

"Diana and Griffin's slow-burn closed-door passion is authentic."

—*Kirkus Reviews*

"*Cinder-Nanny* is a definite must-read. This cute play on the age-old fairy tale will surely worm its way into your heart and leave you feeling all warm and fuzzy."

—*Harlequin Junkie*

"Wilson's ability to weave a sweet tale of two people, each of whom needs what the other has to offer, is magical."

—BookReporter

The Paid Bridesmaid

"Combining a fast-paced plot with a slow-burning romance, this is sure to give readers butterflies."

—*Publishers Weekly*

"Wilson's (*Roommaid*) funny, sweet stand-alone about marriage, friendships, and mistaken identities is full of witty dialogue, endearing characters, and fast-paced narrative. Will appeal to fans of feel-good romances, rom-coms, and plots about weddings and social media."

—*Library Journal*

The Seat Filler

"Wilson (*Roommaid*) balances the quirky with the heartfelt in this adorable rom-com."

—*Publishers Weekly*

The Friend Zone

"Wilson scores a touchdown with this engaging contemporary romance that delivers plenty of electric sexual chemistry and zingy banter while still being romantically sweet at its core."

—*Booklist*

"Snappy banter, palpable sexual tension, and a lively sense of fun combine with deeply felt emotional issues in a sweet, upbeat romance that will appeal to both the YA and new adult markets."

—*Library Journal*

The #Lovestruck Novels

"Wilson has mastered the art of creating a romance that manages to be both sexy and sweet, and her novel's skillfully drawn characters, deliciously snarky sense of humor, and vividly evoked music-business settings add up to a supremely satisfying love story that will be music to romance readers' ears."

—*Booklist* (starred review), *#Moonstruck*

"Making excellent use of sassy banter, hilarious texts, and a breezy style, Wilson's energetic story brims with sexual tension and takes readers on a musical road trip that will leave them smiling. Perfect as well for YA and new adult collections."

—*Library Journal*, *#Moonstruck*

"*#Starstruck* is oh so funny! Sariah Wilson created an entertaining story with great banter that I didn't want to put down. Ms. Wilson provided a diverse cast of characters in their friends and family. Fans of *Sweet Cheeks* by K. Bromberg and Ruthie Knox will enjoy *#Starstruck*."

—*Harlequin Junkie* (4.5 stars), *#Starstruck*

SARIAH WILSON

 Montlake

Published by Montlake, Seattle

www.apub.com

Amazon, the Amazon logo, and Montlake are trademarks of Amazon.com, Inc., or its affiliates.

ISBN-13: 9781542039260 (paperback)
ISBN-13: 9781542039253 (digital)

Cover design by Philip Pascuzzo
Cover image: © dwph / Shutterstock

Printed in the United States of America

For Hayden,
my first grandchild—
you are light and joy and I adore you

CHAPTER ONE

"Jane?"

The barcode that was supposed to stick to the book was instead stuck to my finger. I shook my hand hard in an attempt to dislodge it. It didn't work. I yanked the sticker off and slapped it on the back of the library book before it could launch another attack. "What?" I asked, only half paying attention as I reached for another book and another barcode.

I glanced up and stopped mid-movement. My sixteen-year-old assistant, Connie, looked shell-shocked. I wondered if something had happened to her beloved YA section. It was the entire reason she volunteered at the library—the ability to curate a collection of her favorite young adult authors was an opportunity she couldn't pass up.

"Nick Haddon's publicist is on the phone. For you."

While I technically recognized the words she was saying as English, the order in which she'd said them made no sense.

Nick Haddon. Television/movie star. Literally named as the Most Handsome Man Alive. His publicist was calling me? Why? My face went slack and my expression probably mirrored Connie's. This had to be some kind of prank, right?

But not many pranks happened in our small town of Patience, Ohio.

My very pregnant sister-in-law, Gretchen, had been lying on a couch near the circulation desk, fanning herself. She'd overheard us, and her fan went still as her eyes grew wide.

"If I could leap to my feet in triumph, I would," she told me. I was still trying to process the fact that Nick Haddon's publicist was on the phone. "It worked. I told you it would. You know how much I love being right. And I was sooo right."

My brain started to fit all the puzzle pieces together. Auditors from the governor's office had shut down our entire local government due to embezzlement and fraud being committed by the mayor, Wilfred Newcastle, and he'd emptied the city's bank accounts.

The library system operated on the county's budget rather than the city's, so that made the librarian the most senior city employee, as the library was the only branch of the government still open. That meant the librarian had to step up and take charge of the fall harvest festival, which couldn't move forward without a city employee to officially oversee everything.

And the only chance to refill the city's coffers and reopen the government was through raising money from the festival.

That librarian was my mom. She had just taken over the festival planning when my father had a heart attack. I came home to help and ended up being drafted into taking over her job and the festival.

I had zero experience doing either one.

Fortunately (although sometimes it felt unfortunate) I had a very active team of "volunteers" to help—mostly former city employees hoping that the profit made from the festival would reopen the government and give them back their jobs once the investigation ended.

Gretchen had been the head of the tourism department. (I repeatedly reminded her that she was the only person in the department, but that didn't seem to matter to her.) She would have helped me regardless of her former job because, in addition to being my sister-in-law, she'd also been my best friend since we were five years old.

To give credit where it was due—Gretchen was the one with the big ideas. Which included making a video inviting Nick Haddon to come and visit Patience in time for the festival. The video had gone viral. (I was particularly proud of the music I'd written for it, but the other embarrassing things she made us do, including dressing up as Greek gods/goddesses in honor of Nick's most famous TV show—those were things I never wanted to speak of ever again.) She'd managed to get #ImPatienceForNick trending on every social media platform; my mom had pointed out that it technically didn't make grammatical sense, but nobody seemed to care.

I'd told Gretchen that Nick Haddon would never see it, as any reasonable person would assume. Now Connie was telling me that Nick's publicist was calling. I glanced down at the phone in front of me, and Line 2 was blinking alongside Line 1. Line 1 was Mr. Schmidt, calling in with his weekly list of books he thought should be banned (never due to content—solely because he didn't like the covers) and Line 2 . . . was Nick Haddon's publicist.

"Pick up!" Gretchen said. "Put it on speakerphone. I need to find out just how right I am. Like if this is something I have to bring up on my deathbed just to make sure you remember all my rightness."

Annoyed, I put it on speakerphone. It couldn't actually be his publicist. Surely it would end up being one of my older brother's idiot friends, and Gretchen would have to eat her words.

"This is Jane Wagner," I announced loudly and with authority, expecting whoever was on the other end to just hang up.

There was silence and then a woman responded, with just as much actual confidence as I'd been faking. "I'm Shanice Johnson of Johnson & Associates. I'm the lead publicist for actor Nick Haddon. We saw your video, and we would like to send Nick to your town."

This was not one of my brother's friends. This couldn't be happening, could it?

Everyone in the room was staring at me. Well, almost everyone. Gretchen had gotten up and was dancing around while pumping her arms triumphantly in the air.

Nick Haddon was actually going to come to Patience? Population 5,384?

It might be 5,385 soon—if Gretchen kept jumping up and down like that, she was going to make my nephew be born early.

Connie took out her cell phone and typed quickly. Our slow internet delayed her search, but she turned the screen toward me and showed me a photo of a Black woman in an expensive pantsuit captioned *Shanice Johnson of Johnson & Associates*. If this was a prank, it was a very elaborate and specific one.

Which was so far out of reach of my brother's drinking buddies that I knew it had to be real. The weight of that felt a little oppressive. I didn't want to mess this up.

"Hello?" Shanice asked, jolting me back to reality.

"Yes. I'm here. Hi." I winced. Not at all awkward.

"Do you have a moment to chat with me?"

I nodded, then remembered that she couldn't see me. "Yes. I do. Yes. Uh-huh."

She paused again. I wondered if she was evaluating me. "My understanding is that you're in charge of the Patience harvest festival." Shanice said this like she found it hard to believe.

Couldn't blame her. "I am."

"Then you're the person I need to speak with. There are several logistical things we need to arrange. Mr. Haddon will be arriving with his own documentary crew. They will be filming all of his interactions with the festival and townspeople for a streaming service. The deal has already been made; this crew must have access to Mr. Haddon at all times."

"Oh. Okay." That was fine with me. The more eyes we had on Patience, the better. Once word got out that Nick Haddon was coming to the festival, every single ticket was going to sell out.

I felt a little like one of those cartoon characters whose pupils had turned to dollar signs. We were going to make a fortune. Enough to right our sinking ship and get the government back up and running.

Everything would go back to the way it should be.

"We've already made arrangements for the crew's accommodations. The issue will be with finding a place for Mr. Haddon to stay."

"There are several excellent B and Bs in town," I told her. "The old paper mill was actually converted to—"

She cut me off. "That is not going to work for us. Mr. Haddon needs to be . . . watched."

Watched? Both Connie and Gretchen exchanged weird glances with me. A tritone, the dissonant sounds of "the devil's interval," started up in my head. Like I was scoring a horror movie.

Before I could ask about her meaning, his publicist continued. "Normally, I would make you sign a non-disclosure agreement, but everything I'm about to tell you is easily discoverable online. He has had some issues in his past and has had a sober companion, but he feels as if he's in a better spot now and doesn't need one. His team is concerned that he might get into trouble if he's left alone."

"In Patience?" I asked incredulously. Not a whole lot happened here. In fact, the last time the sheriff had been called was after the graduating seniors had dyed a bunch of cows blue in honor of their mascot, Babe, the Big Blue Ox.

I had never understood how we got Paul Bunyan's sidekick as a mascot out here in Ohio, but I tried to rein in my wandering mind. It didn't help when Connie showed me her phone again, with picture after picture of Nick Haddon partying and making out with a bunch of supermodels. In one of the images, he was punching a paparazzo.

Not much danger of those things happening here. "We're not really a place where people get in trouble." Other than Wilfred Newcastle, I meant.

"You'd be surprised," she said with a touch of sarcasm. "I'm assuming you have women and alcohol there."

"We do. Have those things."

"Then I need you to personally take responsibility for him."

"You want me to babysit a movie star?"

"In a manner of speaking. Do you have somewhere that he could stay?"

Gretchen must have been able to tell that I was about to deny it and completely lie to this person, because she spoke up. "Hello, Gretchen Wagner here. I'm the head of tourism for Patience. Or, I was the head of tourism."

"Yes, I understand that you're having some issues with your local government." It made me wonder just how much research Shanice Johnson had done on us. Had she run a background check on the people in town? On me? For all she knew, I might be the kind of person to tie him up and stick him in a basement. As if she could read my mind, Shanice continued, "I've done my research. I know he'll be safe in your hands. I'd prefer that he be watched by someone in a position of authority and with a vested interest in this going well. Mr. Haddon will be coming to show the world how he has changed. None of us can afford a scandal."

Ah, mutually assured destruction. I'd keep her actor safe because I needed him for publicity, and he'd behave because he needed the positive press.

"Understandable," Gretchen said. "Jane is just who you're looking for. She is in a position of authority and she has quite a bit of room at her place. It's a renovated bed-and-breakfast with several spare bedrooms. And a guest suite on the first floor."

I tried to shush her, but she put her hand in front of my face. I had been living in my grandmother's pink Victorian-inspired house since I'd returned. My parents were halfway through with renovations to turn it into a B and B, but they hadn't finished, given my dad's medical situation. I'd offered to stay at home with them when I came back, but they'd apparently turned my bedroom into a sewing room for my mom and we all decided it would be easier for me to stay at the Pink House (the very imaginative and descriptive name my parents had chosen for the B and B), especially since there was a baby grand piano that I could play all evening if I wanted and not bother anyone else.

I hadn't been composing much lately, though. Instead, I'd been working on the house whenever I had the chance. My parents had offered me the opportunity to run the B and B when it was finished. My dreams of going to Los Angeles and being mentored by a famous composer seemed like such a far-fetched fantasy that ever since I'd come back home, I had felt like I needed to start making plans that were based in reality.

Even if I'd spent my whole life planning to leave Patience behind.

"That will be acceptable," Shanice said. "He's going to be arriving tomorrow and will stay until the end of the festival."

Gretchen gave me a triumphant look. Tomorrow? And then he was going to stay for two weeks? With me? The whole situation seemed weird and made me feel a little panicky. I couldn't just let some strange man move into my house, even if he was a movie star.

I pushed the mute button. "Couldn't he stay with you?" I asked my sister-in-law.

"Heath is almost done with the nursery. He assembled the crib last night." Gretchen and Heath lived in an adorable little two-bedroom cottage on the lake. I knew they didn't have the space.

"There has to be another solution," I said. "It doesn't seem safe to have a stranger come stay with me."

"That's what you'll be doing when it officially becomes a B and B—letting strangers stay in your house every night. You can lock your door," Gretchen told me.

I supposed that was true.

"Why would you lock your door?" Connie asked, sighing as she scrolled through pictures of Nick. "I wouldn't lock my door."

"Which is why he's not staying with you and your family," Gretchen said in a reprimanding tone.

"He's only ten years older than me."

"I do not have time to explain all the reasons why that is a huge deal at your age, but please know that you should not be dating actual adults until you are one," Gretchen said, unmuting the phone. "Were there other logistics that you needed to discuss?"

It took me a second to realize that she was talking to the publicist and wasn't speaking to me. Like I had no say in the matter. Even though I was apparently in charge of the logistics.

"We will be happy to compensate you for his room and board," Shanice said. "But the most important thing is keeping him away from any sort of scandal."

There was a strange note to her voice that made my worried feeling intensify. And when I got panicky, that was when inspiration would strike. "If you're so concerned he might do something, why don't you just have him make a large donation? He could repost our video on his social media, say he donated to help the town, and that could be the end of it."

And no handsome men would be staying with me, alone, in my house.

Because I'd had my fill of wealthy, handsome men. I was done with that particular species.

There was another one of those pauses that made me think there was so much she wasn't telling us. "Mr. Haddon is not in a position to make a donation. The only thing he can give you is his time."

Another round of open-mouthed stares passed between the three of us. Nick Haddon was broke? The son of two of Hollywood's greatest stars didn't have any money? How was that possible?

Hadn't he starred in a bunch of movies? Anytime I watched a film, most of my attention was geared toward the music, so I couldn't name anything he'd been in over the last few years.

There was his most famous role, of course—he'd played Zeus in a TV adaptation of a YA book about the Greek gods being stuck in high school, deprived of their powers. It had been a runaway success but had gone off the air five or six years ago.

And I couldn't think of a single role he'd played since then.

Huh. Maybe he had blown through all of his money. "Can't your office just send someone to keep an eye on him?" I had no idea what Nick Haddon would be like in real life, but given his publicist's subtext, I didn't want the responsibility of making him behave.

There was too much riding on this for me to screw it up.

"Mr. Haddon specifically asked that we not send any members of his team with him. He agreed to the documentary crew and photographers, but that was it."

Again, that made no sense to me and I liked things to make sense. To be ordered and flow from one note to the next in a logical pattern. He would rather come and stay with some potentially obsessed fan than someone he knew he could trust?

Why?

That intrigued me, which also annoyed me.

I didn't want to be intrigued by someone who was going to blow in and out of my life like a tornado. I didn't have time or the emotional capacity for that kind of devastation.

"The documentary crew will send us clips every day that we will post on his social media. The whole world will know that Nick Haddon is in Patience, Ohio, for the festival. You couldn't ask for better publicity. Are those terms acceptable to you?" Shanice asked.

Gretchen kept mouthing whole sentences at me and Connie looked up with pleading eyes, begging me to say yes.

I still couldn't believe any of this was happening.

So I said the only thing I could say. "Yes."

Connie put her hands to her mouth to silently scream while Gretchen resumed dancing around.

"Oh, there's one more thing," Shanice said, and that ominous music returned in my mind. "You can't let him know that I asked you to watch him. He would be furious."

I wasn't going to lie to the man. I opened my mouth to say as much when Gretchen elbowed me in the side and said, "No worries."

It was noncommittal, probably in recognition of the fact that I wasn't going to agree to that condition, but it was enough to placate his publicist. Shanice gave me her contact information in case I needed it, and Gretchen gave her my cell phone number in return.

My best friend hung up the phone before I could say anything else.

"I'm going to tell him," I said.

"You don't have to say anything right away," she said. "At the very least, give us time to get the information out there that he's here. Let us enjoy this first-class publicity before you and your annoying honesty blow the whole thing up."

Maybe she had a point.

Before I could respond, Connie dramatically announced, "This is the most exciting thing that has ever happened!"

She was right. I sat down slowly in my chair, tuning the both of them out. The full implication of what was happening hit me.

Nick Haddon was coming here.

He would be staying in my house.

It was easily the most exciting thing that had ever happened in our sleepy little town. Even more exciting than the Newcastle embezzlement scandal, which had nearly destroyed Patience. But nobody beyond the people who lived here seemed to care about that.

We'd never been a touristy kind of place. Most people just drove through on their way to Amish villages.

But Nick Haddon? People would be coming here in droves just to breathe the same air that he did.

And I had to keep an eye on him.

CHAPTER TWO

"Is that him?" someone called out.

It felt like half the town had gathered in my front yard. The Pink House had several acres, but with so many people there, you couldn't tell that it was a wide-open space. Instead, the crowd felt suffocating. I wondered if people here actually knew who he was or if their teenagers had just dragged them out of the house and forced them to come.

There were professional photographers, clumped together in a tight formation away from the townspeople. The documentary crew had arrived early that morning and had already set up.

Gretchen had offered to do my hair and makeup, like she used to do when we were younger. I had accepted, mostly because the thought of being on camera while looking washed out didn't appeal to me.

I didn't want to embarrass myself.

"It *is* him!" someone shouted, and everybody broke into cheers. I heard my old high school band director call out to the marching band, and they started to play the theme song of *Olympus High*, Nick Haddon's TV show. It didn't sound great, mainly because I'd called the director yesterday afternoon to give him the heads-up and they hadn't had much time to rehearse.

At least the tune was recognizable. Cringey, but recognizable.

Not that I'd actually needed to call the band director. Word had already spread through town like wildfire. Gretchen had been standing next to me when Shanice texted Nick Haddon's arrival time, and Gretchen had immediately texted Heath, who told my parents, and then everybody knew.

And now they were all here.

A black SUV came up the long driveway as people cheered and called out, holding up hastily made signs welcoming him. The crowd was electric with excitement and anticipation.

All I felt was a faint sense of dread. I knew that I should be just as excited as everyone else, but this whole thing unnerved me. I'd spent most of my morning explaining to Patches (my calico cat) that we were having an unexpected guest. It was a good way for me to talk out some of my anxiety, and she'd given me the courtesy of pretending to listen with her leg extended midair and then went right back to licking her butt.

Gretchen stood close to me and leaned in to say, "I think you should have a fling with him."

That struck me as so supremely stupid that for a second, I couldn't respond. "No. One, I need him to make this festival a success. We're going to have a purely professional relationship. Two, you know I don't date men like him."

"He could be really nice. You don't know."

"Yes, the spoiled son of Hollywood stars is really down-to-earth and sweet," I responded sarcastically. Of course that possibility existed, but I found it hard to believe. I expected him to spend most of his time working out and being on his phone.

I'd never admit this to her, but I'd thought about what he'd be like. If I went off internet gossip alone, he was a hothead who wouldn't let crew members look him in the eye while filming. Maybe he was reserved. Or artistic. Or a snob. Or selfish. It would be kind of nice if he was self-centered. Then I one hundred percent would not be attracted to him.

The few dates I'd had over the last six months were obviously coloring my perceptions, but I'd never considered myself to be an optimist. Better to be prepared for the worst possible outcome than have all your hopes and dreams shattered.

Again.

"For all you know, he's dating someone," I added.

"I think I would know if he had a girlfriend," she responded. That was probably true; she'd always loved reading celebrity gossip. "Think of the stories you can tell your grandchildren about that torrid affair you had with the most famous man on the planet. I'll be there to back you up as proof."

There would be no affairs, torrid or otherwise. But she'd just argue with me if I disagreed with her, and knowing her, we'd still be going back and forth about it when Nick Haddon arrived. So instead, I settled on a safer topic. "Not the most famous."

She frowned at me. "Yes. Everyone in the world knows who he is."

"There's that group on North Sentinel Island that doesn't allow outside contact. I bet they haven't heard of him."

"I'd take that bet," she said.

I sighed. Gretchen was particularly single-minded when she thought she was right about something.

"You're assuming he would be interested in me." It seemed so farfetched that I didn't know how she couldn't see the delusion for the trees. I was definitely not the kind of woman he apparently dated. And I was okay with that.

I didn't have to question why Gretchen was doing this, though. Ever since she'd married my brother, her number one priority had been marrying me off. There weren't a lot of available men here in town, so I had been relatively safe from her scheming.

But now an attractive man was coming to stay in my home and I suspected my friend would be relentless.

Good grief, this wasn't something I'd thought I was going to have to worry about. I was more concerned with keeping this guy happy and having the festival be a success. Gretchen needed to keep her nose out of it.

She quickly let me know that that wasn't her plan. "Of course he'll fall in love with you! You're amazing," she said. "That Nick Haddon won't know what hit him. I'll make sure of it."

"Don't—" I said, but then the SUV came closer, distracting both of us. There was a lump of nervousness in my throat that I couldn't swallow down. The band got louder, as did the cheers and whistles. The car came to a stop right in front of me and the next part happened in slow motion.

The main theme from *Superman* began to play in my head as the back passenger-side door opened and Nick Haddon got out.

He didn't even look real. It was like a character from the big screen stepping down to sit next to you in the movie theater. He was all broad shoulders, blinding white teeth, lightly tanned skin, and dirty-blond hair. He sported his trademark too-perfect stubble on his sharp jawline. He had on jeans and a plain white T-shirt, just like half the people here, but on him it looked like high fashion.

A large crystal hung from a leather band around his neck, accompanied by a tiny blue beaded necklace. He had on several thin leather bracelets, and there was this definite overall effect of a stereotypical California surfer / womanizer, but somehow he made it work. Like, yes, he would break your heart into microscopic slivers, but you would thank him for doing it. He waved to the crowd, turning to make sure that he faced and waved in every direction.

It struck me as thoughtful, like he was considerate of the people who had shown up for him. Or vain, basking in their attention and the limelight. I wasn't sure which.

He wore aviator-style sunglasses and I wondered if his eyes were really as blue as they seemed on-screen or if it was movie magic.

Gretchen nudged my shoulder, as if to remind me that I was basically like the mayor here and it was my job to greet him. I took a step forward and pulled in a deep breath. As I walked down the steps from the front porch, I shivered slightly. And whether that was due to the cool September air or the absurdly handsome man in front of me, I wasn't sure.

Tall. He was tall. I'd expected him to be short. Didn't most of the men in Hollywood lie about their height? I was 5'10" and thought he'd be a good three or four inches shorter than me. Nope. Three or four inches taller.

Then he took off his sunglasses. He probably did it normally, but again, I was hearing the swelling of an orchestra and it was all happening in slow motion.

No movie magic here. His eyes were definitely a bright aquamarine. Suddenly a torrid affair didn't seem like such a bad idea.

I stood there, awestruck, and he took a step forward. "You're Jane Wagner? I didn't realize it would be you."

Me. He was talking to me. There were flashes and the photographers were approaching, taking photos. I became aware of Gretchen taking her phone out and pointing it at us. The crowd quieted down, the band stopped playing.

Or maybe that was just my head drowning them all out because I was so focused on him, although I couldn't quite make out what he was trying to say. He didn't think it would be me? What?

He held out his hand and I instinctively stuck my right hand in his. An electric charge surged through me at his touch, spreading throughout my entire body, lighting up cells I didn't even know I had. Then he made it worse by using both of his hands to enfold mine. Double contact, double currents flowing through me and illuminating my nerve endings.

"Yes," I choked out. "I'm Nick Haddon. I mean, I'm Jane, and you're Nick Haddon."

So much for not embarrassing myself.

He gave me a grin full of mischief and delight, and I realized very quickly that I did not possess any sort of defense against a smile like that. I was going to have to build some kind of wall very quickly so that I didn't get sucked into anything.

Which was just as presumptuous of me as it had been of Gretchen. The man had not flirted with me at all and I was acting like he'd strolled up here, asking to speak to my father so he could declare his intentions.

Having an overactive imagination and a determined best friend was not a good combination.

"Nice to meet you, Jane."

Grateful that he overlooked my speaking lapse, I pulled my hand away as I said, "Nice to meet you. Welcome to Patience." I flexed my fingers, like I could still feel him holding them and wanted to chase the sensation away.

It wasn't working.

"Thank you," he said and, after a beat, added, "I didn't expect you to be this pretty."

I could feel my cheeks flushing, and it had nothing to do with the nippy air. What the freak was I supposed to do with him saying that? What had his publicist told him? He had expectations? The way he'd said it made me feel like he somehow already knew me and found me to be different in person from what he'd thought I would be. I felt confusion, quickly followed by minor embarrassment that he'd said it and also hoping that other people had overheard. Well, not Gretchen. She didn't need the encouragement.

But Mrs. Schumacher wasn't standing very far away, and it would make me happy for her to run home and tell her daughter, Brenda, that Nick Haddon had said I was pretty. It would absolutely wreck my nemesis and I was petty enough to want her to be as annoyed as possible.

Then I wondered what I should say back to him. My brain apparently settled on, "It's just makeup."

Wow. Masterful speaking there.

Gretchen stepped in to save me. "Hi! I'm Gretchen, Jane's best friend slash sister-in-law. I used to be the head of the tourism department."

Nick Haddon shifted his attention toward her and it was like a spotlight being turned away from me. One second, I was basking in the glow and attention; the next, it was focused entirely on someone else. I didn't like that, and my reaction concerned me.

He shook her hand the same way he had mine—enclosing her hand with both of his—and given her expression, I actually worried that Gretchen might pass out and I was going to have to explain to my brother why his wife was in the ER. Somehow it would be my fault that Nick Haddon was so much more charming and handsome in real life than any of us could have possibly predicted and caused Gretchen to faint.

Maybe it's all an act. He is *an actor,* a tiny voice inside me said in protest. True. He might have been doing this for the crowd's benefit, and things would be very different once we were alone together.

But there was this air of sincerity about him that made me want to believe.

Maybe finally recognizing the danger she was putting herself in, Gretchen disengaged and nodded toward Connie. "This is our friend, Connie Yi. She's a big fan."

Connie did not deal well with the Nick Haddon–attention spotlight. She opened and closed her mouth several times and was unable to speak.

She finally said, "Oh my Zeus."

"Hey, don't take my name in vain," he said in a teasing tone, and it seemed to be too much for her. She just nodded, her eyes bright with unshed tears.

That triggered something inside me. I could not afford to be like that. I couldn't allow him to reduce me to a teary teenage fangirl. I got the impulse, but I was supposed to be an adult. It hardened my resolve. The point was to help Patience, not to throw myself at a movie star.

Even if he had said I was pretty.

The problem was, I had no idea what to do next. Was I supposed to introduce him to everyone here? I could, it would just take forever.

As if he sensed my indecisiveness, he walked up onto the porch and waved to the crowd again. "Thank you so much, everyone, for coming out to meet me. You've made me feel so welcome! I'm looking forward to getting to meet as many of you as I can. I may not remember all of your names, though. And my name is Nick, in case you didn't know."

The crowd laughed appreciatively.

We stood there a moment. Was there something more I should do or say? Was I just supposed to let people gawk at him? It was then that I noticed that Nick Haddon had stuck both of his hands into his pockets and was slightly shivering. Duh. He'd come here from California and wasn't wearing a jacket. I hoped he'd packed one.

"Let's get you inside and settled in," I said. He waved goodbye to the crowd, and Gretchen headed over to the nearest busybody and said to tell everyone to head out.

"Wait." A man from the documentary crew approached us. He held out his hand to Nick and they shook. "I'm Steve Yardlin. I'm directing the crew. Could we get some footage of you going into the house?"

Nick Haddon smiled at him, but it was easy to see that it didn't quite reach his glorious blue eyes. "Could we grab it another time? I'm a little tired from the flight and the drive."

Steve looked annoyed, but what could he do? "Sure thing. We'll be in touch."

The driver had brought over Nick Haddon's luggage—a couple of expensive-looking duffel bags. I reached for one, but Nick got there first. "Don't worry about it. I've got it."

Trying not to register just how close he was standing to me and how good he smelled, I took a step back and cleared my throat. "If you want to follow me."

He hefted up the bags, putting one over each shoulder. I was pretty sure he had more muscles in his shoulders than I had in both arms. Wow, was he nicely formed. He really would spend all of his time here working out.

I had locked the door and I wasn't sure why I'd done that. Patience wasn't the kind of place where people locked their doors. Maybe it had something to do with the crowd that was barely dispersing; I hadn't wanted to risk somebody sneaking inside.

Although I was starting to be concerned that the person I had to worry most about was me. I had to get a grip, and fast.

I pulled my key ring out and couldn't remember which one was the house key. Why did I have so many useless keys? I had no idea what any of these did.

As I thumbed through them, trying not to feel self-conscious, I glanced up to see Nick taking in the outside of the house. When he noticed me looking at him, he said, "This kind of looks like the place where Barbie grew up before she moved out to Malibu."

I found the right key and inserted it into the slot. "What can I say? My grandma really loved pink. She wore it every day. She requested that we all come to her funeral in our finest pink outfits."

"When did she pass away?" he asked as I walked inside.

"About ten years ago. She left this house to my parents and we're turning it into a B and B. I'm supposed to run it."

"You don't sound excited about that."

Didn't I? I mean, I wasn't unexcited about it. It was just . . . whatever. How my life was going to turn out. Not how I'd hoped, but this was good, too. I lived near my family, including a soon-to-arrive nephew whom I planned on spoiling rotten, and I was comfortable here. "It's . . . fine," I said as my response. "Your room is this way."

He continued to take in his surroundings as I pointed out the living room, the parlor, the dining room, and the kitchen. Giving him a tour of my home was feeling a little dreamlike—as if all my teeth were about to fall out or I was going to glance down and notice that I was naked. I actually checked. Nope. Clothes still on.

Patches was curled up in her bed on the kitchen counter, lying in the sunlight. She woke up at our approach and sleepily blinked at us.

Then she did something that surprised me. She jumped down and came over to Nick Haddon and started rubbing against his legs, wrapping her tail around him.

She had been my cat for ten years, and I'd never seen her do that before.

He really was charming everyone.

"Who is this?" he asked, sounding amused.

"Patches."

"She's cute."

I would not be jealous of my cat. "You're not allergic, are you?" I asked, suddenly worried about what kind of arrangements I'd have to make if he was.

"Not as far as I know," he said.

That was good. I reached down to grab her and put her back in her bed. I mean, I understood the inclination to want to wind around the movie star, but he needed to get unpacked. "This way," I told him.

I took him to the suite on the first floor so that he'd have his own space. So far it was the only room with a private bathroom, even though it still definitely needed further refurbishment.

I opened the door. "This is your room. You're my only guest—I mean, besides Patches. But she's not really a guest. She thinks she owns the place and I'm just here to feed her and give her chin scritches."

"Smart girl," he said, taking in the room. I tried to imagine how it looked through his eyes. It definitely had a little-old-lady feel to it. I'd done my best to update it, but there were some things I couldn't swap out until we got a moving crew here to help.

"Patches isn't that smart. She is constantly burning her tongue by licking light bulbs. She hisses at it and then does it again. I keep hoping at some point she'll figure it out, but so far that hasn't happened. So just be careful about which lamps you use."

A smile curved his mouth. "When I thought of what it would be like to come here, I wasn't expecting Barbie houses and licking cats."

"Nobody ever does," I told him ruefully. He laughed, and the sound did something to my insides.

He set his bags on the bed and realized what he was dealing with. "A waterbed?" he asked, sounding like coming to my house was his own personal carnival—one unexpected delight after another.

"There are other rooms in various states upstairs. This is the only one with a private bathroom, though. We do have plans to replace the bed. Maybe when my dad is feeling better."

His eyes widened slightly, questioning, but he just said, "This will be fine. You just don't see waterbeds anymore. The phrase 'motion of the ocean' is running through my head, though."

My mouth went dry. He'd probably meant it innocently enough, but my mind went to some not-suitable-for-work places. I gripped the doorknob tightly and twisted it. I needed to change the subject. "This door locks. Just so you know."

Why had I felt compelled to tell him that? Because my thoughts about this nice man who wasn't flirting with me at all were becoming increasingly inappropriate and I had to reassure myself that he had refuge from me?

"Here are the keys." I held up the keys to his room and to the front door, explaining which one went where, and then placed them on the dresser, which was within arm's reach of the door.

"Are you worried for my safety?" he asked, like he knew exactly what I was thinking.

"Someone should be." Hopefully he'd be up to the task, as self-control had never really been one of my strong suits. Although knowing there was still an entire multitude of people standing on my lawn helped me to curb my impulses.

"Am I in danger from you? I'm assuming you have the key." His voice was definitely teasing, but it honestly felt like he was taking a stroll through my brain.

When this whole idea of him staying here was first proposed to me, I'd been worried about the position it put me in, having a strange man staying downstairs in my house. I'd glossed over the position it potentially put him in.

Not just from me but everyone in Patience. I thought movie stars were supposed to have bodyguards.

I supposed this was something else that was going to have to be up to me. Although this tall, broad man obviously didn't need my protection. Maybe I'd give Sheriff Jones a call and see what we could arrange.

"You are not in danger from me," I told him, realizing that I'd been standing there quietly for too long. Did that sound normal? I hoped I sounded normal. I stepped into his room and immediately stepped back out. This had to be his domain. "Sorry, I don't want to infringe on your space."

It really had been too long since I'd dated someone if I was being this weird over being near a hot guy.

"You're welcome to come in anytime you'd like. It's nice to meet someone and know you can trust them." There was a tone to his voice that made me think he didn't have much trust in his life.

His words and tone unintentionally stung me. Obviously I wasn't planning on tying him up and forcing him to answer questions about his former show or have him demonstrate what he'd meant by "motion of the ocean," but I wasn't exactly trustworthy.

Not yet, anyway.

Maybe I should rectify that. "When you get settled in, I'd be happy to take you on a quick tour of the town." Where I would tell him what was going on. He should know the truth.

"Sounds good. We should wait for a bit—I want the documentary crew to clear out first."

"Why? Shouldn't they get footage of you touring Patience for the first time?"

"We can do it later. I'd like to experience it without feeling like I'm playing it up for the camera."

That made sense. "I hope you won't be disappointed. There's not much to experience."

"There's beauty in everything."

I waited for him to finish, like he was quoting some New Age philosopher and was about to name-check them. He didn't say anything else, though, and the silence stretched between us into awkward territory. I cleared my throat. "Cool. Well, when you get done in here, I'll be in the kitchen. There's something I need to talk to you about."

He nodded, looking intrigued, and I closed his door. As I walked toward the kitchen, I found myself listening, wondering if he'd lock the door.

He didn't.

Why did that make me smile?

It was imperative that I get a hold of myself and my runaway thoughts. I didn't want to date or fling him, and I had to remember that and what we were both here to do. I needed to be more serious so that I wouldn't forget myself.

Because I got the definite impression that Nick Haddon was the kind of guy who made the rest of the world just fade away.

I had opened a kitchen cabinet and just reached up to grab a mug when I heard a very angry feminine voice behind me demand, "Just what do you think you're doing?"

CHAPTER THREE

I turned around to see Gretchen glaring at me. "Getting something to drink?" I offered as explanation to her question. I was in trouble—I just didn't understand why.

"I'm not talking about that." She slammed her purse down on the kitchen table. "What was with all that 'we need to talk' nonsense you were just spouting off to Nick Haddon?"

Oh. "I don't want to lie to him."

She crossed her arms, resting them on top of her large baby bump. "You agreed to keep quiet."

"Technically, you agreed to keep quiet. I did not." I set my mug down on the counter. I'd planned to brew some coffee, but considering that Gretchen had had to give it up for the pregnancy, I tried not to drink it around her.

"The problem is, as soon as you tell him, he'll go back to California."

True. Maybe that would be the best thing for me, though. Giving in to my attraction would be a mistake of epic proportions. I'd been down a similar road before—I knew exactly how this was going to turn out. I couldn't be tempted by him if he went back home. We had footage of him showing up to Patience and that might be enough to increase ticket sales.

That was a selfish thought, though. I didn't want to be selfish. I wanted the festival to succeed. "I don't think he'll take off. I get the impression he values honesty."

"Did you somehow intuit that in the three minutes you've been alone with him?" she asked.

She sounded snarky, which was very unlike Gretchen. Figuring she was hungry, I opened another cabinet. I quickly located the emergency marshmallow stash and passed her the bag. She looked at it grumpily. "The doctor says I'm not supposed to be eating this stuff. That it's just empty calories."

"I won't tell him," I said.

She sat down heavily in the chair and tore the corner off with her teeth. "Just two." Two quickly turned into four, which turned into eight, but if it was going to tone down her bark, I was all for it.

Once the sugar had hit her bloodstream, she sighed and seemed more like herself again. "Did I tell you I have a great idea?"

"The last great idea you had landed me in zoo jail," I reminded her.

She waved her left hand as if that were inconsequential. "The last great idea I had got a handsome, famous actor living in your downstairs suite, and he's going to publicize the festival and make it a success. You're welcome for that, by the way."

I sat down at the table across from her. I wasn't sure if I should thank her. I still didn't know what was going to happen with him being here. It felt . . . precarious. "Out with it," I told her.

"I think you should ask Nick Haddon out."

"What? Like on a date? Are the marshmallows messing with your brain? No."

She grinned at me.

"Stop smiling at me like that. You look like the Joker."

"You think he's hot. Admit it."

I really, really did. But it didn't matter and Gretchen did not need any more ammunition. "He's not really my type."

She pretended to choke. "Sorry about that. A little irony just went down the wrong way." Then she held up her finger. "One, he is *absolutely* your type. I know your entire dating history, remember? And two, you are a liar and your pants are most definitely aflame. Thirdly, that man is everybody's type. I'm pretty sure every woman in this town with a pulse is head over heels. I might even have to include the ones buried in the church cemetery."

She started typing furiously on her phone and we had to wait, wait, and wait for whatever she was trying to download. Our Wi-Fi was ridiculously slow. Supposedly, the mayor had nearly finalized a deal to get us fiber-optic cable, but given that he was busy spending all the town's money and couldn't pay the company, it hadn't happened.

"Here." She pushed her phone toward me. "Look at these pictures and please point out what part of him you are not attracted to."

It was a black-and-white photo shoot. He was shirtless, and someone had very wisely poured water on him and his muscles were glistening, his hair slicked back and . . .

Oh my.

I pressed my lips shut so that I wouldn't make a sound and just shrugged one shoulder as my response.

"I'm not really buying your supposed lack of attraction," she told me, reaching for her phone.

I curled up my fingers so that I wouldn't try to snatch it back. "I'm not trying to sell it to you."

"You're trying to sell it to someone." Her tone indicated that she meant me, but she didn't say it out loud. "Because, objectively speaking, that man is like a delivery from Amazon."

At my confused expression, Gretchen continued, "He's the total package. An American Hemsworth."

"'The total package'? Really? How did you come to that conclusion?"

She started raising fingers at me again. "First, he came here. Maybe it's a mutually beneficial situation, but the reality is that he didn't have to. His publicity team could have put up some post and had that be the end of it. Or promised he'd visit someday and then never show up. It says something that he paid his own way here and is covering his room and board. Especially if he's broke."

I tried to interject, but she shook her head. "Nope. Not done. Two, he has been nothing but considerate, polite, and gracious since he got here."

"That could be an act. I feel like his hotness is clouding your judgment."

She gasped in delight. "You just admitted he was hot! And why do people slam on clouds? I love clouds. They bring rain and thunderstorms, shade, adorable fluffiness that turns into shapes. Like hot movie stars."

I crossed my arms. "Well, if we're speaking objectively, then yes, he is handsome. I'm just not interested in him. Again, we don't know anything about him."

Now it was her turn to shrug. "I feel like I have good instincts about people."

I didn't say anything about the fact that she'd never been more than fifty miles away from Patience, and that was only to attend cosmetology school. All the people she knew, she'd pretty much known her whole life.

She took my silence as an invitation to keep talking. "And if you don't want to date him, you could just flirt with him. Catch and release. It could be really fun. You should go out with him. And Heath and I could come. I've already pictured it—the four of us on a double date."

"When you pictured this, had Satan moved to Ohio because hell had actually frozen over?"

"You're no fun," she told me. "I don't understand you. I'd nail that man down like a very enthusiastic hammer."

"That's . . . a mental image I did not need. You're happily married and pregnant," I reminded her.

"It's not my fault my hormones are making me so—"

"La, la, la," I chanted as I plugged my ears. I did not want any more information about her sex life with my brother. She had always been too much of a sharer. She smiled, letting me know she had finished whatever gross thing she had been saying, and I uncovered my ears. "Are you done?" I asked.

"Possibly."

"This is such a pointless conversation," I told her. "You're acting like Nick Haddon doesn't get a say in any of this."

"He gets a say. He's already had it. When he said you were pretty."

That strange pang was back. I'd worried about Gretchen overhearing, and my fears had been justified, because now it was coming back to bite me in the butt. "He was being nice."

"He didn't call anyone else pretty."

Growing up, I'd never felt like the girl who guys wanted to date. I was not as pretty as Gretchen or Brenda Schumacher. It hadn't been a competition thing with me and Gretchen—she had been in love with Heath since she and I were twelve years old, and he had always been the only one for her. It had taken him a long time to figure it out—it wasn't until he came back from his first year of college during my senior year and realized that she was gorgeous and he'd been a bonehead not to have noticed her before.

She had always been the beautiful one, though. That's why I'd been as shocked as everyone else junior year, when Teddy Newcastle asked me to the prom instead of Brenda. Although if I'd known how it would all turn out, I would have told him no.

Maybe that was the lesson here—to not get sucked in again. I was going to have to figure out how to behave like a calm and rational adult around Nick Haddon, who was like Teddy Newcastle but a million times more attractive.

"Plus," she added, "I saw him check you out."

That sent a jittery flutter of excitement straight to my heart. "He did not."

"He did. And he wasn't the only person I was watching. You were like that emoji with heart eyes. You're definitely interested."

"No."

"Yep. I'm not teasing you about it, just stating a fact. Well, maybe I'm teasing you a little. But even if your mind is objecting, the rest of you was game."

I rested my face between my hands. She was going to torment me for the next two weeks. I just knew it. She'd told me a couple of months ago that she wished that I could get married and pregnant so that our kids would be close in age and be best friends, too.

While I understood and appreciated the sentiment, neither Nick Haddon nor I needed to be her sacrificial lamb.

Gretchen just kept talking. "It seems like such a waste. Somebody should be taking advantage of this situation."

I looked up at her. "You can't, so I should take one for the team?"

"That's the kind of thing good friends do."

She was being so irrational that I didn't know how to make her see sense, but I tried anyway. "What if I pursue him and it freaks him out and he leaves?"

"That's why you'd have me to watch over you and give you advice. Think of me as your own little guardian devil. Looking out for you but also leading you straight into temptation."

"The festival is the most important thing here, and I'm not going to chase the nice movie star away by being inappropriate with him. You need to remember that." So did I, for that matter.

We were interrupted by the sound of a closet door shutting and dresser drawers opening and closing. If I could hear him doing that, I wondered if he could hear us and the kind of discussion we were having in here.

I hoped not.

"It sounds like he's building shelves in there," Gretchen commented.

"Or putting his stuff away." I'd never met anyone who actually put their clothes in dressers and closets when they traveled. I always just kept my junk in my suitcase. Mostly because I lived in fear that if I put my clothes in drawers, I would forget and leave without them.

"Do you smell that?" she asked me. Her sense of smell had definitely heightened since becoming pregnant.

It took me a second, but then I caught the scent. "What is that? Incense? Great. I'm going to get a contact high from secondhand hippie."

"It smells nice," she protested. "And I'm kind of the expert these days."

True. If it had smelled bad, she would have been running for the bathroom. It was kind of light and refreshing. Why was I jumping to snarky conclusions? It had to be because Gretchen's campaign to elect Nick Haddon as my boyfriend / fling / torrid affair was annoying me and I was leaning toward grumpy.

"I don't think it's incense. I think it's a candle," she observed. "You should ask him what scent it is."

Yeah, I'd get right on that.

She shifted uncomfortably in her chair and then said, "Sounds like he's settling in just fine. What did he think of the waterbed?"

I opened my mouth to answer and then immediately shut it again. I was not going to tell her that the words *motion of the ocean* had come out of his mouth or else she would move in here and devote her entire life to trying to get us to hook up.

When I didn't say anything, she leaned in and asked, "Did he invite you to go skinny-dipping in it?"

"Maybe we could just sit here in silence," I said.

She gave me a knowing look, topped off with a self-satisfied smirk, but we both fell quiet.

Which ended up being a mistake.

Because a few moments later, I noticed a thumping beat. It was music. What was he listening to? I strained my ears to hear it better, and at first I thought I was having some kind of hallucination.

"That's the *Raiders of the Lost Ark* soundtrack," I said incredulously. That movie was the reason I had wanted to become a composer.

"Are you sure?"

"To quote Indiana Jones, 'Pretty sure.'"

"Who sits around and listens to the soundtrack of *Raiders of the Lost Ark*?" she asked.

"I do!"

"I mean besides you," she said. Then her face lit up. "It's a sign."

"It's really not." Then a thought occurred to me. "Did you tell him to do that?"

She cocked her head to the side and grimaced. "Yes, in the few moments you were away from him, I somehow managed to quietly sneak my hugely pregnant body into his room to tell him that the way to win your heart was to listen to this soundtrack."

"Your sarcasm is both noted and ignored."

"It's my body's natural defense against people saying irrational things."

Gretchen needed a task. She was the kind of person who always had something going on, but she'd been unable to work for the last couple of months due to the government shutdown. She had done hair before getting the tourism job, and she wanted to return to doing that, but the doctor wouldn't okay it because her blood pressure was elevated. He didn't want her standing all day.

Leaving her with all kinds of unstructured time.

It hadn't been an issue before, but now I could see that it would be. Heath was busy running the store and she was getting bored. She had been spending time hanging out with me at the library, but apparently setting me up was about to become her new project. The same thing had happened in high school when she got mono, only back then she'd tried to get me to go out with Billy Dreskin.

He'd asked out Brenda Schumacher instead.

"There's something I do need your help with," I said to her in a conspiratorial tone.

"Yes?"

"I noticed that Nick Haddon didn't bring any security with him. Which seems strange. I'm going to talk to him about it, but I'm kind of worried about what people might do. We all need to keep an eye on him and stop strangers from harassing him." Because if our plan worked, Patience was about to be overrun.

I half expected her to tell me that was a waste of her time, but instead she sat straight up in her seat. "You're right. He's here as our guest and we need to keep him safe. I will spread the word."

Relieved that she agreed, I just nodded.

"And that's safe from everything. Including things that might hurt his pride. Like that he's being watched over. By the town. Or by you."

Not this again. "I don't like lying."

"You've literally been sitting at this table and doing it for the last twenty minutes."

There was a difference between self-preservation and heading off a very determined best friend and what Shanice wanted me to do with Nick Haddon. "I dislike the idea of being dishonest just to trick someone into doing something that I want them to."

"You didn't trick him. He came here of his own free will."

"Am I interrupting?" Nick Haddon came into the kitchen, putting on a black faux-leather bomber jacket.

My face flamed as I wondered both if he'd overheard us and how it was legal for a man to look that sexy. I hadn't realized that I had such a weakness for bomber jackets. I had to swallow twice before I could speak. "Not at all. Gretchen was just leaving."

I knew her way too well. I could see that she was torn between wanting to ask Nick Haddon very personal questions and giving us a chance to be alone together. "Yes. Leaving. That's what I was doing."

We both stood up and that struggle was still there, but she overcame it. "Good to see you again," she said.

"You too."

Then she was gone, and she'd gotten one of her wishes. I was alone with Nick Haddon.

"I'm glad you brought a jacket." It was the first thing I could think to say.

"Of course I did. You think I'd come to Ohio in the fall without one?"

It would be rude to point out that he hadn't been wearing one when he arrived, wouldn't it?

"You didn't expect me to have one. I can see you've formed a high opinion of me," he said.

"I don't really have an opinion about you one way or the other." My statement shifted the energy in the room. Like my words had surprised him. Or hurt his ego. That probably didn't happen very much in his life.

Changing the subject was always a good way to get out of an awkward situation. Or so I'd heard. "So, Nick Haddon, are you hungry?"

"Starving."

He said it in a way that made my own appetite roar to life. And not the eating-food kind.

I put my hand on the back of the chair. My life had gotten to a particular level of patheticness if someone saying they were hungry was making me feel weak-kneed.

"We could, uh, get some breakfast in town. All I have here is cereal. Fruity Pebbles and Cookie Crisp, mostly. The diner is pretty good, if you want to go there."

He took a step closer to me. What was that scent? All clean and masculine? I wanted to bury my face in his neck and get a better whiff.

I had to get a handle on things.

I'd like to get a handle on him, an inner voice whispered. Great. Now I had not only my sister-in-law conspiring against me but also my own stupid libido.

My weak-knee situation did not improve when he smiled sexily and said in a low tone, "Jane Wagner, are you asking me on a date?"

CHAPTER FOUR

Had I asked him out? It was entirely possible and I hadn't realized it. Especially since Gretchen had been pressuring me to do just that. "I'm offering to show you where to eat food here in town."

Nick Haddon laughed. "I'm sorry. I was teasing you."

What was the joke? That he wouldn't want to go on a date with me? "Good to know the idea of going out with me is funny."

His face fell. "That wasn't what I meant."

"It wasn't?"

"No. I was just joking about the vibe between us. Don't worry—I've caught your signals loud and clear."

Again, I panicked. What signals? That I had wondered just how much chocolate it would take to completely immerse him before I licked it all off? "What do you mean?"

"I think you haven't stopped glaring at me since I got here."

Great, I was making him feel unwelcome. That was the opposite of what I wanted. "No, I'm so grateful that you're here. That's just my face. It's how I look. I have resting *everyone annoys me* face."

"Oh." He paused. "You know, they say that smiling takes less muscles than it does to frown and—"

Ugh, I hated when people said stuff like that. "You know, they say stabbing someone in the neck takes less muscles than it does to choke them out," I said. Then I added, "Socrates."

He laughed. "So I might have misread this. Thanks for clearing that up. I'm doing this thing where I'm trying to be straightforward with my intentions so that there's no confusion or misunderstandings."

Was he giving me advice or just telling me about himself?

And what did he think he'd misread?

"I don't like when there's unanswered questions. Or secrets," he added.

So much guilt. "Secrets are the worst. They eat you up. Especially when they involve someone else." Apparently, I wasn't even trying to be subtle anymore.

Nick Haddon seemed to realize this. "What are you trying to say, Jane Wagner? Are you keeping secrets from me?"

"Well, I . . ."

Gretchen came back into the kitchen, breathing heavily and holding a rolling pin aloft. For a second I thought she was going to hit me over the head with it just to keep me quiet. "Rolling pin!" she announced.

"What?" I said.

"I borrowed your rolling pin and I forgot to return it and I saw it in the car and here I am. Making sure that things get back to the people they belong to and nobody shares things that they shouldn't share."

Was this going to be my life now? Gretchen popping up in random places like a Whack-A-Mole in an attempt to keep me quiet? Her fears were unfounded. Nick Haddon was a reasonable person. Anybody who listened to the *Raiders of the Lost Ark* soundtrack had to be someone you could reason with.

But Gretchen knew as well as I did that the rolling pin didn't belong to me. I'd never baked a day in my life. "That's not mine."

"I'm pretty sure it is. Maybe you can carry this around to keep Nick Haddon safe."

She was trying to truth block me.

"What is happening?" he asked, and I realized how weird this must all seem to him.

"What's happening is Gretchen is leaving and she's going to stay gone. Right?"

She frowned but handed me the rolling pin. This was obviously Heath's, and now I was going to have to give it back to him. One more thing on my to-do list. I set it down on the table.

"Right," she finally agreed, and I let out a breath I hadn't realized I'd been holding. "I just like to check in on Jane as much as I can since she lives here alone. All alone. Because she's single. What about you, Nick? Are you single?"

It was humanly impossible for Gretchen to be more transparent than she was being right now. I was afraid to look him in the face.

"I am single." Why did everything seem to amuse this man?

And was that relief that I was feeling?

"We will walk you out to your car," I told her loudly. Where I would make sure she got in it and drove away. "Come on, Nick Haddon."

He trailed behind me, and I fought off the urge to rage whisper at my best friend. She, thankfully, knew to stay quiet.

The lawn was mostly empty when we got outside, but there were a couple of photographers left who started taking our picture as we headed to our cars. Gretchen waved. "See you soon!"

It sounded more like a threat than a casual goodbye.

Too bad for her, though. No one was putting me in that position. If Nick Haddon was going to stay in Patience, it would be with all the facts.

"I'm over here," I told him, walking with him to my car. I went to the driver's side while he slid in on the passenger side.

As I started up the engine, he asked, "What was the rolling pin about?"

Was he more perceptive than I'd given him credit for, or were we just really obvious and inept at being subtle? Obviously, Gretchen had more holes in her story than a slice of swiss cheese, but I thought I had somewhat managed to cover things up. Apparently not. I opted to stay close to the truth. "We were worried about your safety," I told him. "Since you don't have bodyguards with you."

"I requested to not have them. I wanted to come here and just . . . feel like a regular person."

"I'm sure the paparazzi and camera crew are really going to help with that."

He grinned at me as I headed down my long driveway. "Good point."

I glanced in the rearview mirror and saw that the photographers were still taking photos of us driving off. It was unnerving, and I'd only been putting up with it for a little while. I wondered how he dealt with it all the time.

Then I noticed how good he smelled in this tiny, confined space we were sharing. He was still adjusting his seat, leaning it back to fit properly. I wondered what that scent was—some combination of expensive cologne, soap, possibly that candle of his.

Maybe it was just him.

"It really is beautiful here," he said, taking in the maple trees that lined my driveway. His words shocked me out of my reverie on how good he smelled, and I forced myself to pay attention to the road again. He added, "We don't really have leaves that change color where I live in Southern California."

"They're a dime a dozen here," I said.

"It looks like the trees are on fire. Gorgeous."

He was right. It was funny how you got so accustomed to something and it took a person with a different perspective to come along to remind you that you were missing out on some cool stuff you were taking for granted.

I turned left onto the main road and headed toward town. "Speaking of fire, my sister-in-law wanted me to find out what type of candle you were using earlier."

Yes, it was all about Gretchen. It had nothing to do with me and how much I was responding to his delicious scent.

"It's one of my favorites—it's called Santiago Huckleberry. And just so you know, I put it out before we left."

"That's good. My dad was a volunteer firefighter for a few years when I was younger and I got yelled at a lot over candles. Plus, in addition to licking light bulbs, Patches also enjoys a good candle flame. So if you're going to light it again, just make sure she's nowhere around. She can't afford to lose any more whiskers."

"Will do. I only lit it because it's part of my ritual."

"Ritual?" I repeated, feeling a bit alarmed. What kind of ritual was he participating in that needed a burning candle?

"I stayed in a lot of hotels growing up. My parents were always bringing me and my nanny on location with them. My nanny, Erica, taught me how to make the hotel rooms feel more like home. So I have this routine—I always unpack all of my clothes, I have a blanket and pillow I bring with me everywhere, and I light a candle and play some of my favorite music. It helps me settle in."

"That's . . ." It struck me as so sad, that a little boy had been forced to try to find a way to make his own home. A wave of sympathy cascaded through me and I pushed it aside. I did not need to look for reasons to feel bad for this fallen angel. I should focus on something else. "The music. You were listening to the *Raiders of the Lost Ark* soundtrack."

Oh, yeah. That was going to help. Talking about the one thing that would probably make me like him even more.

"I was," he said, sounding a little surprised.

"It's my favorite soundtrack of all time. It's the reason I wanted to become a movie composer."

"Really? You want to be a composer? Like John Williams?"

I let out a little laugh. "There's only one John Williams. That kind of brilliance comes along once in a generation. But yes, I'd love to do what he does. When I was six years old, my parents had sent me to bed and were going to watch *Raiders of the Lost Ark* together. I remember hearing the music and sitting at the top of the stairs, just listening. The music made me feel so many things, and it amazed me that the soundtrack was conveying all these different emotions to tell a complete story. I decided then and there that that's what I wanted to do with my life."

"I think that's amazing."

And despite the admiration in his voice, I felt self-conscious. That was a story I didn't share very often. Even when I'd studied music composition in college, I didn't tell anyone why I hoped to be a composer. Mostly because the other students had these very sophisticated reasons for wanting to write music. They had loftier aspirations.

Not that it mattered much these days. It wasn't like I was going to do anything with my degree.

"Thanks," I said.

"Do you plan on moving out to LA, or are you going to compose from here?"

"Oh, I don't think I'm going to be composing anytime soon," I said. "I'm not good enough."

"Would you mind sharing some of your work with me?" he asked. "This is sort of my industry. I love soundtracks, too. Obviously. It reminds me of what's possible in my profession. What movies are meant to do." He sounded wistful and I wondered what he meant by that. His tone shifted and he said, "I know people. I can make an introduction, if you're interested."

That was really generous of him, but I already had my Hollywood in. Honestly, some part of me wanted to impress the movie star, and I found myself saying, "There is this mentorship that I was offered, but I had to defer. It was with Maxine Portman."

"Impressive. She's a legend. Why did you defer?"

"My dad had a heart attack, and I came home to help out."

"I'm so sorry," he said.

"He's okay now. In fact, I think he's probably fine to get on with his life, but my mother insists on coddling him. I took over her job to help them and now . . . I'm here with you."

"How did that happen? You being in charge of all of this?"

He seemed genuinely curious, and it had been such a long time since a man wanted to know anything about me that I found myself telling him the whole story. I filled him in on the Newcastle embezzlement scandal. "The Newcastles are the wealthiest family in Patience. They own Newcastle Paper, which employs half the town." It was slowly going out of business, which probably meant that they were having money issues. Someone probably should have noticed that the mayor's lifestyle didn't change one bit despite that, though. "Wilfred Newcastle emptied out all of the money in the town bank accounts he had access to. So he's being investigated and his family is hiding him behind an army of lawyers. But regardless of how that turns out, the government can't reopen until we have the funds to start operating again. The fall festival is one of our main sources of revenue for the town. So it's all shut down, which made the librarian the most senior official position in charge of the festival, which was my mother's job and I took over, and now you're all caught up."

"You're the librarian?" Again with the delight.

"Yes. Temporarily."

"Like Marian?"

It felt familiar, but I couldn't place it immediately. "Who?"

"From *The Music Man*. The librarian's name is Marian. There's a song about it."

"I've seen it, but it's been a really long time." I noticed that he was humming a little bit and drumming his long fingers against his leg. "You're not going to start singing to me now, are you?"

Because that would end me. Music had always been my weakness and the idea of someone who looked like him serenading me would make my brain explode.

"I could."

"That's okay," I said, swallowing hard. I gripped the steering wheel so tightly I was worried about breaking it.

"We should watch it some night."

I was tempted to tease him like he'd teased me and put him on the spot—and question if he was asking me on a date, but he was probably just being polite and I had already done enough today to thoroughly embarrass myself. I did not need to be adding to the list. So I just said, "Sure."

We arrived in the downtown area. It was one of those quaint little main streets, very Disney-esque. I pointed out all the major businesses and restaurants as we drove to Tony's, then parked behind the diner.

"It's like a movie set," he murmured after listening to everything I'd said.

Giving that tour was a good distraction because all I could think about was that Nick Haddon liked movie soundtracks and listened to them for fun. I'd never met anyone else who did that before. Not even in college.

And he seemed attentive and actually listened to me and seemed to care about my interests.

It was all unnerving, and the day continued with that dreamlike feeling—as if none of it could actually be happening.

As we climbed out of the car, I said, "Follow me, Nick Haddon."

"It's Nick." He fell into step next to me.

"That's what I said."

"No, you said Nick *Haddon*. You always say Nick Haddon. I'm just Nick."

Had I been saying his full name? As I ran through my recent memories, I realized that not only did I call him by his entire name, but I did it in my head when I was thinking about him, too.

That was because it was how I thought of him. He was Nick Haddon, Hollywood star. Not a regular man with a regular name.

It probably also explained why he had been calling me Jane Wagner. Like he'd been holding up a mirror to show me what I'd been doing, and I hadn't picked up on it.

In my defense, he was really hot and distracting.

"Sorry, Just Nick."

"You're not funny, Just Jane," he said with a smile.

I pulled open the door to Tony's and there was a moment when everyone in the diner paused to stare, but it passed quickly.

Which let me know that Gretchen had been successful in getting the town to calm down. It was a good thing our gossip network was so efficient.

I led him to a booth in the back and sat. He took a seat across from me, and Shirley came over to welcome us and hand us our menus. I didn't bother looking at it because I already knew what I was going to order. Shirley promised to return with water.

"What do they have here?" he asked. "Food poisoning?"

He was joking, but I still felt defensive. "I knew you'd be a snob." I was teasing, too, but there was probably some conviction in my words that he picked up on.

"Put your knives away," he said, trying to suppress a smile. "I surrender. Mental note—don't make jokes about the town or anything in it."

I decided to forgive him. "Good note. Plus, Tony makes the best pancakes you'll ever eat."

"Oh, I don't eat carbs."

Didn't eat . . . I was aghast, my mouth hanging open slightly.

How was that possible?

"Ever?" I whispered.

"Mostly. But there's this role I want, and I'm going to have to be in perfect shape, and that means chicken breasts and broccoli while I'm on set and no carbs leading up to it."

This just didn't make sense to me. "I don't know what I'd do without sugar."

"I promise you'd live."

I would probably be in better shape, that was for sure. But nothing was worth giving up cookies for.

Not even Nick.

"Do they have any vegan options? That's usually a safe bet," he said, holding the menu up. I found myself hoping he wasn't planning to eat vegan during his whole visit, as cheese was far too important in my life.

Although maybe it was a good thing since it meant there would be no future for us whatsoever; I couldn't imagine an existence without cheese, and therefore I could put an end to these inexplicable pangs of attraction I was feeling for him. "I think the vegan option is probably to go back to California and eat there."

He laughed, and I really liked being the reason for it. I found myself saying, "If it makes you feel any better, I think the pig who provided the bacon was a vegetarian."

Another laugh. I could spend all day listening to the musical tones of his delight.

Shirley gave us a couple of waters, and Nick Haddon—er, *Nick*—made the mistake of asking if he could make substitutions.

Before she could answer, I said, "Oh, no, Tony doesn't do substitutions."

"No, he doesn't." Shirley nodded. Tony's kitchen temper was pretty legendary, and we all did our best not to do things that would make him start throwing pans through the pass window.

"Could you find out if he has keto bread?" Nick asked, in such a charming and persuasive way that Shirley couldn't resist.

I completely understood.

"Sure thing, sweetie. Be right back."

"You probably shouldn't have done that," I told Nick.

The next thing I heard was Tony yelling in the back, "Keto bread? What's a keto bread?"

Nick leaned across the table and asked, "I'm guessing that's a no? Do you think I'd be pressing things too far to ask if he does avocado toast?"

I put my head near his as Tony kept shouting. "You would be taking your life into your own hands. I'm pretty sure the only vegetables Tony is even familiar with are tomatoes and lettuce, and that's only for the hamburgers."

That blinding smile of Nick's made my toes curl. "Technically, tomatoes are fruit."

"Does that mean ketchup is technically a smoothie? Because I could get behind that."

We stayed there in that moment, smiling at each other, and I liked it. Sharing something with him, being in our own little world, if only for a moment. I should have backed off but I didn't.

A pan clattered on the floor, breaking the bubble, as Shirley scooted over to our table. "No luck, sweetie. You could get the omelet."

Nick handed her the menu. "That sounds great. I'll try that."

Shirley took it and then turned toward me. "The usual for you?"

"Yes, thanks."

"The usual?" he asked as Shirley left.

"A stack of pancakes with maple syrup."

"Sugar on sugar."

"It's delicious," I insisted. "You are missing out."

"Maybe you can share a bite of yours with me."

Just as Tony didn't do substitutions, I didn't usually share food. But I would have given him my entire plate of pancakes if he'd asked for it in that charming way of his. "Okay."

There was more yelling in the kitchen, but I had learned long ago to tune Tony out.

Nick paid close attention, though, and then commented, "The cook has some anger-management issues, it sounds like."

"I don't know if I'd call them issues, because that implies it's something he could fix. Tony is only that way about food here at the diner, though. Like a temperamental artist. He is the nicest man you'll ever meet. He worships his wife, and when someone needs something, he's the first person on their doorstep with a tray of food. He also sponsors all of the soccer and Little League teams in town. The Girl Scouts know to come in here because he'll buy every box they have. Current situation notwithstanding, he's a great guy."

Nick looked at me thoughtfully and then pointed at a booth near the door. "What about that woman over there? Do you know her story?"

"Virginia? She's amazing. She's an astronomer who taught at the University of Cincinnati for years and then retired here to Patience. She opened a no-kill animal shelter."

"Do you know everyone in here?"

I glanced around the diner. "Yes."

At that, he shook his head. "You are so real. And everyone here. Real."

Funny how he made me feel like everything around me was a dream, while apparently I made things real.

It felt like there was some kind of implication there that I wasn't quite comfortable with, so I made a joke instead. "Are the other people you know *not* real? If that's the case maybe you should see a doctor."

He grinned at that and then turned more serious. "The people in my life are not real. They are consumed with money and fame and publicity stunts."

There was a moment when I told myself not to do it, but the words came out anyway. "Isn't you being here a publicity stunt? You're not concerned with fame?"

"I'm trying to change perceptions. People are more interested in who I'm dating than the work I'm doing. I want to be taken seriously."

"You could have built homes for orphans or worked at a food kitchen."

His aquamarine eyes fixed on mine, and those unsettled tingles were back, low in my abdomen. "There were a lot of things I could have done. This one appealed to me the most."

Some part of me didn't want to give him the benefit of the doubt. That might have been due to the tingles I was trying to wish away. "Or our video went viral and your team knew you'd get the most attention if you came here."

He leaned back like he was evaluating something. "If that were true, I could have come in the day of the festival and left. I didn't do that. This is more to me than just a photo op."

"Why?"

Nick had this mysterious smile, and for a second I was worried he wasn't going to answer. "I noticed you in the video."

My heart slammed so hard against my rib cage it felt bruised. "What?" For some reason I had assumed his publicist had seen the clip and gotten him on board. It had honestly never occurred to me that Nick had watched it. Wasn't he too busy for things like that?

"Everybody else looked like they were having the time of their lives, but you looked uncomfortable."

Oh, sure. That would be what he remembered. It was true, but still. "Those Greek togas Gretchen made everyone wear—it was too short on me."

The memory of that day, the thought that Nick had seen me . . . It made me nervous. I picked up my water and took a big drink.

"I thought you looked cute."

Cute. He'd called me cute.

While my heart was swelling at his words, that contrary voice inside me said, *He called your cat cute, too.*

So it didn't mean anything, right?

But then, why did I feel like I was choking?

Did he just flirt with everyone? Was he one of those people where it was some kind of natural instinct? Like how breathing was for me? I did it without thinking.

Only now I was thinking about it because I might actually be choking. I forced the water down, willing air into my lungs.

"Are you okay?" he asked, concerned.

"Yep." Good. I could talk. I wasn't going to choke.

I was fine. Just fine. I could sit here and pretend like famous actors called me cute every day of the week. To be honest, I don't think anyone had ever said I was cute before in my entire life, but it was fairly awesome.

And maybe he was just being polite. Or nice. Either way, he seemed to be a kind person. Guilt coursed through me, making me feel slightly sick to my stomach.

Guilt, or lack of oxygen from almost choking.

Either way, Nick deserved to know what he was getting into—what his publicist had asked me to do.

Maybe he'd be okay with it and maybe he wouldn't.

Only one way to find out.

"Nick? There's something I need to tell you."

CHAPTER FIVE

"You called me Nick." His smile was so . . . well, cute.

"Er, yes. But that's not what I have to tell you." How did I prepare him for this? He had come to Patience with the idea that he would get to be a regular person. Regular adult men did not have people who were watching them to keep them out of trouble.

I vacillated for a second. Maybe I shouldn't say anything to him. I could hear Gretchen yelling at me in my head to stay quiet. That I shouldn't risk him leaving town. Honestly, revealing this secret didn't seem like it should be that big of a deal. I didn't know the dynamic between him and his publicist. I could be risking a lot without having all the facts.

But it had been on my mind since Shanice had called. I didn't want to keep it from him and have it all blow up in my face later.

He should know. I would just deal with whatever the consequences were.

My hands felt a little shaky and I tried to breathe slowly, in and out. "Okay. I know this sounds weird, but I'm supposed to babysit you," I told him.

"What?"

It was hard to make out his tone. Was that anger? Surprise? I pushed on. "When your publicist called, she asked me to keep an eye on you, to keep you out of trouble. She also wanted me to stay quiet about it and not tell you."

His expression was closed off and I couldn't tell what he was thinking. Several long moments passed, my pulse pounding in my throat, before he asked, "So why are you telling me?"

"I feel like you have the right to know. Plus, I didn't agree to it." He raised both eyebrows, questioning my statement. "It was Gretchen who said yes. She's kind of a human steamroller."

More long, quiet moments. "Basically, what you're saying is that you have to spend time with me. Even if you don't want to. So that you can watch me."

Why did that make my heart race? He was just asking questions to better understand what was going on. "That's the deal."

"We'll be in close proximity all the time."

My heart beat even faster. "Yep."

He finally smiled, and relief flowed through me like a flash flood. He jokingly said, "Where I'm from, we call that stalking."

I wanted to tell him he was free to go, but I couldn't. We needed him and his star power. "I can be as far away or as close as you want."

His eyes seemed to darken and his smile turned into something sexy and dangerous. "Good to know. That I can keep you close."

The air in my throat solidified at the look on his face, the smooth charm in his voice, but we were thankfully interrupted by Shirley bringing out our food.

I attacked those pancakes like a lion pouncing on a gazelle. Mostly because I needed to stop having this conversation, which was doing funny things to my internal organs, and eating was an excellent distraction.

Or it was, until Nick Haddon decided to make things worse.

A minute or two passed while we were eating and I probably should have asked if his omelet was okay, but I was letting sugar, butter, and syrup soothe me.

"Does that offer of yours still stand?" he asked, and I wasn't sure what he meant.

"Offer?"

"To try your pancakes."

"Oh. Sure." I immediately cut through the stack of pancakes to get a bite-size chunk and held it out toward him.

It was then that I realized he had his fork up, presumably to get some himself.

I'd probably grossed him out by offering him food from my fork. I started to apologize, but then he leaned forward and closed his mouth around my fork, and I felt it in my toes.

He pulled back slowly, his lips trailing over the tines until the bite was gone.

Then he did something that made my stomach flip over—he licked the syrup from his lips.

"You're right," he said. "Delicious."

Yep. That was definitely the word I would have used.

Flustered and feeling a tad dizzy, I went to get myself another bite of food, trying to block out what had just happened. I was behaving like a giddy middle schooler.

But as I ate my pancakes, that same middle schooler part of my brain told me that my mouth was now touching something his mouth had touched and that was almost like kissing him.

I was twenty-two years old. I was supposed to be more mature than this. I should not feel sweaty just because I'd shared my fork with him.

This was all Nick Haddon's fault. I swallowed my bite and then asked, "I'm now personally responsible for you eating carbs. Is your trainer going to kill me?"

It was a shot in the dark, an attempt to change the subject—and fortunately, it was a good one. "Sergei? No. He's always telling me to practice moderation." He paused and then added, "Moderation is hard for me."

"Weren't you the one who said you don't eat carbs? That's pretty good moderating. I wouldn't be able to do it. I would probably last about six hours before I demolished a sheet cake."

He smiled. "I've never been good at denying myself things. Sugar is a little bit easier because I need to for my job. But everything else . . . I overindulge."

I wouldn't mind overindulging with him, some feverish part of me thought, and I tried to tamp it down. Because as much as I said out loud that I was done with men who looked like him, my lady bits still found him attractive.

"I'm on a new path," he continued. "I need to make new choices. Better choices. To not act like I used to. I want to be more authentic. A better man."

What exactly had he done? "What do you mean?"

He looked at me like I'd been living under a rock.

Or in a small town in Ohio.

"You haven't heard about me?" he clarified.

I was not going to tell him how I'd been a huge fan of *Olympus High* because I had the feeling he would tease me relentlessly. And just because I was a fan of the show, and particularly of him as Zeus, that didn't mean I knew anything about his personal life. "I'm woefully behind on my celebrity gossip. Most of what I know about you, I've learned against my will."

"Gretchen?" he asked knowingly, and I nodded. He added, "Let's just say I've done a lot of stupid things. And karma has found a particularly effective way of forcing me to change. In Hollywood I'm known as . . . a jinx."

I blinked at him. Did that mean something different there from what it did here? "What?"

He leaned in, like he was sharing a very big secret with me. And maybe he was. I'd told him something significant and it felt a little like he was returning the favor. "A jinx. It means that despite being given a new series to star in or having a movie specifically written for me, every project I've been involved with since *Olympus High* has tanked."

Was that true? I was so on the periphery when it came to things like that. I enjoyed the television shows, movies, and soundtracks that I liked and didn't think much about them beyond that. "Really?"

"I've lost a lot of very rich people a lot of money."

Including himself, according to his publicist.

"So nobody wants to hire me and I'm not able to get new work. I need to turn things around. Both on a personal and professional level. That's part of the reason why I'm here. I'm trying to rehabilitate my image and myself. No more going to extremes. No more taking everything that's offered to me."

Again, I knew I should probably keep my nose out of his business, but I couldn't help myself. "Like what?"

He put his fork down and folded his arms across his chest. "Like . . . a lot of things. It means I'm not drinking anymore. I don't think I was ever out of control with it, but I definitely flirted with that line."

Not surprising. As I'd already discovered, he flirted with everything.

"I realized that, outside of work, everything in my life has been too easy. Anything I want I've gotten. Want to be an actor? Done. Want to star in the biggest series on TV? It's yours. Want to fly to Paris this weekend? Here's my private jet. If I see an attractive woman at a party, there's no question who she will be going home with at the end of the night."

I didn't doubt that, and it somehow managed to make me slightly jealous. I was worried that if I spoke, he would hear it in my voice. I stayed quiet.

"People generally don't tell me no. Including studio executives, even when I'm losing them money."

I tried to imagine what that would be like—to have everything you ever wanted, to never be denied anything—and I . . . couldn't. That was so far from my reality. He leaned his head to one side, studying me.

Did he think I wouldn't reject him either?

Because I would. I didn't care if he was pretty.

"No," I blurted out, because I was me and that was the kind of thing I did.

His eyes lit up. "I didn't ask." He said it with a knowing grin, like he understood me in ways that I didn't understand myself.

Yep, he had seen right through me. "Well, if you did, my answer would be no."

Nick held up both of his hands. "Message received."

And yet it seemed like it hadn't been. He kept eating and smiling like he didn't believe me.

Which was annoying.

Fair and probably a bit correct, but still annoying.

He ate a few more bites of his food while I tried to process some sort of quippy response to show that I didn't like him, but I had nothing. *Nothing.*

Then he asked, "So you studied musical composition at Miami University?"

That surprised me. I was pretty sure I hadn't told him where I'd gone to college.

He confirmed I hadn't when he said, "Which is here in Ohio and not in Florida, as I'd initially assumed?"

In disbelief I asked, "How do you know where I went to college?"

At least he had the decency to look embarrassed. "Shanice's company did a background check on some people here in town, including you."

When I'd first spoken to his publicist, I'd considered that she might do a background check. But imagining something and then being confronted with the reality of it being done were two totally different things. "That's . . . creepy. Weren't you just saying something about me being a stalker?"

"Or it's necessary. Especially if you're me and doing what I'm doing right now."

I tried to imagine being him but knew that I'd probably just Evil Queen from *Snow White* it up and stare at myself in a mirror all day. "Yeah, I guess that makes sense." He was here without security, staying in what was essentially my house. He and his team should know things about me.

Although I wasn't sure how my alma mater and credit score would make any of them feel better about his safety.

"Where did you go to college?" I asked, as my way of letting him know that I understood and wasn't upset.

"I didn't go. I always wanted to, though."

"Why didn't you?"

"Because I was stuck playing an immortal teenager on TV."

Right. Should I pretend that I didn't know anything about *Olympus High*, or did I admit to the fact that I had organized my entire Thursday around his show?

"Jane, were you a Zera shipper?"

My eyes widened. I absolutely had been. I'd never been able to resist a good enemies-to-lovers story and had rooted every second for Zeus and Hera to get together. Unfortunately, the show had been canceled before they admitted their love.

"Possibly," I admitted. Nick really made me feel like I was made out of glass. Slightly breakable and all too easy to see through.

"Do you have any questions about the show? People usually do."

I tried to keep it in, but I couldn't. "So many! Why did the Greek gods all have British accents? Shouldn't they have had Greek accents? Or American ones because it took place in America?"

He slid easily into Zeus's accent and made goose bumps break out on the back of my neck. "Because someone in Hollywood decided that British accents either mean sophistication or a period piece. Plus, British accents tested better with the fans. Especially the teen girls."

I needed a moment. I wished I could have fanned my flaming face. I'd had a serious crush on Zeus when I was younger and those three sentences had brought it all back.

This was not good.

He was looking at me expectantly, unaware of the fact that he had caused a mini–nuclear meltdown inside me.

Nick is not Zeus, I told my excited hormones. We had to talk about something else. I could not sit here calmly and discuss the romantic pairing that he'd been part of. "Um, were Persephone and Hades actually dating in real life?"

He shifted out of the British accent. "Believe it or not, that's the question I get asked the most. No. It was nothing but a showmance meant to promote the show."

"Oh. Have you ever done that?"

"Lots of times. Hollywood will do anything to sell a movie or a TV show, and nothing sells better than a pretend 'real-life' romance between two of the main characters. Most of the celebrity romances you see are heavily orchestrated by publicists. The actors go along with it for the attention."

Gretchen had never told me that before. It made me wonder if she even knew. Her head was going to explode when I told her.

But now was not the time for that. Now was the time to find out as much about his time on *Olympus High* as I could. "What did you like best about being on the show?"

He put his fork down on the plate in front of him and pushed it to the side. He rested both of his elbows on the table and again leaned toward me. "It was my first real job. I loved everything about it. For most of my costars, it was no big deal. Just another day at the office. But I think making shows and movies like that is . . ." He paused, searching for the right word. "Magical. The way you can tell a story and have this audience that collectively experiences it and engages with it, enjoys it—that means a lot."

"That's why I love music," I told him. "The way it connects people, makes them feel something. How you communicate without even speaking and cause an emotional and social experience."

"Exactly," he said, and there was a look in his eyes I didn't quite recognize. Appreciation? Understanding?

Connection?

Chopin's "Ballade No. 1 in G Minor" began to play in my head, as if I were searching for a way to musically express what I was feeling.

"Who are your favorite composers?" he asked, interrupting me.

But it was a welcome interruption. First, because I could get too caught up in that sort of situation, composing whole scores to complement a situation happening in my life, and I did not need to do that now. Nick was temporary. I couldn't let my musically inclined brain or my ovaries forget that fact.

Second, talking about the composers I liked best was one of my favorite things in the world to do. I tended to get more than a little bit wound up about it and could speak on the subject for a long time.

Which was exactly what I did. Until I realized that I'd been doing it for a while. Not because he gave me any indication that he was bored—in fact, he looked interested—but because I'd glanced at my phone, seen the time, and realized that I'd gone far beyond the point when most people's eyes would start to glaze over.

"I'm sorry," I said. "I just get really excited about this stuff and no one ever wants to talk to me about it." Including my ex-boyfriend, who used to complain if I ever even so much as mentioned music to him. "I know it's boring."

"I don't think it's boring. I enjoy listening to you. People who are passionate about things are interesting."

It felt like a compliment even if he hadn't worded it that way. It had been a long time since a man had given me one of those.

He added, "You're easy to talk to. I like talking to you. I like you."

My inner middle schooler was back. He liked me? *Like* liked me?

He did say you were interesting, that voice then helpfully added. *And pretty. And cute.*

That didn't necessarily mean anything, though. He seemed to be a nice man, and it could be that he was only being polite.

Maybe I wanted it to mean more and I was reading into it. That was entirely possible.

Or he's just an honest person and doesn't want to play any games.

Argh. I had no way to evaluate any of it and I was honestly scared to tell Gretchen because she was already making herself available to plan my and Nick's wedding based on our limited interaction. If I told her that he'd said he liked me, she'd probably spontaneously give birth just so that her son's birthday would mark the day when she was Completely Right About Everything.

I then realized that I'd been quiet for a long time and I wasn't sure what to say back, because I didn't want to make a nice situation into something awkward by misreading things. I settled on, "I like talking to you, too."

It was true, and it had the added benefit of sidestepping his saying he liked me and maintaining a pretense of not being obsessive by demanding he explain himself and what precisely he meant.

Win-win.

There was a moment when I thought he was going to put me on the spot, as he was sporting that knowing grin. "Can I share something with you?" he asked.

My pulse started pounding in my temples, my lungs tightening. I meant to say *okay*, but it came out a slightly garbled mess of consonants. I could think of oh-so-many things I'd like to share with him.

Even though I knew better and should have had more control over my hormones.

"Do you know . . . that not one person has stared at me since we sat down?"

Did he mean other than me? Because I felt like I hadn't been able to take my eyes off him since he stepped out of that car. I blinked rapidly, my breathing returning to normal.

"No one has taken a picture of me or asked for a selfie since we got here. It's very . . . refreshing."

"Welcome to real life," I said. "We have sugar here."

He laughed and then asked, "Should we get the check?"

"Oh, they'll put it on my tab. I heard you weren't rich." Why did I say that? It was like I was implying something about his financial status and I honestly had no idea how much money he did or did not have in his bank account and it was rude to bring it up.

My mother was going to die of embarrassment specifically so that she could roll over in her grave at my mistake.

Mortifying. What was wrong with me?

"Relatively speaking, yes." His gaze flickered away and then back to mine. If I'd upset him, he didn't show it. "I'm assuming you have to get to work."

I debated what to say. Did I tell him that I had taken today off in anticipation of his arrival and to help him get settled in? Although from his "making a strange place feel like home" story, it didn't sound like he needed any help in that area.

Or should I agree and flee to the library so that I could get my head on straight? Because he was knocking me for a serious loop. He was not at all what I'd expected him to be, and with that outside packaging of his, it was overwhelming. It might have been scrambling my brain just a teeny, tiny bit.

Okay, a lot.

Which was evident when I said, "I'm free. What did you want to do?"

How did he manage to look so mischievous and sexy all at the same time? "I can't tell you that because you've preemptively told me no."

He's teasing, I told my overexcited glands. *He likes to tease you and make you turn that particular shade of red.*

To distract myself I cleared my throat and said, "I could take you to the grocery store so that you can pick out whatever you need. Because I'm pretty sure that everything in my house is laced with sugar. I could drop you off and pick you up later."

I was trying to give both of us an out. I'd said I was free, but maybe he'd forget that part; I wasn't sure it was that great of an idea for me to keep hanging out with him.

He didn't forget about my availability, though. "Only if you come with me."

It was just grocery shopping, the most mundane of basic errands, but his words sounded like he was promising adventure and fun and like I'd be a fool to turn him down.

It might not have been the smart move, but I found myself powerless to resist.

CHAPTER SIX

We walked from the diner to the store. It didn't take long, but I hoped he didn't notice how heavily I seemed to be breathing. White, misty clouds lingered near my mouth. I was both walking quickly and trying to stave off this overwhelming attraction I felt for Nick.

He kept up with me fine, and I noted that he was not out of breath. Stupid in-shape Nick Haddon.

The front doors of the store slid open and we walked inside. "Here it is. This is the grocery store. My parents own it and my brother, Heath, is currently running it."

"I've never actually been grocery shopping before," he confessed, and I only had a second to try to process that bizarre piece of information before he continued on. "Heath? That's the brother who is married to Gretchen," Nick said, taking in our tiny store. Bigger than a convenience store, but not the kind of grocery stores people were used to in larger cities. Just a good place to get the necessities and some fun extras.

"Yes, Heath is married to Gretchen."

"So this is the family business?" he asked, picking up an apple. He turned it one way and then the other, studying the bright redness.

Why did Nick look so hot standing there with a piece of fruit? I was suddenly getting the whole Garden of Eden–temptation thing.

Thankfully, he set the apple back down on the display. I remembered that he had asked me a question. "It is. It was started by my great-grandparents."

"I know a little something about that. Being in the family business."

"It must have been weird to grow up with two huge celebrities as parents." I wasn't up on my gossip like Gretchen, but everybody knew about Sheila Starr and Bradley Haddon—how they had been married to other people, fallen in love on the set of one of the worst movies of all time, and been blissfully happy for the last thirty years.

Nick shrugged. "It was my normal. That was my life—people taking my photo everywhere I went. And we had a lot of money. I never knew anything else. Even when I went to school—most of my classmates had famous parents. It was their normal, too. It wasn't until I was older that I realized just how different other people's lives were." He looked at the sweet corn, and I made a mental note to grab a couple of ears. They would be so fresh this time of year.

It was *not* because I thought Nick might enjoy it and I wanted to share a piece of Ohio with him.

Was. Not.

I was just making a shopping list. Yes, that was it. A shopping list. I was not imagining a private and maybe romantic dinner at my house with Nick Haddon. Mostly because that would be wildly unrealistic. Both the romantic part and the thought that I could make something I wouldn't burn. That might be one way to scare him off. Let him taste my cooking.

As I was coming up with other possible ways to keep him at bay, Nick asked, "Do you only have the one brother?"

"Yes, and he's as annoying as you'd expect an older brother to be. We're closer now than when we were kids, but he still thinks he has to protect me." That someone had hurt me badly and made Heath feel that way was not really any of Nick's business. "You're an only child, right?"

He made a soft scoff of disgust and then said, "As far as I know."

What was he trying to say? It wasn't my place to question him, but I found myself asking, "What do you mean?"

"Let's just say that Bradley is not quite the devoted husband the world imagines him to be. I found that out the hard way when I was twelve. I might have several half-siblings, for all I know, but my dad is the king of non-disclosure agreements."

I felt so bad for him. That was awful. "Does your mom know?" I asked in a stage whisper. This was all so shocking to me. His parents had the most famous love story in Hollywood.

"She knows. But she pretends that everything is okay. It has to be for the cameras. Nothing is authentic or real in our lives. If things ever got rough at home, which was basically all the time, my dad would go on location and my mom went off to a six-month-long spa retreat. They left me with a rotating list of nannies."

"That must have been really hard to deal with." This revelation shifted things for me. I'd thought Nick Haddon was some golden boy who had never known a day's hardship in his whole life. That he'd never been grocery shopping before had added to that belief.

I'd imagined that he'd grown up with perfect, talented parents in some mansion, where his life had been easy. Instead, his upbringing sounded really . . . lonely.

It made me sad.

"You're not what I expected," I confessed to him.

"What did you expect?"

"A little more full of yourself, I guess?"

He briefly shrugged and gave me a slight smile. "A few years ago you would have been right. I've been working hard on that, though. Hopefully, there's more to me than meets the eye."

Well, what met the eye was pretty darn good, so that was a ringing endorsement. I reached for one of the mini–shopping carts. "This is a shopping cart. Put the stuff you want in it and bring it up to the cashier when you're done."

Now he looked offended. "I understand how the process works."

"Because you've seen it on TV?"

His expression made me think that hit close to home. "I've always had an employee who did all the shopping. But even though I've never done it myself, I get the basics of it."

"Okay, poor little rich boy. You can get your own groceries. Have fun. But just wait until I tell you how to combine coupons with sales. Your whole world is going to shift."

"Promise?"

Why did everything he say sound like some kind of come-on? It had to be because I hadn't been on a date in so long.

Maybe that's what I needed to do. Go on a date with a regular guy so that I wouldn't buy into the fantasy of what it would be like to date someone like Nick.

There was that nurse practitioner at Gretchen's ob-gyn, Wells. He'd hinted around about asking me out, and my best friend had repeatedly told me that it wasn't like a conflict of interest because I wasn't a patient. It still seemed a little strange to me, so I'd been polite but hadn't really responded.

Perhaps it was time to change that.

"This way," I told Nick as I led him over three aisles. "You might be interested in our health food section. It's Gretchen's idea. She pushed Heath into it when she got pregnant, because she had lofty expectations. Instead, she got really sick in the beginning and pretty much could only keep marshmallows and saltine crackers down."

He reached for a box on the shelf and handed it to me. "Hey! Look at this. It's one of my favorites."

"Seaweed squares?" I asked, trying to keep the disgust out of my voice. "Somebody actually made a snack out of the worst thing in the ocean? What's next? Microplastics bites?"

He laughed and took the box from me and put it in his cart. "I'll have you know that seafood is a superfood."

"What's its superpower? That it's inedible?"

There was a ding as the front doors slid open and a customer walked in.

Only it wasn't a customer.

It was the actual devil.

"Brenda Schumacher," I grumbled. I couldn't remember the last time she'd stepped foot in my parents' store.

"Who is that?" Nick asked. "You just said 'Brenda Schumacher' the same way Lex Luthor says 'Superman.'"

"I am not the supervillain in this scenario," I told him. Brenda made eye contact with me and headed straight toward us. Whatever was about to happen was not going to be good and I definitely didn't want Nick to witness it.

"Go shopping," I told him, pushing against his shoulders. Why was he so solid? He was like a brick wall with eyes. I wasn't able to move him even a little.

"You're very bossy," he said in a playful tone, not picking up on my panic.

"I'm just aggressively helpful," I said, still pushing against his shoulders.

Then he seemed to realize something was going on. "What's happening?" he asked.

"Please." My voice broke slightly. I didn't want to beg, but I was prepared to. I knew what Brenda was capable of, and the last thing in the world that I wanted was for Nick to be here.

I wasn't sure why that was so important to me, but it was.

"Okay," he said and, thankfully, left.

She might have been the actual worst, but even I had to admit that Brenda was like a perfect little doll come to life. She had always managed to make me feel too tall and frumpy. She was tiny, with dark black hair, and had the tiniest waist I'd ever seen on a person. She also enjoyed clothing that left very little to the imagination. I knew I wasn't supposed to judge her for that, but . . .

Judging, judging, judging.

"Jane Wagner. I haven't seen very much of you lately," she said in a fake-friendly, high-pitched voice.

"Really? I feel like I always see too much of you." I glanced down at her low-cut top, but she wasn't insulted. She smirked at me.

My hackles went up. She was here for something specific. I could feel stomach acid rising at the back of my esophagus.

There was only one logical explanation. My gaze inadvertently flickered over to Nick.

So did hers.

I stepped into her line of sight, towering over her even though she had on four-inch boots. "What are you doing here, Brenda? Did somebody forget to lock the gates of hell?"

"How long have you been holding on to that one? Did you practice it in your mirror at night?"

I had come up with it a few weeks ago, but I wasn't going to dignify her accurate guess with a response.

"What's the matter, Janie? No prepared quip to hurl back at me?"

Her whiny falsetto voice grated on my very last nerve.

"Why do you always sound like someone pressed your fast-forward button? I know that's not your actual voice."

"You're so mean, Janie. I can't help how I sound."

I saw red. Literally saw red. She had said it just to rage bait me, and yet she had still successfully baited me into a rage.

I'd never make fun of something that someone couldn't control, but in Brenda's case it was entirely within her control. She'd adopted this tone and pitch when she tried to steal Teddy Newcastle from me in high school. I had held on to a horrible voice mail she'd sent me years ago as evidence of her bullying, and she'd used her regular octave in it as she raged at me and called me names.

I had finally deleted the message a few years ago when Gretchen convinced me that it wasn't in my best mental health interests to hold on to it. She had been right, but now I wished I had it just to play it for Brenda. To prove that she was lying to my face.

This baby voice of hers was one of the many things I couldn't stand about her.

Correction, *hated*. I knew I wasn't supposed to hate anyone, but I really did hate Brenda Schumacher.

She easily picked up on my Hulk-level anger and tsked at me. "So sad. And pathetic."

I should have walked away. I knew I should. Instead, I stood there, fuming. Wanting her to stop eyeballing Nick. "If you have something to say, you can look me in my kneecaps and say it."

"The crush you have on Nick Haddon. Everyone is talking about it. It must be so awkward for him, having to live with you when you're publicly throwing yourself at him."

My first instinct was to react. To protest. Because I hadn't done anything of the sort. Yes, there had been things happening inside my head, but I was sure that there wasn't anything I'd physically done that would make people jump to that conclusion.

And it had only been a couple of hours since he'd arrived.

News definitely traveled fast in our town, but this was ridiculous.

Or she was making it up, trying to rattle me. Which was entirely possible.

She continued, "Maybe I should offer him a place to stay."

"Where? In your lair?" I would run Nick Haddon off myself before I'd see him staying with Brenda.

"Oh, you haven't heard? Wilfred bought me the Fairchild place."

What?

The Fairchild place was a small inn just outside of town. Brenda's "boyfriend," the former mayor of Patience, had bought her an entire building. Possibly with embezzled money.

I had no way of knowing that, of course, but it wouldn't surprise me.

Why didn't anyone know about this yet?

Then it hit me that my friends probably already knew and were keeping it from me. Because the idea that I was going to be in competition with her when the Pink House officially opened for business was enough to send me into a rage spiral.

I would not give her the satisfaction.

"Worried?" she asked. "You should be. I'm going to take your customers, and I'm going to take that yummy man from you."

"You mean like you tried to do with Teddy and you had to settle for his uncle? A man old enough to be your grandpa? How is Oldielocks, by the way? Are you at all concerned that your relationship might be considered elder abuse?"

Anger flashed in her eyes, and I felt a small thrill that I'd finally managed to shake her calm exterior. Her voice was steady, though, as she said, "You do understand that Nick Haddon is out of your league? Tell me that you understand that."

That was such an obvious thing to say. Of course he was. In other news, water was wet and the sky was blue. Did she think that would hurt me? That I hadn't already realized that myself? My voice was equally steady as I asked, "Why would you want Nick? He doesn't have any liver spots, still has his own hair and teeth, and doesn't take heart medication. I don't see what the attraction is. Unless you're just looking for another rich guy to hitch your wagon to?" If that was the case, she was going to be sorely disappointed.

She crossed her arms. "I think someone like Nick Haddon wants a woman he can relate to. That's on his level. You know what they say. Behind every great man is an even better woman."

"I wouldn't know. I've never stood behind a man. Or let one buy me an inn."

"No, you just let your daddy do that."

"My parents didn't—"

"Hey, hey, hey." Gretchen came over and joined us, a fake smile plastered on her face. "Voices. You two are getting loud."

I could feel everyone in the store staring at us, including Nick. I didn't dare turn around to make eye contact with him, though. I hoped he hadn't heard what we were saying.

I should have stopped, but I did not. Instead, I rage whispered to Brenda, "Does your grandpa know that you're trolling for a new man? I'd hate for him to take his present back."

She gave me a serene smile that made me want to punch things. Mostly her. "Wilfred and I have an understanding. You and I should have one of those, too. Because I'm like the Canadian Mounties."

I blinked at her and decided to be deliberately obtuse. "You wear a red suit and a funny hat?"

"You're thinking of Santa," Gretchen interrupted, picking up on my vibe. "He wears a red suit and a funny hat."

"That's not what I'm—" Brenda hissed, balling her hands up into fists. "What I meant was, I always get my man."

"Are you going to make a list and check it twice?" I asked. "Because that's Santa, too. You should try not to get the two confused."

Brenda didn't know what to say to that as she vibrated with anger. We had already made a pretty big scene, and I was done with this conversation. So I announced, "As much as I'd love to stay for more of your witty and delightful banter, I'm just not that good of a liar. I don't want to keep you from your busy schedule of kicking puppies and sucker punching babies."

At that, she went completely calm and still, and that was somehow more terrifying than her visible anger. "You're right. I am busy. I'm actually here on official Newcastle business."

Warning sirens started sounding in my head.

"I hate to be the one to tell you this"—her smile indicated that was a total lie and she was loving every single second—"but your little orchestrated publicity stunt is doomed to fail. You can get your picture with Nick Haddon in every magazine in the country and pretend to be a couple, but no one's going to buy it. And no one's coming to your little festival. There won't be a festival at all because Newcastle Paper is pulling out as the official sponsor."

Boom. She had just lobbed a nuclear bomb at me. Newcastle Paper had agreed to be the sponsor of the festival almost a year ago, as they had every year prior for the last forty years.

How had she done this? I knew Wilfred Newcastle sat on the board of that company. Had she convinced him to revoke their sponsorship? That had to be some kind of conflict of interest or something, but I wasn't a lawyer and didn't know what we could do to get them to pay up. I assumed there was a contract, but the Newcastles were notorious for getting out of their promises.

Something I knew all too well.

She was right about one thing—without the money that they'd promised, we would never be able to pay the vendors, and there wouldn't be any festival.

We wouldn't be able to save Patience.

With a terrible, nasty smirk on her face, Brenda turned on her extremely high heels and walked back out of the store. I stood there, shaking, my breathing turning panicky.

Gretchen asked aloud what I was thinking. "What are we going to do?"

CHAPTER SEVEN

I had to calm down. I couldn't deal with this problem if I was freaking out. There was a solution. There had to be. I was going to find it. I couldn't get this jittery, frantic feeling to go away, though.

I told Gretchen, "We need to call an emergency meeting of the festival-planning committee. Text everyone. I'll take Nick back home and join you at the library."

"Got it," she said and jumped on her phone.

I texted my mom to ask for the Newcastle Paper contact—a woman named Julie Eliason—and then immediately called her. She picked up right away and when I asked her about the situation, she informed me in a very cold voice that the information I'd been given was correct, that Newcastle Paper wasn't going to sponsor the festival this year and would be looking to invest their charitable dollars elsewhere.

It was a very measured and calculated response, and then she hung up on me. I wished I could slam down my phone instead of swiping futilely on the screen that indicated the call was over.

They wanted to spend their dollars elsewhere. Ha. They didn't have any. If there was one thing everyone in Patience knew, it was that Newcastle Paper was slowly going under. Every year they lost more clients as they continued to switch to digital, and the company was forced to lay off more employees.

It was a slow grind to the end, but it was going to happen.

I'd just never expected that the festival would be caught in the line of fire. Part of me felt bad, like I had somehow caused this to happen because of my lifelong rivalry with Brenda. Had she specifically done what she could to wreck the festival? Not caring how it would affect people she'd known her entire life just to stick it to me?

It seemed so selfish. The worst part, though? She had come here specifically to tell me that the sponsorship had been revoked. She'd wanted to see my face when she told me.

She was the absolute worst. I wanted her to go cordless–bungee jumping.

Gretchen came back, looking frazzled. She wasn't supposed to get stressed, and I felt guilty. "I got in touch with everyone. They're headed over to the library now."

It wouldn't take long for them to arrive. "Do you want to head over there and I'll finish up here with Nick? I'll join you as soon as I can." I put both my hands on her shoulders. "It's going to be okay."

She gave me a watery smile. "I know."

I didn't think that either one of us believed it.

But even if I didn't believe it, I had to find a way to make it be true. Gretchen left and I made my way over to Nick.

There were so many men who would have been oblivious to the fact that I was all hopped up on anger and vengeance, but he immediately asked, "What's wrong?"

"What's wrong is that Brenda the Bad Witch came to tell me that we just lost our biggest sponsor for the festival."

"I take it that's bad."

"Very, very bad."

"What can I do to help?" he asked, and I could tell that he meant it. His sincerity made some of my bloodlust subside.

"You're already doing it. You're here. But I have a lot of work to do now and have to figure some stuff out with the committee, so we need to finish up."

"Sure thing. And my offer to help stands. Just let me know."

We went up to the checkout lane and I handed my things to McKayla. She greeted me cheerfully but didn't make eye contact with Nick at all. She was maybe taking the "leave him alone" thing a little far, but he didn't seem to notice.

"Where are you going to find a new sponsor?" he asked me. "Do you have someone who can step in?"

"There's no other company here in town that has that kind of resources," I said. "We're going to have to make a list of companies we might call. Maybe some that have employees that live here."

Two weeks. We had to find a new sponsor in two weeks.

"I really am happy to help," he said. "I could make a donation."

"It's okay," I told him. He didn't have the money we needed, and he wasn't familiar with the nearby businesses. "We'll figure something out."

McKayla scanned our things quickly and said, "Do you want me to put this on your account?"

"Yes, please."

Nick was in the middle of taking his credit card out of his wallet and looked at me, confused.

"It's fine," I said. "Your publicist is taking care of it. Plus, this way they'll deliver everything to the house."

"Are you sure?" he asked.

McKayla put our bags in a cart and wheeled it off to the back to get it ready for delivery. I was about to tell Nick that we had to go when I glanced up to see my brother standing at the cash register, glaring at both of us, his arms crossed across his chest.

Uh-oh. What was this about?

"Nick Haddon, this is my brother, Heath Wagner. Heath, this is Nick. The actor."

Nick held out his hand and said it was nice to meet him, but Heath didn't respond. He just kept glaring.

"Gretchen wanted those marshmallows," I told him defensively. "That was not my fault."

"Buying someone's groceries?" he asked me sarcastically.

Oh. It was about that. "You don't understand the situation. This is all covered. His publicist has already deposited the money up front and if we go over that amount, she'll send more."

Nick winced, and I wondered what that was about.

Heath didn't seem convinced, though. "You shouldn't let men like him take advantage of you."

I probably shouldn't tell my brother that I wouldn't really mind all that much if Nick tried to take advantage of me. "I'm not. It's fine. You can turn off your overprotectiveness."

Heath continued to glare, but after a few moments, he finally headed back to the bakery. It was what he really loved—baking. He'd even gone to culinary school and was excited to use his skills here in the store. I didn't think he loved the managerial aspect of running this place, but he was the only one who could do it until my dad was back on his feet.

McKayla returned, giving me a drop-off time for the groceries.

Nick picked up a pack of gum. "Sorry, I just realized I'm out of gum. Can we grab this, too?"

"That's why they keep it next to the register," McKayla told him, finally being her usual bubbly self. "It's an impulse buy."

"I can pay for this," Nick said, getting his card out again.

"Oh, I'm sorry," she said. "The card reader is down. We're having internet issues. Do you have any cash?"

"I never carry cash," he said.

"It's fine," I told him. I grabbed a dollar out of my purse and put it on the counter. "We should go."

I said goodbye to McKayla and handed Nick his gum. He offered me a stick, but I shook my head. He popped a piece in his mouth and began to chew.

"You and your brother look alike," he observed as we walked out of the store and headed back toward the diner to get my car.

I supposed we did—we were both tall and had the same light brown hair and dark brown eyes, but I felt like that's where the similarities ended. He looked more like our dad and I took after our mom. "A little bit," I said.

"Is Heath short for Heathcliff?"

"Yes. Our mom loves books and we're named after two of her favorite characters from literature. Heathcliff from *Wuthering Heights* and Jane from *Jane Eyre*."

He nodded. "Your brother doesn't seem to like me."

"It's not you. I used to date someone. Teddy Newcastle. He thought being part of the Newcastle family and my boyfriend entitled him to take what he wanted from the store and that he didn't have to pay. He said it was no big deal. I always covered for him and paid for it later."

Nick looked a little sick. "Like you did for me today."

"It's not the same thing. We have an arrangement."

"Not for the gum. I'm going to pay you back."

"That's not necessary," I told him. "It's just a dollar."

He shook his head like he disagreed with me, but he didn't immediately respond. "Are you going to tell me about Brenda? And why she sounds that way?"

"Like she's been sucking on helium? Or is about to become the newest Chipmunk? It's because she thinks that men will find that voice sexy, and she's been doing it for so long I'm not sure she even remembers how to speak normally."

"I meant more of the anger part of it."

How much had he overheard? "Brenda Schumacher is what would happen if someone tried to make evil from concentrate but forgot to add water."

It looked like Nick was trying not to smile. "I'm getting the feeling that there's more of a story here."

"You mean other than being all pretty on the outside but an evil succubus underneath? She should eat some makeup. Maybe that would help beautify her ugly insides. Or, like, get some Botox injections for her heart."

"I'm fairly certain that if you did that, it would poison her and she'd die."

I shrugged one shoulder. "Either way."

He said, "I feel like I've wandered into some centuries-old feud and I don't even know what the rules are."

"You're on my side, and you should stay away from Brenda Schumacher so that she doesn't eat your soul." I suddenly could see how this might all come across to someone who didn't have the whole backstory, and it felt important to me that Nick understand. "I'm probably coming across, um, not so great here, but she was really awful to me growing up. I mean, as kids we weren't really friends, but we managed to leave each other alone. But then . . ." I realized how I'd have to briefly relive the beginning of where our animosity began. "Everyone our age was in love with Teddy Newcastle."

"The mayor?" He sounded alarmed.

"No, that's Wilfred Newcastle. Teddy is his nephew and heir to the Newcastle fortune. Your stereotypical golden boy. He dated Brenda for a long time and then they broke up. A few weeks later he asked me to prom. Me. I wasn't the girl who got asked to things like that. I'd always had a crush on him, so of course I said yes. That's when Brenda lost her ever-loving mind. She spent our last two years of high school doing whatever she could to ruin my reputation and mental health. She wanted me to break up with Teddy. She bullied me relentlessly—in school, online, anyplace that she could. It's hard to explain just how terrible she was. I never would have gotten through it if it hadn't been for Gretchen. She was my rock. I would do anything for that woman."

He nodded. "Did Brenda ever succeed in getting you and Teddy to break up?"

"No. At least, not at first. Teddy and I dated for a couple of years, and then I went off to Miami University and he went to Columbia. We did the long-distance thing."

"From your tone, I'm guessing that didn't work out."

"Our junior year of college, I found out that he'd been cheating on me for years with Brenda and a large assortment of other women. He ghosted me for a long time after I demanded an explanation. But then, weeks later, he sent me a text that he was dumping me because he had started dating a senator's daughter and he had big plans for his life. He said, 'Sorry, babe, but I have to be serious about my future. I need a girlfriend with connections.' I was devastated. I honestly thought we were going to get married."

"I want to say I'm sorry because you were hurt—but I'm also not sorry, because I'm glad you didn't marry him. You deserve better than that."

That was sweet, but I didn't let myself respond to his kind words. Better to stay focused. Anger was good for that. "I guess I got my revenge. The girl dumped Teddy, and Brenda's been dating Teddy's uncle. The disgraced mayor. And I would like to point out that they were dating when the embezzlement scandal went down. People suspect she might have been involved."

"People or you?"

"People!" I insisted. "Fine, me. And Gretchen."

He chuckled. "I have to admit that earlier I looked the mayor up. He's older than I expected."

"Well, what he lacks in looks and youth, Brenda more than makes up for with her total lack of a soul."

We arrived at my car and I unlocked it. I was glad there was an automobile between us, because part of me wanted to go over and hug him tightly. Which was an inappropriate impulse.

To thank him? Because I was feeling vulnerable and wanted to be comforted?

Because I felt like he wasn't judging me for what had happened with Teddy, as so many other people in our town had?

Or was it that I just wanted an excuse to wrap my arms around that broad chest of his?

I settled on using my words. "Thanks. You know, it's kind of refreshing to be able to tell this story to someone who doesn't already know every intimate detail. It's been a long time since that's happened."

"Trust me, I get it. You live in a small town and everyone knows your business. The whole world is my small town. Everybody knows my name and what's happening in my life, and it's really hard to keep things private."

I could only imagine. At least in college, I'd been able to escape into anonymity. I had my friends, I socialized, but I had mostly lived my life quietly.

Nick had never been able to do that.

Thanks to his parents, it had never even been his choice. I got into the car, unsure of what I was feeling at the moment. Sympathy? Concern?

Something else?

It was difficult to tell with this veneer of rage that still coated my other emotions.

"What's the plan now?" he asked.

For a second I thought he meant with Teddy or Brenda, but I realized he meant in this actual moment. "I'll drop you back off at my place, and then I need to go to an emergency committee meeting at the library to figure out what to do next."

"I can come with you. Not to the meeting, but I can hang out in the library until you're finished. It should save you some time."

"Okay," I said. That was thoughtful of him. "Thanks."

We both climbed into the car, and I might have slammed my door shut harder than necessary. Stupid Brenda.

As I started up the engine, Nick asked, "Did you really date someone named Teddy?"

He was not going to tease me out of my bad mood. "According to E! Online, you dated someone named Peaches."

"It was just for the publicity. Not a real romance."

"Turned out mine wasn't, either."

He kept quiet for a few beats and then said, "I have to admit that I'm curious as to what's running through your head right now."

"I was thinking assault should be legal if the other person is a jerk."

"You could always run for office and make that a new law."

"I should run for office," I agreed with him. "Maybe I could become the new mayor and kicking that birch Brenda Schumacher out of town would be my main campaign promise."

I'd at least get Gretchen's vote.

"Did you say *birch*?"

"Yes. I don't like using the other word to describe women, even women like Brenda that deserve it—but I did call her that once in a text, and my phone autocorrected it to *birch* and it sort of stuck."

He smiled at me. "Can I offer you some advice?"

"Sure."

"I have to deal with a lot of infuriating people. Temperamental artists and demanding executives. The best thing to do is to calm your body down with deep breathing. My therapist taught me this technique called Four, Seven, Eight. You inhale through your nose for four seconds. Then you hold your breath for seven seconds and exhale for eight seconds."

"And that works?" I asked skeptically.

"Try it. Here. Breathe in." He counted to four and said, "Hold for seven." He counted while I held my breath and then counted to eight when I let the air out. Eight seconds was a long time to exhale, but I did it. We went through the breathing exercise three more times until I pulled into the library parking lot.

"Did that help?" he asked as we walked toward the building.

"Strangely enough, I think it did." I was definitely feeling less stabby than I had a couple of minutes ago.

"Good. And once you're calm, it'll be easier to forget about Brenda. You can be the bigger person."

"That shouldn't be too hard, considering that technically she's not a person."

When we got into the library, he headed toward the fiction section and began perusing the new releases. I put my bag down behind the circulation counter and checked to see if there were any messages for me. I noticed him choosing a book and making himself comfortable in one of the chairs.

I was holding my breath, but it was for a lot longer than seven seconds. Because him sitting there reading? Unbelievably hot. It was honestly one of the sexiest things I'd ever seen.

There was something seriously wrong with me. When that man held inanimate objects, I was ready to throw my whole life away for him.

I hurried over to the meeting room and found the committee waiting for me. They'd been talking but went silent when I entered the room.

"Seems like I have everyone's attention," I said.

Phyllis, our senior citizen liaison and a woman without any sort of filter, said, "Yes, we were just talking about you, so now that you're here, we obviously stopped."

Connie looked guilty, as did Gretchen. Dee-Dee was getting some water from the dispenser and seemed unexpectedly chill today. She was typically like if a Caps Lock key had been turned into a real person. She was a few years older than me. Michelle, a middle-aged mom, still had her coat on—she was usually stressed out and cold no matter how warm we made things for her. Phyllis was looking at her phone, complaining that the internet was too slow and the font was too small.

I wondered what they had been saying about me but knew my best friend would fill me in later.

"We know everything," Phyllis informed me. "And I'm trying to look up businesses that we can contact to find a new sponsor. We are not going to let the festival be canceled."

"Good. I feel exactly the same way," I said. I wasn't going to let Brenda win.

Dee-Dee sat in her seat next to Gretchen and said, "Can we talk about that in a minute? I feel like we need to have a discussion about Nick Haddon."

"What about him?" I asked, feeling very uneasy. Now I knew exactly what they'd been talking about earlier. "Like how we plan on utilizing him to publicize the festival?"

"Girl, no. I meant we need to discuss what is going on with you two," Dee-Dee responded with a smile. "Obviously, the festival is our number one priority, and we will a hundred percent talk about it and figure it out—but right now all anyone wants to discuss is how you've been making googly eyes at him all day."

"I have not!" I responded indignantly.

Michelle spoke up. "I have to be honest, I don't really get the hype."

At that, Gretchen turned so quickly in her seat that it was miraculous she didn't knock something over. "A, he's literally the hottest man alive, and B, please refer to A."

"I'm telling Heath you said that," I told her.

"Not if you want to keep breathing, you won't."

Dee-Dee nodded. "Nick Haddon is s-e-x-y."

"You can spell that again," Phyllis agreed. "If I was fifty years younger, he'd be in trouble."

"Shh," I told them. "He's sitting in the library right now. I need you to be respectful to the movie star."

"Why are you only looking at me?" Phyllis protested.

"Because you're the only one I'm talking to." Everybody else would behave themselves.

Mostly.

"And you and Nick Haddon fell in love at first sight," Connie said with a sigh.

"Wait, what? That didn't happen."

Gretchen didn't let me explain. "It's not love. They're just attracted to each other and the more time they spend chatting, the more they'll realize how much they like one another as people, too. They'll banter and laugh and enjoy each other's company, and things will progress from there. They're not in love. Not yet, anyway."

"You are not helping," I told her.

"I wasn't trying to," she said pointedly. "You have to admit that you're at least attracted to the guy."

"Nope." Maybe if we'd been alone, I might have been more forthcoming, but I wasn't interested in sharing with the class.

"It must be nice to be so delusional," she responded.

"It isn't bad," Dee-Dee said with a grin. "Delusion's always been my sweet spot. What I do know is that I'd be all under that guy."

"Don't you mean 'all over'?" Phyllis asked.

"Yes to both."

Gretchen said, "My guess is that, at least for now, the only thing Nick Haddon's getting under is Jane's skin."

"The man eats seaweed. Please be serious." Did I sound as annoyed as I felt? He was not under my skin.

Was. Not.

But whether my annoyance was from Gretchen always being right or lingering feelings from my Brenda encounter, I wasn't sure.

"Relationships are about compromises. Let the man eat his sad green squares and you can introduce him to the wonder of chocolate chip cookies. Also, you do realize that you just proved my point, right?" she asked.

Connie stood up, preventing me from arguing with Gretchen further. "I think love at first sight is a real thing."

"See?" Phyllis said, pointing her thumb at Connie. "This is what happens when you let kids read too many YA books."

They all started arguing and were getting louder and louder. "He is going to hear you!" I hissed, but no one was listening to me, and they kept noisily discussing whether love at first sight was a real thing.

Then my worst fear came true.

"Do you ladies mind if I join you?" Nick asked as he opened the door.

My heart jumped up into my throat, making it hard for me to breathe.

Oh no . . . this was going to be bad.

CHAPTER EIGHT

There were so many ways this could go wrong, and I couldn't expect these women to behave. I had no way to mentally prepare or head off every inappropriate thing they might say.

Nick might be on his own here.

"I thought I heard my name," he said.

"You did!" Phyllis said. "We were just talking about you, so now that you're here, we—"

"We were talking about the festival!" I quickly interrupted so she wouldn't pull the same thing she had with me. "And finding a sponsor."

Dee-Dee was sitting straight up in her chair, beaming at Nick like he was personally responsible for the invention of chocolate. "Please join us! I'm Dee-Dee."

He walked over to shake her hand and that was it—the others swarmed him.

Gretchen came over to stand next to me, sporting a knowing grin that made me uncomfortable. Who knew what she'd say in front of him?

"What's with the smile?" I asked. Better to let her get it out now than risk the chance of her making comments to Nick.

"I can't just be happy for no reason?"

"I think we both know you can't."

She shrugged, not answering right away. We both watched as Nick introduced himself to each member of the committee, the way he instantly charmed all of them, how they hung on his every word.

See? He didn't just have that effect on me. He had it on everyone, expertly casting some kind of spell that made all of us feel enthralled.

"There are a lot of pirates circling that booty," Gretchen observed. "Are you sure you don't want to get in there and stake your claim?"

"My 'claim.'" I scoffed. "As if. But speaking of pirates, he's probably got the morals of one."

"You mean like he makes people walk the plank?"

Again with the obtuseness. "I meant he's probably known for his wenching."

"Wenching?"

"You know, he has a different woman in every port."

"Do you know that for a fact?"

"How would I know?" I asked her. "No, Nick Haddon and I have not had the all-important 'how many women are you currently hooking up with' conversation. Because I don't plan on being another notch on his belt. I've seen the stuff on the internet. All the women he's dated." I had never been a short-term-fling kind of person. I craved the stability and connection of a relationship.

Obviously, Nick was not the kind of man who could give me that, and despite Gretchen saying I was the delusional one, I thought I was thinking pretty clearly. There was only one way for all of this to end and it was smart to protect myself.

"You're not really giving him the benefit of the doubt," she said. "You don't know if he's seeing anyone else or how many notches he has. Gossip is just that—gossip."

"You mean like how you all decided that I was in love with him?"

"Something like that. And you're saying that our speculation isn't true. So why do you think that people who make up stuff for a living have the inside track as to what's really going on in Nick Haddon's life?"

She probably had a fair point.

As I thought about that, Gretchen said, "He really is like the Pied Piper or something, leading all the rats with his magic flute. You want to tell me again how he's not attractive?"

"The way he looks at apples is sexy." The words were out of my mouth before I could stop them.

"What?"

"Nothing." Was my face all red? I couldn't tell. I kind of felt like I'd been flushed most of the day—either from being around Nick or fighting with Brenda.

"Something's definitely changed," she mused. "Do you want to tell me what it is, or should I just loudly guess?"

I wanted to tell her. I couldn't help it. I knew she'd be biased, but I needed another opinion. Plus, I'd never been any good at keeping secrets from her, even when I'd wanted to. "He's different than I thought he'd be. He's really . . . nice. Funny. Smart. Intuitive." Honestly, those were the traits I was looking for in a partner. Admitting those things was almost worse than just saying he was hot, like she wanted me to.

But Gretchen didn't seem to notice. "And?"

"Fine. He's really attractive."

She gave me a "that wasn't so hard, was it?" look and then said, "Welcome to the club. We meet on Tuesdays. And I know you think I'm making a lot of assumptions, but I do think he's interested in you, too."

Apparently, the confessing wasn't over. "Don't overreact to what I'm about to tell you." I glanced around us to make sure the coast was clear and then said, "He told me that he likes me. I mean, there wasn't more context to it, so I'm not really sure what he meant exactly, and I haven't asked him, obviously, but he said it and now I don't know what to do with it. I mean, who just says, 'I like you'? Like we're in kindergarten or something. It's weird. Right?"

Gretchen's eyes just got wider and wider, her mouth turning into a large O. She looked like a volcano about to burst.

"It's happening!" she whispered. "I knew it! I knew it, I knew it, I knew it. I knew it!"

"Are you done?"

"Not yet. I knew it! There. Done. This is meant to be. You are so going to get together."

No one could jump to illogical conclusions faster than my best friend. "I know it may appear that way—"

"—and is that way," she helpfully added.

"But I don't even know how to interpret what he said. It could have just been a platonic thing. As in, he likes me as a friend and host of the place where he's staying. I don't want to read into it."

"I think you should completely read into it. Like one of those library-book-marathon things we used to do as kids. Read into all of it! What does the poor man have to do to convince you?"

I couldn't believe we were having this conversation. "Part of me is afraid that this is all just an act. It's like we all forget that he's an actor, and he knows exactly what to do and what to say and in what tone to make himself seem . . ."

"Sexy," she said.

I ignored her. "It's more than that. His expressions are always . . . and his voice is just . . ."

"Sexy."

At that, I groaned. I couldn't explain to her what I was thinking, because my brain hadn't had time to figure out what felt off to me. But this wasn't just as straightforward as she seemed to believe. "There's something else there. Something that's not quite right."

Gretchen said, "Do you think he's being fake?"

"No, I don't think that's it. He's not fake." That seemed like one thing I felt sure of—that he was genuine. Although I had nothing to base that on.

"So we agree that he's not fake and therefore he's not acting when he's with you, and you're just responding to the real him and you like him, too."

"I didn't say that."

"You didn't have to. Not yet, anyway. He's got some time." Gretchen left to join Nick and the rest of the committee, and I kept mulling things over in my head. I still didn't know what specifically about my situation was bothering me. The whole thing, probably. There were so many reasons to steer very clear of Nick Haddon.

And then he smiled at me, like we were sharing some kind of private inside joke, and my organs melted into a pile of goo and I forgot my own name.

So it took me a second to realize that Michelle was calling me. "Jane, do you think we should get started?"

"Oh. Yes. Sure." We all sat down and I noticed Dee-Dee jostling with Phyllis a bit in order to claim a seat next to Nick. They ended up sitting on either side of him. Our chairs were arranged in a circle, and he was directly across from me. It had probably been an accident, but it felt intentional.

Everything about Nick Haddon was worrisome.

And dangerous.

He was like a stick of dynamite with biceps.

"We're all aware of what Newcastle Paper has done, and I think we agree that canceling the festival is not an option." They all nodded; Phyllis and Michelle made sounds of assent. "So we need a new sponsor. Any ideas?"

In between wishing for bad things to happen to Brenda Schumacher, I had been trying to come up with another company who could match Newcastle Paper's promised funds.

I was coming up blank.

Apparently, so was everyone else in the group.

This was not good.

Nick raised his hand.

"You can just talk," I told him.

He smiled sheepishly and then said, "One of the things I noticed today was how many small businesses you have here in town. Would it be possible to get them to donate?"

There was a reason we never took this path. I told Nick the dollar amount we had to raise. "Even if every local business gave us a thousand dollars, it wouldn't be enough. And a lot of them couldn't swing even that amount."

"You could see what they could offer and then keep looking for a bigger sponsor to cover the rest of the budget. I've worked on movies where they've essentially done that."

Nick said it like it would be easy, but I knew it was going to be a lot of work. "That's a good idea," I told him. "What else can we do?"

We brainstormed as a group, coming up with ideas for how we could possibly raise money. There was that old saying about there being no such thing as a bad idea, but it turned out that wasn't true. There were lots of ideas pitched that wouldn't work / were sketchy / were possibly illegal.

Dee-Dee did have one that sounded interesting—selling photo ops where Nick would pose with ticketed fans at the festival. He said he'd be up for it, and I made a note on my phone.

Gretchen turned to me and mouthed, "Kissing booth."

I just shook my head at her. If she didn't know why that was a bad idea, I would explain it to her later in private.

As the meeting started to wind down, Nick's suggestion still seemed to be the best one to raise money in a short amount of time. Especially since we needed that money now and couldn't afford to gamble on whether enough fans would buy tickets to get a photo with Nick.

And, as Nick had pointed out, it might be easier to find a bigger corporate sponsor if the amount we asked for was smaller.

The group agreed with me. I tried to suppress a sigh because I knew it was all going to be on me to make this happen.

A half hour later I ended the meeting and told everyone I'd be in touch with an update when I had one. Gretchen asked Nick if he would help put the chairs and tables away. That seemed very clever of her, and I was just about to settle in to watch the show when Phyllis said, "Jane, would you mind walking me to my car? It rained a bit."

"Sure!" Weather in Ohio was always unpredictable. The locals always joked that if you didn't like the weather, just wait a few minutes. I had escorted Phyllis to her car before on rainy or snowy days. She was worried about slipping.

When we got outside the ground was definitely still wet. She slid her arm through mine, and I helped her carefully down the steps and walked toward her car. "Did I ever tell you about my first husband?"

I knew Phyllis had been married before, but it was before I'd been born. "I don't think so."

"My first husband, we had this overwhelming physical connection. I confused it for love, but we didn't really like each other as people. My second husband was the opposite—I thought I had learned from my mistakes and I married a nice man that I liked spending time with. But I wasn't in love with him; we didn't have that spark. But my Mikey"— her current husband—"he's perfect for me. We don't have everything in common, but we like being together. I'm curious about his interests and he's curious about mine. And the physical connection!"

I leaned over to open her car door. I did not need those kinds of details. "You don't have to tell me everything," I said.

She got in slowly and settled into the driver's seat. I probably should have asked why she was sharing that information with me, but I already knew. Everybody in this town thought they had some sort of heaven-mandated calling to interfere in one another's lives. Better to send her on her way than prolong this any further. "Drive safe!"

She narrowed her gaze at me and said, "I know you didn't ask me for advice, but I'm old enough that I get to give it whenever I feel like it. That Teddy Newcastle was never right for you. I know he hurt you, and it feels like you've closed yourself off ever since then."

I bristled at her words, but I couldn't say anything to defend myself, because deep down? I knew she was right. "I'm not trying to close myself off. I just need to find someone more my speed. A nice man. Someone solid and reliable." I hadn't exactly been looking for it, but it had been all too easy to neglect my social life out of fear that I'd be hurt again.

"Don't settle," she told me fiercely. "Maybe this movie star's not right for you. But swing for the fences, Jane. You never know."

I could only nod, then closed her car door. She started it up and drove away slowly.

This was very bad. Now it wasn't just Gretchen trying to hook me up with Nick; I had no idea how many townspeople she'd roped into her scheme.

I really hoped that no one had told my mother.

Gretchen and Nick came out of the library, and I didn't like the two of them talking. Because who knew what Gretchen would tell him? It occurred to me that I hadn't told her yet how I'd confessed the truth to Nick about watching him. I should probably do that soon, before she found out from him.

At least she wasn't right about everything. He hadn't run off once I'd told him.

I glanced at the library doors. Connie would stay to keep the library running until closing time. I felt a bit guilty for leaving her, but I was glad I had the rest of my day free. There was going to be a lot to do if I was going to save this festival.

"Okay, we'll talk soon," I said to Gretchen. I stood close to Nick like I was a sheepdog who would herd him away from danger.

"Before you go, Nick, my husband and I are celebrating our anniversary in a couple of days. We'd love to have you join us."

I had honestly forgotten about the anniversary party. It was like it had fallen out of my brain. I was a bad sister-in-law / friend.

But why on earth was she inviting Nick? "What are you doing?" I mumbled to her.

"Us a favor," she whispered back.

Apparently oblivious to our whispered exchange, Nick said, "I'd love to go."

"Excellent. It's cocktail dress and starts at seven. You can go with Jane."

"Thanks for the invitation."

"Of course. You're doing us such a big *favor*," she said, emphasizing the last word for my benefit, "that you're basically like family. See you there!"

Before she could make any more of her oh-so-not-subtle comments or invite herself to be a bridesmaid at our wedding, I said, "Shouldn't you be getting home? And resting?"

"I should," she agreed all too cheerfully. "See you soon, Nick!" She waved and started walking toward her car.

"Just a second," I told him and followed after her. When we were out of earshot, I said, "What was that? How is inviting him a favor for us?"

"Duh, now we all get to see him in a suit. And I got you a date, which is specifically a favor for you. Don't worry about it—we'll have a fun time, and I will definitely include this story and claim full responsibility for getting you two together in my matron of honor speech at your wedding. You're welcome." She kissed me on the cheek and practically skipped the rest of the way to her car.

I felt guilty that I had basically forgotten about the party, but I could only fit so much shame into my current schedule. I knew her mom and my mother had spent a lot of time working on it together. I had been looking forward to an event that I hadn't had to help plan, but I didn't think there'd be much relaxing with Nick there with me.

Did this mean I was going on a date with Nick Haddon?

CHAPTER NINE

I just wouldn't think about it. There wasn't going to be a date of any kind, and I had other things to concern myself with.

Important things.

I couldn't recall any of them at the moment, but I knew they mattered.

"We should go," I said when I rejoined Nick, and we walked to my car together. I got in quickly and started up the engine. As soon as he closed his door, I accidentally peeled out.

"Sorry," I said, willing myself to calm down and drive better. The festival wouldn't matter if I crashed Nick Haddon into a telephone pole.

He said, "I want to help."

There were so many things that could be in reference to. The anniversary party? Our pseudo-date?

My bad driving?

"Help with what?" I finally asked.

"The sponsors for the festival."

Oh, that. I breathed a tiny sigh of relief. "I told you, you're already helping."

"I can do more. I literally have nothing else going on at the moment. I am all yours. Please use me however you'd like."

That put some images in my head that were not conducive to my resolution to drive well.

"I think calling up small businesses was a good idea," I said when I could speak again. "I'm honestly kind of dreading it because I know how much work it's going to be and I'll have to do it alone."

"Why? You had a roomful of people wanting to help."

"Normally, they'd be getting paid but with the government getting shut down, they're all volunteering. And they have so much going on in their personal lives already. Dee-Dee is taking care of her elderly mother. Gretchen is supposed to be taking it easy"—and not spending all of her time coming up with ways for me to date him—"Connie has school and Michelle has a teenage daughter with some mental health issues, and Phyllis's oldest son had to move back home with his kids. I'm the one who has the free time. I can take this on. They would do the same for me if our situations were reversed. We take care of our own."

"Now I'm definitely going to help you out with this, and I'm not taking no for an answer." There was a long pause and then he said, "It must be nice to have people in your life that care about you the way you all do for each other."

"Sometimes it's annoying because they want to interfere out of some misguided notion of what's best for me, but I know deep down it does come from a place of caring." It took me a second to realize the implication of his words. He was saying he didn't have something like that in his life, which I found hard to believe. "You must have people who care about you."

I glanced at his profile as he looked straight ahead, watching the road. "I have people who depend on me for their livelihoods and parents who may get in touch with me from time to time when they remember that I exist, but no, I don't have what you have."

My fingers flexed against the steering wheel as I was struck with the impulse to reach over and take his hand to comfort him. "I'm sorry. That seems so sad."

"I don't need your pity," he said in a tone gruffer than any he'd used before with me.

"It's not pity. I just wish . . . I don't know. That I could share my friends and family with you so that you'd know what it felt like."

I felt his gaze on me and I didn't dare look at him for fear of what I'd see in his eyes. "I think I'm starting to get the idea."

That made my heart speed up, and the desire to reach out and touch him was overwhelming. I wrapped my fingers around the steering wheel tighter and said, "Has anyone told you about the Amish communities nearby? Maybe one of the days while you're here, you can take a trip out there and do some exploring. You might enjoy that."

Yep. Supersmooth transition and not at all awkward.

Taking the hint, he asked some questions about other things to do in and around Patience, and we chatted about it all the way home.

When we got inside the house, I wasn't sure what to do with him. I definitely had a sense of obligation to entertain him, but that was ridiculous. He was a grown man.

We went into the kitchen and I noted that Heath had let himself in and had unpacked our groceries for us. That was very thoughtful of him. I showed Nick where everything was kept. "My home is your home. Please help yourself to whatever you need."

"I'm not great at cooking," he admitted.

"Me neither," I told him. "Mostly because you have to pay attention when you do it, and I always have this music running through my head and I get distracted and start writing down notes on a paper towel and then whoops! The eggs are burned."

"Maybe we can try a couple recipes together. I'll watch the oven," he said.

I didn't like the little domestic scene he was conjuring up in my head. I walked across the room so that the kitchen table was between us. That felt safest. "I should probably start working on that list," I told him, still feeling awkward.

He showed me his phone's screen. "I pulled up a list on the website under the Chamber of Commerce section. It took a long time, though. Why is your internet so slow?"

I quickly explained the fiber-optic situation to him. "My understanding is that there's not much more that needs to be done, but there's no one in charge right now who can get it finished."

"Okay, then I'll continue to use my Stone Age Wi-Fi, and I thought I could expand the search. Contact some small businesses in towns nearby who would benefit from increased tourism here in Patience due to the festival."

"Oh. That's actually a really good idea. You seem to be full of those today."

"Thanks. People don't generally see that part of me."

"Why not?"

He shrugged one shoulder. "No one wants me to contribute. My job is to sit there and say the words they tell me to say and look pretty."

My first thought was if that was his job, I'd bet he was employee of the month.

My second was, again, how sad it all seemed. To not be valued for his mind, not encouraged to speak up and give his opinion, to stay quiet and play a part.

I didn't want to be someone else who discouraged him, but he had to know that it was a lot. "This kind of stuff can get overwhelming fast. It can make your life feel like one big *have to*. There's always so many things I have to do that I don't get to, I don't know, stop and smell the roses."

"You should do that. Roses smell really good."

I smiled.

"It's easy to say," he said. "I get it, probably more than anyone. My life is a big *have to* as well. But I'm trying to find ways to carve out time for me and the things I want to do. Speaking of, what's something you don't get to do for yourself very often that you enjoy?"

Several things flashed through my mind, and all of it just seemed like more work. I'd have loved to sit and work on my music, but a sense of weariness made my limbs feel heavy. I didn't have the energy to do anything at the moment. I just wanted to unwind, even if I didn't have time for it. "I really enjoy taking bubble baths."

Something dark and unreadable flickered in his eyes, his jaw clenching tightly for a moment, before his face relaxed. "You should do that. Take the night off. Everything will be waiting for you here in the morning."

I found myself nodding and saying, "Okay." I wasn't the kind of person who liked delaying things until later, but it was like someone was giving me permission to take care of myself, and I needed it.

He followed after me as I walked to the stairs. We stood at the base together, and it almost felt like the end of a date or something.

I folded my arms and tried to fight off the discomfort I was experiencing.

Also because I still wanted to touch him, and that was the best way I could think of to keep my hands to myself.

He shifted his weight from one foot to the other, almost like he felt uneasy, too. He said, "So, I'll see you in the morning. And don't stress about work tonight. Remember that now you have me here to help you. We'll find sponsors in no time."

"Thanks." Still, we stood there. He put his hands in his pockets and I wondered if he was doing it for the same reason I was keeping my arms crossed. "Okay, so yeah. See you tomorrow."

I walked up the stairs slowly, and I could feel his gaze on me the whole way up. When I got to the second floor, I couldn't help myself. I turned to look, but he was gone.

I ignored the sense of disappointment I felt. I went into my room, shutting the door behind me. I gathered up the things I needed for a bath, my mind completely focused on Nick. What was he going to do tonight? Should I be down there, talking to him? Working on this project?

No, he was right. I needed this break before I tackled everything else that had to be taken care of. I slid out of my clothes and into my bathrobe, grabbed my supplies, and went into the hallway and headed toward the second-floor bathroom. I locked the door and started the bath.

I poured in the bubbles and felt the water, adjusting it to the right temperature. I slipped my robe off and stepped into the tub. As the warm water continued to rise, topped off by frothy bubbles, I ran the events of the day through my mind. This felt like a perfect way to cap things off after my marathon twenty-four hours.

But all I could think about was Nick and how I had enjoyed being around him.

Maybe it hadn't been a date, and there had been some definite bad things that happened, but the day I'd spent with him had been one of the best days I could remember.

And that was solely due to him.

～

I woke up in my bed, wrapped up in my bathrobe and shivering. I remembered lying down, wanting to rest my eyes for a second, and now here I was. Patches was meowing loudly and sadly outside my door. I could barely open my eyes. I picked up my phone, which I'd forgotten to charge and was now nearly dead. I groaned when I realized that I hadn't set my alarm and if I didn't get out the door in the next twenty minutes, I was going to be late to pick up Gretchen. I headed to the bathroom, nearly getting knocked over by my cat. I used the facilities, making sure to brush my teeth and put on deodorant.

Patches meowed again when I returned to my bedroom. "I'll feed you in a minute!" I told her, but she was displeased with me.

I got dressed quickly and put my hair up in a ponytail. As I put my hand on the doorknob, the memory that Nick was here in my house struck me. I rushed back over to my dresser and put on some mascara and lipstick just in case.

Then I added the teeniest bit of eyeliner and blush. For reasons. Like, that I might run into him.

He might still be sleeping, although Patches's hunger whining was enough to wake the dead.

I hurried downstairs with Patches attempting to dart under my feet the whole way. I made it down safely and went into the kitchen to grab her some food. She didn't stop complaining until her bowl was full.

"Spoiled brat," I said affectionately, scritching the top of her head as she purred with delight because she had finally been fed.

I headed for the front door but stopped short when I saw Nick in the living room.

He was doing yoga.

Shirtless.

Wow.

To quote Connie, *Oh my Zeus.*

My heart palpitations weren't my fault. I was genetically predisposed to the heart attack I was about to have.

John Williams's "Scherzo for Motorcycle and Orchestra" from *Raiders of the Lost Ark* played loudly in my head, my pulse keeping time to the beat.

Nick noticed me, frozen in the front hallway, and gave me one of his blinding smiles that had probably cost a small fortune and an army of dentists to create. "Good morning, Jane."

He straightened up and walked over to me. The closer he got, the more my heart thudded wildly out of control.

Nick stood in front of me with a fine sheen of sweat covering his very well-defined chest.

It was weird that I wanted to lick him, right?

"What are you up to today?" he asked.

Blood was rushing through my ears and it took my hazy brain a second to process what he had just said. "I, uh, have to, um . . ." He was so distracting.

So. Distracting.

Finish your sentence, some still-functioning part of my brain reminded me. "I have to drive Gretchen to an appointment. Heath has this shipment coming in this morning and so I said I'd take her, and yeah."

That was good, wasn't it? Coherent?

And in English?

I seriously hoped so.

"I'm doing some filming this morning with the documentary crew. Just so that you'll know where I am at all times."

I had been thinking about how, if I took two steps forward, I could press my lips to his throat and see if his skin was as salty as I was assuming it was. His words pierced through my fantasy and I shook my head, as if I could force my imagination to behave. "You, um, don't have to check in with me."

"Yes, I do. That's part of your deal, isn't it? Needing to know my whereabouts at all times?" He was teasing me again, but the word *magnificent* just kept looping through my brain. It was like that word had been invented solely to describe his chest. "I also realized that I don't have your number. I should get it. Just in case."

How many hours a day did he work out to look like this? I wanted to know his workout routine. Correction, I wanted to *watch* his workout routine. You know, for science.

I had once judged him for sacrificing carbs in service of this and it turned out that I was very, very wrong. Giving up sugar was a hundred percent the right decision. "Just in case what?"

That's how far gone I was. I was just echoing his words back at him.

"Just in case someone grabs me and forces me to be Zeus in a re-creation of an *Olympus High* set." Again, teasing, but I couldn't pay very close attention to his words.

Not with so much gloriously sculpted muscle on display.

"Yes, I can see that there's a high possibility of that happening." I had been aiming for sarcasm, but instead it came out all breathy and like I was agreeing with him, mostly because I wouldn't have minded playing a little Greek gods with him.

I was able to tell my hand to give him the phone, although it wanted to disobey and run my fingers over his abs instead.

"You never know," he said as he quickly input his number, called himself, and then handed me back my phone.

It felt like a personal victory that I was able to take it back without grabbing him in the process and throwing myself against him.

"Right. You never know." Back to echoing again. "I'm going to go. Now. So, bye."

My feet were not cooperating. Nick looked at me expectantly, and I said in a rush, "I don't know how you plan on getting around, but the only rideshare in town is Barney, and he might not arrive when the app says he will. He mostly shows up when he feels like it."

Was it my imagination or had Nick moved closer to me?

Or was I moving closer to him because my feet had gone completely rogue?

"That's okay," he murmured. "I'm not in any rush. I'm happy to wait for the things I want."

My blood was somehow both burning and solidifying inside me, making it difficult to move. Or think.

Or breathe.

So close now that I could feel the heat emanating from his skin. My entire body tingled in response. I could see that his chest rose and fell a bit quicker than normal. It wasn't just me who was affected.

Unless I was imagining it.

"Jane," he whispered in a low, rough voice that sent shivers dancing along my nerve endings.

"Yes?"

"Aren't you going to be late?" In the entire history of time, had anyone ever asked that question more seductively?

No. The answer was no.

"Yes," I said, wondering why my voice sounded like that. I really was going to be late and that would make Gretchen angry. Although I'd bet if I explained the reason why, she would completely understand. "I should go."

"You should," he breathed the words softly, angling his head so that his mouth was close to mine. My lips burned in response, longing to close the gap between us.

Was Nick Haddon about to kiss me?

CHAPTER TEN

Patches meowed loudly behind me, and it was a jolt to my system, pulling me back into reality. I took several steps backward.

What was I doing? What were *we* doing?

Or had it just been me? That was a distinct possibility. I'd been so worried about scaring him off by telling him what his publicist had wanted, and instead I was going to be the one responsible for it by harassing the poor man.

I could feel my face turning red and I hoped he wouldn't notice.

"I'm off!" I announced, grabbing my keys from the hook next to the door and fleeing to my car.

Literally fleeing. It was like he emitted some kind of high-grade pheromone that was making it impossible for me to control myself. Running away seemed to be the only solution.

After I buckled up, I plugged my phone into the car charger and immediately called Gretchen. I put the car in drive and again peeled out.

At this rate, I was going to have to replace all of my tires.

She answered and I blurted out, "Yoga!"

"Did you just say *yoga*? Or *yogurt*? *Yoda*?"

"Yoga," I repeated firmly, finally feeling like I had control over my mouth again. "Nick Haddon was doing yoga. In my living room."

"So?" She sounded bored, apparently not able to pick up on my vibe over a phone call.

She was not understanding what I was trying to convey. "Yoga. Shirtless. Shirtless yoga."

It finally seemed to click. "If he asked you to help correct his form on his downward dog, I hope you said yes."

"I don't need you to . . ." I had been about to say *make this worse* but I settled on, "I don't need this kind of input." I wasn't sure what I wanted her to say, but that wasn't it.

"That's fine. I'm nama-stay out of this one." She cracked herself up before turning serious again. "Not really, though. I can't help myself. How was the shirtless part of your morning?"

Stupendous. Amazing. Forcing me to reexamine my entire life and why I hadn't had a shirtless movie star living in my house before now. "I don't really know how to describe it."

She was chewing on something and then swallowed it. "You've seen him without his shirt plenty of times."

"On television. Not in 3D, Technicolor real life. The two things do not compare. Even a little."

"I'm glad you're no longer denying your attraction to him, because we would be way past the point of me suspending my disbelief."

"How am I supposed to resist that?" I asked, unable to keep the words to myself.

"You're not."

"And you're unhelpful. Do you think pepper spray would work?"

She made a "you've got me" sound and then said, "Only momentarily, and then your eyes would be stinging because you'd still make out with him even if he was covered in pepper spray." Before I could protest that I was absolutely not going to make out with Nick Haddon, she added, "You're going to be here soon, right? I hate being late."

"Yes, I'll be there in a couple of minutes."

We said goodbye and hung up. I had honestly expected a very different kind of reaction from her. More "go get him, tiger" and less "so what?" I wasn't sure what to make of it.

I didn't spend too much time thinking about it, though. Instead, it was all shirtless, sweaty Nick in my head.

I tried to concentrate on other things. Attempted to run scales through my mind, pushing my fingers against the steering wheel like it was a piano keyboard. Nope. It wasn't working. Still just Nick.

Gretchen came out to the car when I finally got to her place, said hello, and then launched into a story about something thoughtful Heath had done for her. Before Nick's arrival, this was honestly how a large percentage of our conversations would go. Gretchen was deeply in love with my brother and thought everything he did was amazing. Today he had made her favorite breakfast and left a tray on her bed before he headed out to work.

Which, yes, it was obviously thoughtful and romantic, but I was having my own crisis and didn't want to talk about Heath.

"Isn't he the best?" she asked me, sighing.

"Wow, I had no idea you were married to the most incredible husband in the whole world. You should talk about him more so I don't ever forget."

"Your jealousy is understandable," she said, patting me on the leg. I didn't feel jealous. I was still rattled and didn't understand why she'd underreacted to the information I'd shared with her.

"Why so testy?" she asked.

"I really thought you'd be more excited about my news this morning."

Gretchen knit her eyebrows. "The shirtless yoga?"

"Yes." Did she not get the magnitude of what had almost happened in my living room? Admittedly, I hadn't told her everything about it, but it felt like she should just intuit it like she did most things.

"First off, let me just say, it is excellent that he does yoga. All that flexibility and great center of balance is good news for you. And second, if I'd made a big deal about it, what would you have done?"

I opened and closed my mouth several times, not sure what she was trying to imply.

"Downplayed it," she told me. "I'm letting you sit in your feelings. There's only so much prodding I can do before you totally rebel and do the opposite just to spite me."

That wasn't true, was it?

Part of me feared that it was.

"Obviously, I'm pro you and Nick happening, but Heath pointed out that I should back off a bit and he's right. I mean, don't get me wrong—you should have taken pictures this morning and sent them to me. But this is your life and you get to make all the decisions for it. Even if those decisions are so often wrong."

"Not always," I protested. "I told him about what his publicist wanted me to do, and he didn't care. He's still here. Because I chose to be honest."

"You told him? And what did he say?" She sounded panicked.

"He was fine with it. He's teased me about it a couple of times since, but he didn't run for the hills like you said he would."

"Well, I can't always be right about everything. That would make me an exhausting person to be around."

"I want to say something snarky to you right now, but given that you are very pregnant and I love you, I won't."

"And I appreciate it," she said. "By the way, you never responded to my text last night."

"What text?" I would have bet good money that it had to do with Nick, despite her saying she was going to back off. I usually checked my phone pretty frequently, but this morning I'd been running around trying not to be late and then had to fight with myself not to press my mouth against Nick Haddon's slick, warm skin.

"We're sold out," she announced.

For a second her words didn't quite connect as I was still imagining what it would be like to kiss Nick. "Wait, we sold out of festival tickets?"

"We did!"

"Are you serious?"

"I am!"

At that, I pulled the car over to the side of the road. "Every ticket?" That was so, so many. We'd been dreaming of hitting fifty percent ticket sales, and now Gretchen was telling me that they were completely sold out.

"Heath also helped me set up those tickets for the VIP meet and greet with Nick. Every single one of those tickets are gone, too. And I charged two hundred dollars per photo. There are going to be so many people who stay here and spend their money in Patience!"

My first thought was people staying in town was going to give stupid Brenda money, but then the rest of me was just overwhelmed and excited at the prospect that this "Nick Haddon Coming to Patience" plan was actually going to work. "How? How did any of this happen?" He hadn't even filmed anything yet.

"Those pictures the photographers took yesterday of Nick arriving—they're everywhere. So when I put up a post on Instagram with the links and the name of the town and the festival, well, it blew up. And we are officially sold out. I've even set up a Facebook group for the people who asked to be put on a waiting list. We're going to make so much money. And it's all thanks to Nick."

This was so huge.

There was no way I could afford to let anything happen with Nick now. Whatever this morning had been, whether it had been just me or both of us—and I knew that my lust-addled brain was messing with my ability to recall things correctly—it didn't matter. I couldn't keep drooling over him. I couldn't risk ruining the festival over . . . whatever it was I felt around him. I had to keep this professional between us.

She didn't seem to notice that I was having a mini–existential crisis and kept going. "Even if you had scared him off by telling him the truth, I think it would be fine. We couldn't have done the meet and greet, but people still would have come to the festival in hopes they might see him. I said very clearly on my post and on the ticket page that we're not guaranteeing his appearance at the festival, but hopefully he'll go out and wave a few times to the crowd. I think that will make people happy."

Yes, it probably would.

And that had to be the priority here.

"Why is there a dollar stuck to your leg?" Gretchen asked.

I glanced down, and sticking out from under my right thigh was a dollar bill. I picked it up and saw that in the top-left corner, someone had written PAYMENT IN FULL.

Nick. He had done this. My heart fluttered in response. He was paying me back for the gum and had put the dollar in the car, where I was sure to find it.

Only I hadn't seen it right away because he had thrown me so off-balance with all that shirtlessness. The fluttering stopped and turned into a sinking feeling. I couldn't let stuff like this affect me. The festival had to be my priority.

"Are we going to go?" Gretchen asked.

"Right. Yes." I turned my blinker on and pulled back onto the road. During our drive to the doctor's office, I only half listened to the story about some other incredible thing Heath had done for her. I was too busy thinking about how I was going to make sure that whatever had almost happened this morning with Nick didn't ever happen again.

We got to the OB-GYN office and checked in. We were in the waiting room for a few minutes until they called Gretchen back. I stayed behind, still trying to figure out a way to keep my distance from Nick Haddon.

"Jane?"

I glanced up to see Wells.

Wells! That was how I would fix this. I would date somebody else. Then I could focus all of my attention on him. He was nice-enough looking—almost as tall as me, wore glasses, had dark brown hair. He always seemed kind and would talk to me if I came in with Gretchen and had made it seem like he'd like to take me out, but I'd never really seriously thought of him as someone to date. In large part because I'd never felt much of a connection with him.

But maybe after I'd spent some time with him, I would. "How are you?" I asked. "Do you want to get dinner tonight?"

Wells seemed a bit taken aback, given my sudden proposal—which made sense, considering that I hadn't eased into it and instead just blurted it out. What if he wasn't interested in me? There could also be a dozen different scenarios of how badly I might have misread this situation, including that he might already be seeing someone.

But he smiled and said, "I would love to get dinner with you. Where should we go?"

Tony's seemed as good a place as any. Plus, it had the added bonus of letting everyone in town see me on a date with someone who was Not Nick, and then they could all go back to minding their own business and stop trying to set me up with him.

I had to admit maybe that played a part in this. That I was looking at Nick as a potential romantic partner because so many people were cheering us on.

Even as I was saying it, I knew that was a lie. Whatever bodily hormone/chemical caused this kind of feeling, it only happened when I was around Nick.

"There's this diner in my town that I love going to. I could meet you there."

"Sounds good. Why don't you give me your number?"

Again, I flashed back to Nick putting his number into my phone. Was I going to be cursed this way for the rest of my life? Trying to hang out with some nice man and thinking about the movie star?

We exchanged numbers and made plans to meet at seven o'clock. I told him I'd text him the address.

"I'm looking forward to it," he told me.

"Me too," I said, and tried to mean it.

"I have another patient coming in. It was good seeing you, and I can't wait to meet up with you tonight."

As he walked away, I nodded with satisfaction. There. I had done it. I was going to go out with someone else, and Nick would remain a professional friendship that was just . . . professional.

My phone rang and my heart leapt in response. I wanted it to be Nick.

So much for my "I'm Moving On" speech to myself.

It was my mother.

After I said hello, my mom said, "What's this I hear about you and some actor?"

To be honest, I was surprised that it had taken her this long to call me. She had always enjoyed being in my business. Admittedly, her focus had been more on my dad lately—for obvious reasons—but that didn't stop her from calling and routinely reminding me that she expected me to find a husband and give her grandchildren in addition to the one Gretchen was having.

"I told you about this. Nick Haddon. He's staying at the Pink House, and I'm like the liaison between him and the festival. It's because of that video Gretchen made. It's for publicity. And it's worked! We sold out of tickets."

"That's wonderful. I'm just worried about you being distracted by having this actor living in Grandma's house."

I mean, fair point, as that had already happened, but she didn't need to know that.

She wasn't done yet, though. "I don't want you shacking up with a man like that."

It was pointless to tell her we weren't shacking up, that the Pink House was almost ready to become a B and B open for business and strange men would be "shacking up" there regularly, but I couldn't help but react to the last part of her statement. "What do you mean, 'a man like that'?"

"Like the kind who changes women like he does underwear."

"You don't know him."

"Neither do you!" she protested.

Normally, I'd agree with her, and I realized how weird it would sound if I said it out loud, but I felt like I knew a lot about Nick. "You don't have to worry about him. I've got a date with a doctor."

"Oh, no, dear, they just call those appointments."

I was not going to waste an eye roll when she couldn't even see me do it. "Mom, I'm serious. One of the doctors—well, physician assistant, technically—at Gretchen's OB-GYN practice is having dinner with me tonight."

She gasped. "You're going on a date? With a doctor?"

"Physician assistant."

Then she started squealing and it sounded like she was jumping up and down. She really needed to get out more. "It's not a national holiday, Mom. Put away the ticker-tape parade."

"I'm just so glad that you're getting back out there on a real date. It's been so long."

What could I say to that? It had been a long time since I'd had, as she'd called it, a real date.

"Are you going to bring your doctor to the anniversary party instead of the actor?"

"No, I have to bring Nick." Then I tacked on, "The actor." Just in case she didn't remember his name.

"Why?"

"Because your favorite daughter invited him and it would be rude not to." I teased her a lot about liking Gretchen more than me, and it wasn't helped by the fact that Gretchen was now bringing my mom's first grandchild into the world. She could literally do no wrong in my mother's eyes.

"Okay," she said in a tone that indicated she didn't believe me. "Well, we just want you to be happy."

That seemed to be all anyone wanted. And I was trying to make it happen. Taking a chance, going on a date with a nice guy who seemed interested in me. The festival was going to be a success. The B and B was coming along nicely. I had a new song I was working on.

Then why didn't I feel very happy?

"Your dad's calling for me. I've got to go. Give me a call after your date with the doctor—I want to hear all about it!"

She hung up before I could correct her again. If I really did end up with Wells, my mom was going to call him a doctor for the rest of her life.

I sat and waited for Gretchen to be done, messing around with a game on my phone. I could have been doing work for the festival, but I was finding it too hard to concentrate. Again, I was thinking about Nick.

Wondering what he was doing. What he would think when I told him about the festival tickets.

What he would think about my date with Wells.

Even though that was silly. Nick obviously wasn't going to care.

Why did I want him to?

About twenty minutes later, Gretchen came back to the waiting room.

"Everything is good," she told me with a huge smile. "The heartbeat is strong, and all of his measurements are right where they should be."

"That's great!" I smiled back at her. She rested a hand on her stomach, and I found myself struck with a longing I'd never really experienced before. As much as I told my mom to back off, there was part of me that really wanted what Gretchen and Heath had. What my parents had.

To be in a relationship with a man who would respect and love me.

Maybe Wells could be that guy.

"Guess what?" I said to Gretchen as we walked back to my car.

"What?"

"I asked Wells to have dinner with me tonight and he said yes."

She frowned, which surprised me.

"What's that reaction about?" I asked. "You were all aboard the Wells train last week."

"That was last week. Keep up." Then she added, "I knew he liked you—another thing I was right about. Which means I'm right about Nick liking you, too."

I sighed. I was going on this date to get over whatever crush I had on Nick and was not going to let myself hope she was right and most definitely was not going to do anything that would let the festival be ruined.

We didn't say anything else as we went out to my car. I had just buckled myself in when Gretchen said, "There's something I need to know. Why are you going out with Wells? Are you trying to scare Nick off? Or me? Or yourself?"

Those were questions I didn't have answers to.

Or, if I did, I wasn't going to admit it.

CHAPTER ELEVEN

I took Gretchen home and then headed to the library to start my shift. It felt like a completely normal day with the same patrons I always interacted with. I worked on last-minute details for the festival, but in between phone calls I found myself writing down my newest composition, humming as I added and erased notes to get the right melody.

It was funny—I hadn't been inspired in months, and Nick Haddon came to town and suddenly it felt like I was brimming with music again.

I didn't want to examine that fact too closely.

My phone rang and I didn't recognize the number. Considering the number of vendors I was in touch with on a regular basis for the festival, I'd made it a habit to answer everyone who called me.

"Hello?"

"Hi, Jane."

Nick wasn't even in the room with me but his voice still made my insides tingle. Why didn't he just text like a normal person? I found myself stumbling over his name. "N-Nick. Hi."

"Hey. I was wondering if you had plans for dinner tonight?"

Totally innocent question. He didn't know anyone else and was literally staying at my house. It would make sense that he would check with me. So why was I freaking out? Nick didn't and wouldn't care that I had a date. I was making up this connection to him that I thought I felt.

And I was being helped along in that delusion by my best friend and half the town. I swallowed hard before I answered. "I'm going out."

Was that enough? I felt like I had to explain. What did I say? *With a friend?* Technically, that wasn't true. I didn't even know Wells. "On a date," I finished.

There. That would settle things. Make them perfectly clear.

"Oh." There was a pause that was so heavy and long that I felt a bit crushed by it. "Well, have fun. I'll see you later."

He hung up before I could say goodbye.

This was fine. This was necessary.

For him and for me.

~

When I got home that night, Nick was gone. I wondered where he went but reminded myself that it wasn't my concern. His bedroom door was open and I couldn't help but stick my head inside. The room looked relatively the same with the couple of touches he'd mentioned, along with an air purifier and a humidifier.

I took the dollar bill he'd left for me and put it in one of the air purifier's slots. I imagined his face when he found it, and it made me smile.

Patches again expressed her displeasure at being made to wait to be fed, so I took care of her before I went upstairs to get ready. I found myself not making the kind of effort I used to when I went out on dates.

Or the kind of effort I would have made if I were going out with Nick.

I wished he'd come home before I left, but he didn't. I thought about texting him because I really wanted to know where he was and what he was doing, but I needed to give both of us space.

Well, mostly me. Nick was probably just fine and wanted us to be friends and I was the one making this more than it actually was.

When I got to Tony's, Wells was waiting inside, standing next to the door. That was a good sign—he was on time. I walked up and I waited to feel something—some kind of romantic spark. Excitement.

It wasn't there.

"Jane!" he said, sounding genuinely happy to see me. I felt guilty that I didn't feel the same.

"You made it," I said.

"Should we grab a table?" He started walking toward the booth that I'd shared with Nick, but I walked in the opposite direction.

"There's one right here," I said.

We sat down in the booth I'd chosen and Wells took off his coat. He had on a polo shirt and khaki pants. I couldn't help but wonder what Nick would look like in the same outfit. I held my breath for a second, reminding myself to stop thinking about him. I was here with Wells.

"What do you recommend?" he asked. I listed off some of my favorites, and he interrupted me. "No fish?"

"I think the fish sticks may have fish byproducts," I said jokingly, but he frowned.

"I take my fish very seriously."

"You do?" I didn't think another person had ever said that to me.

"I spend most of my free time fishing." Then he launched into the different kinds of fishing he did, the assortment of bait he used, the various fish that could be caught nearby. The trip he planned to take to Yellowstone next summer to fish there.

And I had never been so bored in my entire life.

Maybe I wouldn't have been if this had been an actual conversation. Where he told me about his life but then asked about mine. Exchanged stories and information about ourselves.

That did not happen.

He didn't ask me a single question about myself or my life. He kept his monologue going as Shirley came over to take our orders and get us some drinks, then continued on while we waited for our food.

I hadn't realized there was so much to know about fishing. I had thought it was putting a worm on a hook and then waiting. Apparently, there was a great deal of technique involved.

It was sad how uninterested I was in all of this. I tried to imagine Nick talking this way about himself or his interests, on and on, and realized that I wouldn't be bored. I loved listening to Nick talk.

Maybe Wells just needed more of a chance. He might have been nervous. I'd certainly been prone to speaking too enthusiastically about a subject most people found boring before. I should be nice.

All Wells needed was my nodding and sounds of encouragement to keep talking. He didn't seem nervous, though. Just very self-involved. I wondered how long he could keep this up, if I could truly go on a date where I didn't tell the other person one single thing about myself.

He was in the middle of telling me about a fishing trip he'd taken down in the Florida Keys when the bells above the door rang and it opened up.

Nick walked in.

My first thought was that he was here to bust up my date and I was excited—nay, thrilled—for him to do so.

But I hadn't told him I'd be here. He couldn't be spying on me or trying to ruin my date. He'd come here to eat. It would make sense that he'd come to Tony's. Where else would he go to grab dinner?

He didn't see me. Instead, he walked over to an empty table and sat down. Then he pulled out a book and began to read.

It was like he was doing it on purpose. I was on a date with the most boring, self-centered human alive, and Nick was sitting there—all scruffy five-o'clock shadow and that bomber jacket of his—sexily reading a book. He had to know how hot he looked when he did that.

Okay, he couldn't possibly know, but I wasn't feeling very rational.

The only thing I wanted to do was tell Wells thanks but no thanks and go over and sit across from Nick.

I had been trying to feel even a tiny spark with Wells and Nick came into a room and without even looking at me it was like I'd been hit by raging California wildfires.

Life was so unfair.

The guy I should like, who would fit well into my life, was making me want to push my utensils into my ears so I wouldn't have to listen to him anymore, and the guy who was like a bright, burning star—who would be here one day and gone the next—was the one I wanted to spend my evening with.

I couldn't do that, though. I had to protect the festival.

And my heart. I didn't need for it to get broken in that particular way again.

Once was enough.

Wells was waxing poetic over bluegill sunfish and Nick seemed to sense that I was staring at him. I should have looked away, but I didn't. He glanced up, caught my gaze, and gave me a secret smile that made my toes curl. Then his eyes shifted over to Wells and that smile widened.

Nick went back to his book.

Tony came out of the kitchen and I wondered if he'd gotten sick of Wells's stories, too. He was carrying something that looked suspiciously like avocado toast. He brought it over to Nick's table, and they chatted like they were old buddies catching up.

Wells's phone rang. "Excuse me a second. I need to take this." He got up and walked outside the diner.

Was it wrong for me to hope that someone had gone into labor and that he needed to go?

Shirley came over to check on us. I asked, "Is that avocado toast?" and pointed in Nick and Tony's direction.

"It is. Your movie star had lunch here today, and he and Tony bonded."

Apparently. "I've never seen Tony smile in the diner before."

"Me neither, sweetie."

Shirley left while I tried to make sense of what I was seeing in front of me. Tony was making Nick special meals? Tony went back to the kitchen and Nick demolished his avocado toast pretty quickly.

He ate sexily, too.

Wells returned, to my dismay. "Sorry about that. It was work."

"Oh. Do you have to go?" I asked hopefully.

"I don't have anywhere else to be," he said and I felt deflated. Wells finally seemed to notice that I wasn't paying much attention to him. He turned around. "Who is that?"

"Nick Haddon." I hadn't meant to say that name and sigh at the same time, but here we were.

"Should I know who that is?"

I shouldn't have felt personally insulted, but I did. "He's an actor. He's here to help with publicity for the festival. Which I'm planning." I didn't add that he might know that if he'd bothered to ask me about my job.

"Right. I always forget about your town's little festival. I keep meaning to stop by, but I never get around to it. Maybe next year."

Did he realize how demeaning that sounded?

The bell rang again and Brenda, the devil herself, entered. It felt a bit like she was stalking or just straight up trolling me. Did she sit at home and think of ways to torture me?

And she didn't help that worry to ease when she came over to my table. "Janie! How are things with the festival going?" Like she wasn't personally responsible for trying to wreck the entire thing.

My blood boiled and flashes of red tinged my vision again. Someone was going to have to call the sheriff because I was about to choke this Smurf out.

"And what's this?" she asked, looking between me and Wells. "Oh, is this like a date? How . . . appropriate for you, Janie. You two seem like a good match. Well, have fun if you can. I'm off to enjoy my evening plans."

"Good luck with that!" I yelled after her as she walked away. I had meant it to be sarcastic, but it came out sounding supportive. That's how much she had infuriated me.

"Were we just insulted?" Wells asked, finally aware of something besides fish. I probably should have congratulated him on not being totally oblivious, because yes, Brenda had indeed insulted us.

I didn't know what I expected to happen next, but it wasn't Brenda going over and sitting down at Nick's table.

That rage turned to an all-consuming jealousy. I actually felt like I was going to suffocate from it. What was Nick doing with her?

Were they here on a date?

I should have felt bad about being inattentive to Wells, but he didn't seem to notice. He was currently explaining to me the weight of each big fish he'd ever caught and how each one was measured.

I grabbed my phone and put it under the table. I found my latest text message to Gretchen and typed:

I think Nick is on a dinner date with Brenda!!!

It was a good thing I had perfected the art of texting without looking in high school so that I could keep nodding at Wells. He was actually being the perfect cover right now; I could observe whatever monstrosity was happening across the room without looking like I was spying on them.

This was so pathetic.

I glanced down to see Gretchen's response.

Maybe it's a coincidence. Maybe Nick was just hungry.

That wasn't going to be the case for much longer because I was sure Brenda would be all too eager to offer him a steady diet of her tongue.

Ew. I was grossed out by even imagining him kissing her. I wouldn't survive having to see it in real life.

It doesn't mean they're on a date.

Gretchen was right. This might be a coincidence. If we were talking about it in person, I would have used air quotes around *coincidence* because Brenda had never coincidentally done anything in her life.

A thought occurred to me that gave me new levels of anxiety.

What if she's trying to sabotage the festival? Getting Nick to back out. There will be hell to pay if she screws this up for me.

Good thing she already has a line of credit there.

I was not in the mood for jokes.

I'm being serious.

She tried to reassure me.

I don't think you have anything to worry about.

Nick and Brenda stood up, and I saw him putting cash on the table.

I didn't even pretend like I wasn't watching them. Brenda shot me a triumphant look on her way out. She'd told me that she was going to steal Nick away from me and here she was—leaving with him. Nick gave me a friendly wave. I couldn't wave back. What was he doing?

They went to Brenda's Jeep, and I hoped that Nick was just being polite and walking her to her car.

But then he climbed in! They drove off!

He just left with her. He. Left. With. Her!!!!!!!!!!

Gretchen didn't seem to understand the enormity of what I'd just witnessed.

Maybe she's just giving him a ride.

I bet she'd like to give him a ride, I mentally grumbled. But I wasn't going to dwell on it. Nick Haddon was free to date any evil troll he wanted to. I didn't have any kind of say over his life.

Gretchen sent another text.

Still don't think you have anything to worry about. Aren't you supposed to be on a date of your own right now?

It's not going well.

Because you like Nick. I could practically hear her smug smile in that message. I responded:

Because Wells would be happier dating a largemouth bass than me.

I don't understand what that means.

I'll explain later. I have to get out of here.

Wells was midsentence when I said, "I'm sorry, but I'm not feeling too great. I think we should call it a night."

"Oh. Are you sure?"

I was so, so sure. "Yes." I flagged Shirley down. I didn't want to wait for a check, so I told her to put it on my tab. I grabbed a twenty from my wallet and left it as a tip for her. I took my coat and stood up.

"That's a fifty percent tip," Wells said. "Are you certain you want to do that?"

If I'd had any doubt at all before about not wanting to see him again, he had just erased it. I didn't care what his reasons were for saying it—whether it was an aspersion on my calculating skills or being stingy when tipping someone who had waited on us, it didn't matter. Either one did not reflect well on him and his character.

"Yep."

"You paid this time; I'll have to make sure to get it next time," Wells said as he climbed out of the booth. I realized that I'd never been in this particular situation before. I'd never gone on a date with someone who I didn't ever want to see again. I wasn't sure how to end this night.

Especially since I was the one who had initiated it.

"Thanks for coming out with me tonight." I should have said, "It was fun!" but didn't have it in me to lie at the moment. I hurried outside and went over to my car, Wells trailing behind me. I did not want any end-of-date awkwardness with him. I texted Gretchen that the date was over and I was leaving.

When I got to my car, I unlocked it. I turned toward Wells and said, "Good night. Thanks again. Drive safe."

There. That should cover it.

He said, "I'll call you," and I just didn't respond to him because I knew it would be so rude to say, "Please don't." I hoped he got the hint and wouldn't call, because I needed our encounter to be over, never to be repeated. I was getting a tension headache.

I settled on nodding at him. He took that as some kind of encouragement and came toward me. To hug me? Kiss me?

No, no, no. I got into my car and locked the door, waving at him so that he understood this was done. He stood there for a moment, but then walked toward his car.

Letting out a sigh of relief, I felt my phone buzz. Another Gretchen text. I expected her to want an explanation, but her response was:

Do not go home and obsess about what Nick and Brenda are doing.

I didn't reply because that was exactly what I was going to do.

CHAPTER TWELVE

What I ended up actually doing—in addition to obsessing over Nick and Brenda falling in love and getting married here in Patience and having to witness them as a happy couple—was playing with Patches, feeding her, and then going into the music room. It was a space that had been specifically designed for acoustics and had a large baby grand piano in the center of it. I had always loved playing in here. When I was a little girl, it had made piano lessons feel like a reward instead of a *have to*.

I was toying with the tune I'd been working on the last couple of days, playing bars on the piano, writing notes on the paper I had propped against the stand.

"That's beautiful."

My heart slammed into my throat, and I jumped, my fingers slamming into the keys. "Nick. You scared me."

"I'm sorry. I didn't want to disturb you, because I'm enjoying listening to you play. Did you write that?"

"I did."

"You're really talented," he said in a way that made it seem like he was impressed, and that thrilled me in a way it shouldn't have.

Especially because I was still angry with him.

I glanced at the clock. He had been out with Brenda for two hours. Despite Gretchen telling me not to, I had very much spent that entire time wondering what they were up to. I should have been working, but instead I had fixated on him. Again. "Did you and Inspector Gidget have a good time on your date?"

That knowing smile of his was back as he came into the room. He grabbed a chair and set it next to the piano bench. He sat down. "I wasn't on a date."

"You say that like I didn't just see you with your hand in the evil-wench jar."

He didn't say anything, just gave me a look that made me feel unnerved. Like he could read my thoughts and found all of this amusing.

"I hope for your sake you let her sniff your hand before you tried to pet her." My voice was seething. Actually seething.

"If I didn't know any better, I'd think you were jealous."

"I'm not jealous!" I immediately protested. "I just really hate Brenda Schumacher."

"Yeah, I caught that." He folded his arms, still studying me. "I wasn't on a date. Brenda offered to give me a ride home."

"It doesn't take two hours to get from the diner to here." It was like I couldn't keep the words from coming out of my mouth. By basically demanding an explanation and revealing that I knew exactly how much time they'd spent together, I was proving that I was every bit as jealous as he'd accused me of being.

"She took me for a drive and just kept talking and talking and talking."

"We're aware of her condition." And boy, could I relate to how annoying it was.

"We went out to some pond that she said was popular with the kids around here."

"Brenda took you to Make Out Pond?" I would not freak out. I would *not*.

"She did, without running it by me first. I think I was a little bit kidnapped tonight."

His calm description of what he'd been doing was making me feel a little bit better. "But you're home safe now. I'm sorry I didn't protect you from her."

"You did warn me," he said with a wry grin. "But the only thing I was in danger of dying from was boredom."

"I get that."

"Things didn't go so well with Mr. Clean-Shaven?"

"I like clean-shaven men," I retorted. Which made no sense because I didn't like Wells and had no reason to defend him. I did usually prefer clean-shaven men, but I had recently discovered a weakness for stubble as well. "But the man I was with tonight suffers from the same talking disorder as Brenda."

"Maybe we should introduce them."

"Wells still has a pulse, so Brenda would never go for him."

Nick laughed. "Does that mean you're not going out with him again?"

"Not unless I get a little bit kidnapped, too. That was a one and done." I ran my finger along the middle C key, wondering if I should ask the question that was burning me from the inside out. Did I want to know? I had to. "What happened when Brenda took you to the pond?"

"Nothing happened." He said it in a way that made me feel like he knew exactly why I was asking. "She did ask me out, but I told her I wasn't interested."

The sheer joy this gave me was unbelievable. "Really? Did you let her down gently, or can I buy a billboard?"

"I was very polite."

Sighing, I said, "That's good, I guess. But now you're going to have to keep an eye out for her flying monkeys. And I'm glad you didn't go out with her, because then someone might have set fire to your air purifier."

"Good thing," he agreed. "I've heard open flames and your cat don't mix."

Now it was my turn to laugh. This was already a thousand times better than hanging out with Wells.

"I have something for you," he said. "Be right back."

What could he possibly give me that was better than turning down Brenda? He came back in with a stack of papers, which was not what I'd been expecting. He handed them to me as he sat back in his chair. "This is a list of every local business in a twenty-mile radius that might benefit from increased tourism here in Patience. I could expand the search further out, if you'd like."

I thumbed through a couple of the pages. "I can't believe you did this." It was so much work.

"I needed something to do after filming today."

There was an unexpected catch in my throat. He had spent his free time working on something that he absolutely did not need to, in an attempt to help the festival succeed.

"Thank you." I wished I could tell him what this meant to me, but I was aiming for professional.

Admittedly, I was falling pretty short in that attempt.

"How did the filming go?" I asked, wanting to change the topic to something I could manage more easily.

"It was fine. I had to spend my day dodging calls from my agent."

"Why?"

"He wants an answer."

"About what?"

Nick slouched in his chair and rubbed the back of his neck. "They want me to do a reboot of *Olympus High*."

"*Olympus College?*" I joked.

"No. Not a sequel. A reboot. They want me to play Kronos."

"The dad?"

"They want all new teens for a new generation."

That made no sense. "It only went off the air a few years ago. There's no new generation to watch."

"I know." He nodded. "But my agent thinks it's a guaranteed hit."

"You don't sound like you agree."

"I'm the jinx, remember? I'll screw it up somehow."

"I think rebooting a show that was just on the air is the screwup here." He looked upset, and this time I gave in to my impulse to comfort him. I reached over and squeezed his arm. "I don't think you're a jinx. I think you're an awesome person."

His gaze traveled down to where my hand rested on his forearm. His very nicely formed forearm, veined and strong and warm.

I jerked my hand away as if I'd been burned.

"Thanks," he said, not bringing up my temporary lapse. "There's this other part, this romantic comedy that I want to do, but my team thinks it will be wrong for me. Not on brand. A step in the wrong direction."

I curled my fingers, as they very much wanted to make contact with his arm again. Honestly, they weren't choosy. They would have been happy to touch any part of him. "You've never done a rom-com before?"

"No. And the script is unlike anything else I've ever read. It's so classically a rom-com, but it turns the whole thing on its head while still giving the audience the happily ever after. It's really smart and funny, and they're going to make me audition." That seemed to amuse him.

It took me just a second to figure out why. "No one is handing it to you. And that appeals to you."

"Very much so." Ha. Evil Brenda didn't even realize what she'd done. She'd made things too easy for Nick. He liked things he had to work for. "But I can't tell if the script is actually good or if I'm just excited by the prospect of having to earn my part. I don't really trust my own instincts."

"Do you have someone you could ask? Besides your agent?"

"Not really. I'm surrounded by a bunch of yes-men that don't like to tell me no."

I thought for a moment. "What about Shanice? She seems really straightforward. Other than the whole 'she wanted me to lie to you about keeping an eye on you' thing. But I think even then, she had your best interests at heart."

"You're right. She does tell it to me like it is, which is why I hired her. But reading scripts isn't really in her job description."

"She is in your industry. She must have some familiarity with stuff like that. And I don't have any special insight I can share, other than I think you should do it just because it's a rom-com and Hollywood does not make enough of those."

"They don't?" he asked.

"Nope. It's like somebody in charge decided falling in love was unimportant. That the only way to be 'art' was to be about suffering or self-loathing when love is the most important thing in the whole world. Someone should show them that it matters. And you could be the one to do it because you're very good at romance."

"I am?" he asked, his voice deep and rough as he leaned forward in his chair. Those pheromones of his were back, sending tingles along my skin. A lock of hair fell forward on his forehead, and it took everything in me to fight the urge to push it off his face.

I gulped. "On-screen," I finally managed to say. "You're good at romance on-screen." He'd had so much chemistry with the actress who played Hera that I had assumed they were really in love with each other when I was younger.

He didn't reply right away, and with each second that passed, I felt more and more like I was making a fool of myself and he was going to tell me he couldn't do this anymore and would go stay at Brenda's inn and then he really would fall in love with her after he invested in a pair of noise-canceling headphones and then—

"Do you want to watch *The Music Man* with me?" he asked, totally derailing my train of thought. "I downloaded it today."

"That must have taken ten million years," I said.

"It did. Do you want to?"

I wanted so many things that I couldn't have.

Things I shouldn't want.

"You did promise Shanice you'd keep an eye on me. That would be easier to do if you're sitting next to me on the couch."

Didn't he know that he didn't have to convince me? That I didn't need to be talked into anything but instead talked *out* of my current impulses?

"You know, when she asked me to do that, I kind of thought you'd be like Bruce Wayne."

He looked confused. "Fighting crime in Gotham?"

"No, not Batman. Bruce Wayne. The womanizing playboy who parties all the time. I can't really imagine Bruce Wayne wanting to watch a musical."

"Sorry to disappoint," he said.

"No, it's a good thing. I wouldn't want a Bruce Wayne or a Batman here. Although you in a black latex suit—" Nope, I was going to stop talking, maybe mentally berate myself for not being able to follow my own boundaries, and I was most definitely going to ignore the delight in his eyes.

"Batman tangents aside, you know you didn't actually answer my very polite invitation."

I knew what I should say. I should go up to my room, where I wouldn't be distracted by his sparkling eyes and rippling biceps, and lock myself in. Give myself time to cool off.

What I actually said was, "Sure."

His whole face lit up, and it was kind of glorious. Even more glorious was knowing I was the reason for it. "Great! I'll get my laptop."

"Wait," I said, reaching out to stop him from getting up. I quickly drew my hand back before I made actual contact. "I wanted to ask you a question."

Because I had to know if this situation was worth fighting myself over. If this was, as Gretchen claimed, meant to be—destined, even—then maybe I should know and just give in.

"When you first got here, you played the soundtrack to *Raiders of the Lost Ark*. Why did you choose that?"

"I always listen to music when I get to a new place. My taste is pretty eclectic—everything from classical to Top 40. But I picked that soundtrack because there was a poster for the movie in my room. Why?"

I couldn't exactly tell him that Gretchen had deemed it a sign and that some small part of me had wanted to believe her.

It wasn't a sign, though—he had only played it because of the poster that I'd forgotten was hanging up. I felt surprisingly let down.

"No reason. I was just curious."

He nodded. "I'll meet you in the living room." He left.

I got up and walked toward the living room, my feet feeling surprisingly heavy. I couldn't date Nick, so it wasn't logical that I wanted a signal from the universe that it should happen.

He brought his laptop into the room and set it down on the coffee table. "Be right back," he said.

I picked up his laptop, wondering if I had the right cables for it to be compatible with my television. I was going through the drawer where I kept my cables when he returned, carrying his box of seaweed and a bowl of popcorn.

"I made popcorn!" he announced, sounding very pleased with himself.

"You mean you opened the plastic wrap, put the bag in the microwave, and pushed the popcorn button?" I teased him as I put the laptop back on the coffee table.

"I've never done it before. This is an accomplishment." He put the bowl next to the laptop.

If it had been anybody else, I would have teased them relentlessly. But I didn't want to rain on his parade, especially not when he was being so cute about it.

He held up his snacks. "You should try one of these. Much healthier for you."

"Uh, no thanks."

"Come on, what if you try it and it becomes your favorite thing to eat in the whole world?"

"Doubtful," I told him.

"You won't know unless you try it. It's salty and crunchy. Like popcorn."

Again, if he had been anyone else, I would have outright refused. I wasn't interested in trying sea trash. He held out what looked like a sheet of thin green paper.

"Okay," I said, letting him know that I still thought it was a bad idea.

"It's nori flavored."

That didn't mean anything to me, but I decided to try to get through this experience as quickly as possible. As could have been predicted, it tasted like strangely flavored chewy paper and was not in any way, shape, or form better than popcorn.

I swallowed and . . . couldn't breathe. It was stuck, lodged in my throat. I attempted to speak and nothing came out. Panic rose in my chest as I gestured toward my throat. I tried to breathe and panicked some more as I realized that I couldn't drag any air into my lungs.

Nick immediately understood the situation and got behind me, wrapping his arms around me and doing the Heimlich. He clasped his hands together, pushing in and up under my ribs. It hurt, but on his second pull against my diaphragm, the seaweed came loose and I coughed it out.

I dragged air into my lungs, and nothing had ever been sweeter. I collapsed against him, relief drugging my limbs. He kept me upright, holding me close.

"Your snack just tried to kill me," I told him when I could finally speak. I wanted so much to stay exactly where I was. It felt . . . right. My brain—recently deprived of oxygen, I might add—asked me, *Who almost dies and all they can think about is how much they like being pressed against Nick's firm body, his strong arms wrapped around them?*

Turned out it was me. That's who.

There was something definitely wrong with me.

Things only got worse when he said, "Are you all right? Are you breathing okay?"

He said those words right next to my ear, which sent serious shivers up and down my spinal column, making sure to hit every nerve ending they came across.

"I'm okay. But I want you to know that that's never once happened with a chocolate chip cookie."

He ignored my joke. "What if I hadn't been here?" There was a tinge of desperation in his voice that made me think maybe I should be asking if *he* was okay.

"I would have been fine because I wouldn't have voluntarily eaten your disgusting seaweed squares."

He smiled against the side of my head and it made the tingles intensify. Warmth spread through my entire body, like he was infusing it into me.

"Thank you for saving me," I said.

He didn't answer, but his arms did tighten around me.

We stayed that way, with me cradled against him, for a few more moments before I realized how weird and pathetic this was getting, and I tugged myself away from him, walking out of his embrace.

My entire body wanted to stage a protest against my decision, but I managed to sit down on the couch, still feeling out of breath. I tried to ignore how much I wanted to go back over to him and keep being held. I tucked my hands under my legs. It was the only way I could make sure I wouldn't try to touch him. "Should we watch the movie?"

He hesitated and I wouldn't look up at him. I was scared to, not knowing what I'd see there. Concern?

Pity?

I couldn't take his pity.

After another few beats he sat on the couch next to me, reaching out to mess with his laptop to get the movie to come up. It started and I leaned back against the couch, keeping my eyes on the screen. It did strike me as funny that his publicist had been so worried about him having wild and crazy nights, and instead we were watching a musical.

I did my best to pay attention to the movie, and I loved the score and the songs, but Nick was too distracting.

Patches apparently agreed with me, as she had curled up on his lap, purring. Her affection was typically very limited but not with Nick. It was like he had been built out of catnip and my little attention strumpet couldn't get enough of him.

Sitting there with him was like being back in high school— watching a movie with a guy and knowing his parents were in the next room.

But other than Patches, there weren't any chaperones here. Just us hanging out, me wanting to touch him but knowing that he didn't feel the same.

I couldn't just throw myself at him. I mean, I could and Gretchen would be overcome with joy, but I couldn't risk the festival.

I had to keep that in mind, but he was making it very, very hard.

He kept looking at me during the "Marian the Librarian" song, but I stayed facing forward. The lyrics didn't mean anything. It was just in reference to the joke he'd made when we first met about me being a librarian. Nothing more.

The movie ended and Nick leaned forward to pause it. Normally, I would have liked listening to the music in the credits, but that didn't seem like a good plan tonight.

I needed to put myself in my room until I could figure out a way to behave.

"Thanks for the movie. Good night." I started to stand up, but he reached out and put his hand on my knee and then both my legs stopped working, so I stayed put.

"Jane, wait. There's something I want to ask you."

CHAPTER THIRTEEN

Calm down, I told my percolating hormones. It was probably something innocuous. Like where I kept the extra toilet paper.

No need to get all worked up over what was most likely going to be nothing.

"What does it take to get you to respond?"

"Respond to what?" I asked, feeling thoroughly confused.

"To me."

Now my hormones were boiling over, doing a frenzied dance, glorying in their rightness. Not about toilet paper. "What do you mean?" I desperately needed clarification because I didn't want to jump to some really bonehead conclusion.

His hand was still on my knee, the other on the couch behind me. "I've done nothing but tell you since I got here that I'm attracted to you and interested in you, and you haven't really given me a response one way or the other."

"I . . . I . . . ," I stuttered, not able to wrap my still-hazy brain around what was happening. My pulse raced so quickly that I was seriously in danger of nearly dying for a second time that night. Was Nick Haddon really sitting on my living room couch, telling me that he, what . . . wanted to be with me?

"You never said that," I said, squeaking the words out. Because I would have remembered if he'd said those actual words.

Gretchen would have had them engraved on my tombstone.

I knew I hadn't missed anything.

Or had I?

"What else do you want me to say? How I spent the last two and a half hours thinking about how much I want to kiss you?"

Somehow my heart managed to gallop even faster, and my lungs were so tight I worried I might pass out. "I thought you were watching the movie."

Why was I saying inane things?

His hand squeezed my knee gently. "I wasn't watching the movie."

"Oh." I didn't know how to respond to that. Because none of the obstacles had been removed. Even if he wanted to make out with me, and my glands were urging me to quickly accept before he changed his mind, it didn't alter anything.

The festival was still going on and I needed him to make the visitors happy.

I didn't want my heart to get broken again.

There were other reasons, but I couldn't think of them at the moment. Most of my self-imposed boundaries had been based on the belief that he couldn't possibly be interested in me, and I didn't want to make a fool of myself.

What was I supposed to do when he erased that line?

He said, "It feels like every time I get close to you, you run away."

"That's . . ." *Accurate.*

At that, he took his hand away and I wanted so much to drag it back. When I didn't finish my sentence, he said, "I'm not trying to make things awkward between us. I just wanted to be honest. You are a very attractive woman and I enjoy your company."

Uh, same. But I didn't say it. Mostly because I was too busy internally basking in the revelation that he thought I was attractive.

"And I know we've been spending time together, but I want to do something, I don't know, more official," he said. "Go on a real date with me."

"I don't think I can do that." It was honestly a wonder that I was able to speak at all.

"Why?" He sounded genuinely curious.

"There are so many reasons why. To start with—I have a policy against dating men like you."

"Men like me? What does that mean?"

"Popular, handsome men." If I had expected a reaction from him over that explanation, it wouldn't have included him grinning. I'd just told him I wouldn't go out with a guy like him. "Why are you smiling?"

"You are attracted to me."

Technically, I hadn't said that, but he wasn't wrong. "You know how you look. And I have to focus on the festival, and I haven't even started calling sponsors because . . ." Because he was distracting me. "Because I'm spending time with you, and this festival has to go well in order for me to save the town. It has to be a success. And if you and I start, I don't know, dating or whatever, and it goes bad and you take off early and go back to California, that screws the festival."

"I won't do that. I promise to stay here through the festival no matter what."

Yeah, that wouldn't be at all awkward, living in the same house after we'd tried to date and miserably failed.

"You're anticipating the worst," he said. "What if things don't go bad?"

"Okay, let's imagine it's all stars and hearts, and then what?" I asked. "We do the long-distance thing? I've done that before and had my heart shredded into tiny pieces. I'm not interested in that happening again."

He didn't have a quick response for that, and I wanted to make sure he understood where I was coming from. "I need to be practical. What could possibly even happen between us? You're leaving in less than two weeks and I'm staying here. It makes no sense."

"I try not to think too much about the future and just live in the present."

At that, I sighed. "Is that part of your fortune-cookie philosophy?" I immediately regretted saying it. "I'm sorry. I didn't mean that. I know you're working on improving yourself and I think that's great, but I'm not a 'live in the now' kind of person. Just because there's something here doesn't mean we should act on it."

"You're not wrong."

I was surprised by how much I wanted to be wrong.

Then he added, "We can have fun and keep things light. It doesn't have to be serious."

"That's part of the problem. I'm not really built for that."

He shrugged. "I think we could find a happy medium. Let me show you."

It was so tempting.

So, so, so tempting.

"I don't want everyone talking about us," I said, trying to justify what was quickly becoming a losing battle.

He shot me a half smile. "At this point I feel like you're trying to come up with an excuse. Did your cat eat your homework? Did you run out of gas on your way to the excuse store and so you didn't have time to pick up a new one?"

Maybe they sounded like flimsy excuses, but they were also reasons. "They're already hounding me. And that's just here in town. What would happen to me if this went nationwide?"

"Why do you care what people think?"

"It's probably the effect of living in a small town." It felt like my life had so often been picked apart—usually out of concern, sometimes out of malice—that I didn't want to do anything to add to the gossip mill.

"As someone who is gossiped about on a massive scale regularly, the trick is to not listen or care. Their opinions are just that—opinions. You can ignore them. Speaking of people here in town, you are forgetting that it would probably really irritate Brenda if you went out with me."

Oh, that was true. I allowed myself to imagine it for a few glorious seconds. That wasn't a reason to do this, though. "That's not playing fair."

"I'm not trying to play fair."

His words did things to my stomach, making it feel like it was sinking and floating at the same time.

"That's . . ." The word came out breathy and I was finding it hard to get air in my lungs to circulate. "You wouldn't care if I went out with you just to make Brenda mad."

"I'd be fine with that."

Again, I allowed myself to imagine her face upon seeing us together. She'd accused me of having a crush, which had turned out to be true, but she didn't think he'd like me back.

She would absolutely die.

But I shouldn't be making major decisions just to piss Brenda off. Because that's what this was—a big moment. It might seem like a small thing, to just go on some dates with the famous actor and then go back to my regular life, but I knew that whatever answer I gave him was about to change everything.

He was still pleading his case. "Technically, we've already got a date planned. Gretchen set it up."

It took me a second. The anniversary party. "That's not a date. She invited you to go and I'm going to drive you because I'll be going to the same place at the same time."

"Okay, then let's go out and do something the day after tomorrow. Just you and me."

"Nick, I . . ." I let my voice trail off because I didn't know what to say. I wanted so desperately to accept, but there was something inside me that wouldn't let me get the words out. That made me resist giving in.

He waited a bit for me to finish and when I didn't, he used that self-deprecating tone that made him even more adorable. "I have to admit that I've never tried to convince a woman to go on a date with me before."

I didn't doubt it.

I was so close to caving. I'd been trying hard to fight my attraction to him and he had just blown up all of my defenses by waving the white flag of surrender and offering me exactly what I wanted.

"You should think about it and then get back to me. You know where to find me," he said.

I nodded and got up. There was no way I could stay here in this room with him, because I would melt faster than an ice-cream cone in an Arizona summer. "I'm going to go to bed."

Commanding my feet to move, I made it all the way to the stairs before I realized that he'd followed me.

He reached out gently, wrapping his long fingers around my wrist, tugging on me to turn around. I turned to face him, afraid of what he might ask me.

Afraid because my resistance was so worn down that there was no way I'd refuse him anything.

"Just tell me this," he said. "Do I have even a glimmer of hope here?"

I should have said no. Protected the things that needed to be protected. But his fingers were on my skin, and it was messing with my ability to think.

So instead, I said, "There's a glimmer."

"That's all I need. We can take it slow. I know you're worried about things changing, but they don't have to if you don't want them to."

Nick released my arm and walked off toward his bedroom.

He couldn't promise me things wouldn't change.

Because they already had.

~

I spent the night tossing and turning, unable to sleep. I couldn't figure out a way to make everything work out. To make sure my heart didn't get broken, that the festival was still a success, while also getting to finally feel what it would be like to have Nick's lips pressed against mine.

It was probably pretty freaking fantastic.

I considered calling Gretchen, but she needed her sleep. I knew she wouldn't have minded me waking her up to tell her about what had just happened, but I didn't think I should.

But texting? That seemed okay. She could call me in the morning. I sent a quick note:

Something happened with Nick tonight. Call me when you get this.

My phone rang immediately. "Gretchen?"

"What do you mean, something happened with Nick?" she demanded.

"Why are you awake? It's like three o'clock in the morning."

"Your nephew has his days and nights mixed up and he's currently kicking me as hard as he can, but I wouldn't be able to sleep anyways because your brother is snoring next to me like someone put a 747 engine in his throat." She sounded really annoyed and I knew better than to interrupt her mid-rant. "But I'm not calling to complain. Yes, I am uncomfortable and exhausted and I need to know what happened with Nick."

So I filled her in, giving her almost all the details. I still didn't tell her about how attracted I was to him, but I wanted her perspective on what he'd said to me. How he wanted us to go on a date.

When I finished there was a lull that made me think that maybe she had fallen asleep, but then she said, "I'm not sure what order I should put this in. First, I was right. I told you he liked you. Second, while I understand your reasons for not wanting to move forward, I think they're dumb and that you should go for it. We're going to have to give you a couple name. Nane? Jick? I'll have to think about it. Nick and Jane. Together at last."

"That settles it. We can't date. Nick and Jane. It sounds like one of those books you give to kindergartners to teach them how to read. 'See Nick and Jane run. See Nick and Jane swim.'"

"See Nick and Jane make out so that Jane's best friend can live vicariously through her," she added.

Gretchen bringing up what our couple name would be set off an internal alarm I didn't know I had. Something had been nagging at me, making me uneasy, and now I finally knew what it was. "Wait, what if that's the whole reason he's doing this? If Shanice thought this would play well in Peoria?"

"It may be because it's really late at night slash early in the morning, but I don't know what you mean."

"What if his publicist told him to find some local girl to date? That the fans would eat it up? What if this whole thing between us is orchestrated? I mean, even Brenda called it out. She implied that this was a publicity stunt." She'd thought I was the one who had come up with the idea, but maybe she hadn't been totally off base.

Ugh. It hurt giving Brenda even imaginary credit.

Gretchen sighed. "If we've gotten to the point in our lives where we're taking something Brenda Schumacher said seriously, I think you know how bad things have gotten."

I sat up in my bed, pushing my blanket off. "Even an evil clock can be right twice a day. This really could all be some publicity stunt. He called them *showmances*. Where the two leads of a project pretend to date to get attention. He's done them in the past."

My stomach turned over and I felt a bit nauseous. What if he was just using me and I was stupid enough to fall for it?

"I'm assuming the actresses he pretended to date knew it wasn't a real relationship."

Getting up, I started to pace. I wanted to go downstairs and play something angry just to unbottle some of these feelings swarming around inside me. But that would wake Nick up, and I needed to sort some things out before that happened. "He's the one who is always telling me he used to be a bad guy. Maybe some of those tendencies stuck. He wants this part in a romantic comedy and has to earn it. What better way to show the producers that he's right for it than being in a public romance with a girl next door?"

"I just think Nick would have mentioned it if that was true."

Patches was on my bed and raised her head to look at me. It occurred to me that Nick might be able to hear me, too. I climbed back into bed carefully and spoke more quietly. "It feels like everything is happening too fast. Maybe this is why his publicist told me to watch over him. She knew I wouldn't be able to resist his charm. You have to admit that all of this came out of nowhere. He suddenly shows up and just starts pursuing me?"

She made a sound of disgust. "You know that happens regularly, right? If a guy at a bar thought you were cute, liked talking to you, it would not be weird for him to get your number and then ask you on a date. Nick just happens to be living in your house, which sped up the process."

"It feels fishy to me."

"That was your date with Wells."

I smiled. My best friend was always able to reach me when I was spiraling.

She continued, "You're making up excuses. You do that when things are getting too intense or too real for you. And I know you kind of swore off men in general after Teddy, but not every guy is like him. I know it's hard for you to believe that Nick Haddon actually likes you, but go along for the ride and have some fun. You don't have to marry this guy."

"Might I remind you that you're the one who said you were going to speak at our wedding?"

"I was teasing you," she said with a groan. "I mean, obviously going out with him is your decision. But I think you should talk to Nick about your suspicions before you make a choice. Or you should just kiss him to figure it out."

"How would kissing him make a difference?"

"Well, it would make me happy and I feel like you should do things to make your pregnant best friend happy."

"Kissing him won't answer my question," I pointed out. "I think you just want me to kiss him."

"You're probably right. But in my defense, he did say that he likes you."

"Give him time. He'll get over it. Men usually do." There was a loud buzzing sound coming from her side of the phone call. "What is that?"

"Like I mentioned earlier, that is your brother snoring," she told me. "I should probably get going before someone *wakes him up*!" She said the last few words loudly, but the snoring continued without interruption. "He sleeps like the dead."

"I remember," I said. We had been late to school many times because of it.

"Make Nick some waffles in the morning. Talk to him about it."

That was a good idea. Waffles made people bare their souls. Although I was going to have to find him the sugar-free kind. I'd make an early trip out to the store to see what I could scrounge up. "Okay, I'll do that."

"Good. The baby has stopped kicking, so I'm going to try to get some sleep," she said. "And, Jane? One more thing—don't let Nick get away just because you're scared."

She hung up and I was tempted to call her back and say that wasn't what was happening here and she'd missed the point completely.

But even I had to admit that she was right.

And I had to stop operating from a place of fear.

CHAPTER FOURTEEN

A few hours later, I headed out. I got to the store quickly, and sure enough, Heath had just what I was looking for in Gretchen's healthy-food section. My brother made a face when he saw me and asked, "What are you doing up at this hour? Trying to impress a movie star?"

My family had always been the best at seeing right through me. Technically, I was using the waffles to have a hard discussion, but did I want to impress Nick? Yes. "It's none of your business, and seriously, you should go to a sleep clinic."

I told him to put it on my account as he sputtered something about sleeping just fine, and I headed back to my car.

On the drive home I tried to think of what exactly to say to Nick but couldn't seem to find the right words. I decided I would figure it out when I saw him.

Bad plan.

Because as I was in the midst of making the waffle batter, Nick walked into the kitchen, looking as if he'd just rolled out of bed. His hair was artfully ruffled, his eyes sleepy, and once again, he didn't have a shirt on.

"Good morning, Jane. What's all this?" he asked.

"I'm, uh, making waffles." I forced myself to look back at the batter and stir it with the whisk so that I wouldn't make either one of us uncomfortable by openly ogling him.

But he didn't help me in this regard. Oh no, he had to go and make things worse. He came over to the counter, leaning his hip against it. If I shifted sideways just slightly, I would have been able to brush my arm against his bare chest.

While I was contemplating whether this was the best course of action, he asked, "What can I do to help?"

"You could get chest." I immediately realized my mistake. "*Dressed!* I meant dressed. You could get dressed."

He gave me a playful smile and started to walk out of the room backward. "Are you sure you want me to do that?"

No. "Yes."

"Okay," he said, drawing out the *A* like he didn't believe what I'd just said.

He shouldn't have, but that was beside the point.

As soon as he was gone, I grabbed my phone and texted Gretchen. I needed to tell somebody what had just happened.

He's shirtless. Again. Am powerless to resist.

Good for him. He did warn you that he wasn't interested in fighting fair.

If that was his strategy, it was a good one.

What does he have against shirts?

She sent me a shrugging emoji and then replied:

Maybe one spontaneously combusted after he put it on and he's been worried about it happening again. I guess you'll just have to get Zeus to it.

It is too early for puns, I told her.

It's never too early for that. Call me when you finish your conversation.

Nick came back in the kitchen, wearing all of his clothes, and I considered that kind of a win. It would be too hard to have a serious conversation if I was lost in his pecs.

"Can you do me a favor?" I asked.

"Anything."

The way he said it gave me that toe-curling feeling again. "You don't even know what the favor is."

"I don't need to. The answer is yes."

Oh, that had all kinds of possibilities that I immediately pushed aside. "There's a waffle iron down in the basement. It's on a shelf just next to the foot of the stairs. Would you mind grabbing it for me?" I wanted to keep stirring the batter, as I needed my hands busy so that they wouldn't go exploring.

"Sure thing."

I heard him run down the stairs and make a weird noise; then he came back up with the waffle iron. He carried it in his right hand and had the other pressed to his cheek.

"Are you okay?" I asked.

"I found your waffle iron, and as an added bonus, something dropped from the ceiling and bit me on the face."

"That could be serious. We have some dangerous spiders out here. I have a pest-control guy who sprays the house every month, but some of those buggers are tenacious. Let me see."

He set down the waffle iron and stepped closer, and I suddenly realized what was going to happen.

That wonderful, possibly deadly spider had made it so that I could carefully examine Nick's face. I moved closer to him than was probably necessary, so close that I could have kissed him.

I still had to have a serious conversation with him, but this was a nice moment.

Not nice. Thrilling. Exhilarating.

"Where did it bite you?" I asked softly.

He pointed at his left cheek. "Here."

I reached up to run the pads of my fingers along his skin. There was no visible bite. Had the spider been venomous, there would have been a raised bump that was possibly red. But there was just Nick's perfectly symmetrical face.

He sucked in a sharp breath when I made contact and held it. I took my time, enjoying the chance to finally touch him again. He exhaled slowly, making me wonder if he found it necessary to do his breathing exercises. I liked that I might be the reason he was doing them. His minty breath mingled with mine and I realized that he had brushed his teeth already.

All I had to do was push up slightly on my toes and I could have experienced that mint freshness against my lips.

His face was smooth, smoother than I would have expected. I let my fingers trail down to his stubble, enjoying the rougher texture there. I wanted desperately to place a soft kiss against his jawline. Realizing the danger I was putting myself in, I said, "I don't see anything. I think you're okay."

His hands were next to my waist, like he wanted to hold on to me but didn't dare. Maybe Nick didn't trust himself, either. I dropped my hand reluctantly but didn't move away.

"Are you sure?" he asked.

"Yep. All good." I was not personally all good, but that wasn't what we were talking about. We were both breathing a little heavier than normal, and my heart was beating so quickly it was like a dozen hummingbirds had taken up residence in my chest. I wondered if his heart was doing the same.

I wanted to just . . . look at him. To take him in. Drink in his gorgeous face without an interruption or somebody making an assumption about us. By standing so close to him, I discovered that his stubble had light blond strands mixed in with the darker brown ones and that his eyes were an even brighter shade of aquamarine than I'd previously thought. The edges of his eyes crinkled up as he smiled at me.

"You're humming," he said.

"Am I?" I had been totally unaware that I was doing it.

"You do it a lot when you're around me. I like it."

If I was unconsciously humming, it was because he made me hear music. A melody that he'd inspired that hadn't left my mind since he'd arrived. I really was totally enthralled by him, both physically and apparently mentally, and I needed to talk to him first before I did something that couldn't be undone. I cleared my throat and took a step back. Needing something to do, I reached for the waffle iron to clean it. He turned to watch me, still so close, and I could feel the heat from his body.

Heat I wanted pressed against me. I scrubbed harder at the waffle iron.

"I thought you didn't cook," he said.

"Both the fire chief and I agree that it's a bad idea for me to do so. But the waffle iron has a built-in timer. I don't usually burn them. And this is supposed to be a bed-and-breakfast, and I figured at some point, I should actually provide you with the breakfast part."

"You're making waffles from scratch?" He sounded impressed.

"That's hilarious. No, I'm making it from a mix, where I added water and vegetable oil. And don't worry, I'm not going to make you drop your carb protest. I got you a keto mix."

He leaned against the counter again, folding his arms across his broad chest. "That's making it from scratch as far as I'm concerned and I'm impressed."

"If you're impressed, that's on you," I told him with a smile. I was rewarded with his full-watt movie star grin in response and I almost dropped the waffle iron in the sink.

I dried the iron off, giving it my full attention. When I'd finished, I plugged it in so that it could heat up.

This was it. Time to chat. "There's another reason I made waffles. In my family we had all our big, serious discussions over a waffle breakfast."

"Should I be worried?"

I crossed my arms, mirroring his pose. "That probably depends on your answers. The first thing I need to know—what you said to me last night, was that for real? This isn't some elaborate publicity stunt organized by Shanice where you pretend to date me to land your part in that rom-com? Some showmance?"

He reached out, putting his right hand on my shoulder, and little mini-fireworks exploded under my skin from the contact. "Is that what you think?"

I was not going to think about his long, tapered fingers, which would have been perfect for playing the piano and, you know, other stuff. "Obviously, the thought crossed my mind."

"Jane, I would never do that. I just wanted to take you on a date. Where I promise not to talk about fish at all."

My face flushed slightly as I realized what he was referencing. "You heard Wells?"

He pulled his hand back, as if he suddenly realized that he'd misunderstood how I would take his joke. "I think the whole diner heard. It was a bit like having to watch someone get waterboarded."

"So . . . you're asking me on a date because you feel bad for me?" That was somehow worse. So much worse than thinking this was all just a setup for his career.

He edged closer to me. "I'm not sure what's making you jump to these conclusions, but let me be very clear. I want to spend time with you. I don't feel bad for you and I'm not trying to manipulate you into dating me for a movie. There is no ulterior motive other than being able to hang out with you. Because the more time I spend you with you, the more I want."

His lips were near mine again, making mine tingle in anticipation. "Want?" I repeated, barely able to get the word out.

"Yes, want. I'm not lying to you, Jane."

I cleared my throat once, twice. I believed him. I did. He seemed so honest, so sincere, it was impossible not to. But even if he wasn't lying to me or using me, there were other considerations. I asked, "And what happens when you go back to California?"

That seemed to cool him down a bit and he pulled his head back so that we were no longer in any danger of accidentally brushing our lips together. "We'll cross that bridge when we come to it."

With some space, I was able to gain some clarity. "Like we'll go our separate ways and say 'thanks for the fun' or something else?"

"I don't know the future. I just know that I want to be with you."

I couldn't understand why he wanted that when I was literally spending all of my time discouraging him. He said it so sincerely, though, that it was hard to continue disagreeing with him.

Or maybe the promise of his kiss was breaking down all of my defenses. "That's just hard to believe."

"It shouldn't be. You are talented, funny, kind, pretty, loyal, and a million other things I can't wait to discover. I should have had to fight my way through a horde of men lining up to date you."

"And yet you did not."

He shrugged. "Their loss."

Everything he was saying was so perfect and romantic, and it was impossible to keep resisting him.

"I've been thinking about our discussion last night," he said. "I have a proposition for you."

Yes. Whatever he wanted, the answer was yes.

He continued, "We need to call up the potential sponsors. I thought maybe you and I could have a competition to see who could raise the most money and wager on which one of us will win."

"A bet. You want to make a bet?"

He gave me that playful smile, full of confidence. "Exactly."

"And when I win? What do I get?" I asked.

"*If* you win, what do you want?"

I wanted to say him. But I understood why he was doing this. He'd found a kind of loophole for my reluctance. I knew what he was going to ask for if he won.

But he wouldn't win. He had to know that. "If I win, then whatever embarrassing thing that Gretchen cooks up for you to do on social media, you have to do it." And I knew my best friend better than anyone. It was going to be a lot. He didn't know what he was agreeing to.

"Done. And when I win, you have to go on a date with me."

I raised my eyebrows in mock surprise. "I told you, I don't date guys like you." He was going to have to work for it.

"What if . . . going out with me would cure cancer?"

"Nope." I pretended to consider it and added, "Maybe to cure cancer. I'd probably do it to feed the hungry and end war. But that's it. That's the line."

He looked like he was trying not to laugh. "So anything short of solving the world-hunger crisis, curing cancer, and stopping foreign aggression, and you won't go."

"And since those things aren't going to happen anytime soon, should you really be throwing away your one chance to ask me out? It's not a fair competition."

"You're right. It won't even be close."

His arrogance was misplaced. "No, it's not fair because I know everyone."

"I'm very charming."

True. "But I have the home-court advantage."

This wasn't a bet. It was a surefire win for me, and it was a little disappointing that he was going to lose.

"Get ready for defeat, Jane Wagner."

"Doubtful, Nick Haddon." Then, determined not to be distracted by his dancing eyes, I asked, "What are the parameters?"

"I don't know—first person to the finish line wins?"

"No, I mean more like, you can't call the CEO of Amazon to be a sponsor. The business has to be within that twenty-mile radius of Patience."

"I think it would be smart to let a huge corporation sponsor us if they wanted to, but you're on. Twenty-mile radius of Patience, and the competition ends when the entire amount is raised or, in case we don't get the full amount, the winner is whoever has raised the most money three days from now."

He offered me his hand and I reached out to shake on it. That electrical feeling engulfed my hand again, sending little tremors of excitement skating across my skin.

The waffle iron chirped at me, and I wondered how many times it had done that while I'd been standing there, shaking hands with him. I pulled away and asked, "Will you set the table and I'll get the waffles started?"

He did what I requested, and I made the batch of keto waffles first. He didn't so much eat his waffles as he attacked them, and it made me a bit faint to think of what he did to things he enjoyed.

I sat down and quickly discovered that his keto waffles had a weird aftertaste.

"Don't like it?" he asked.

"Not really, but everything's better when you drown it in syrup," I said, doing just that. I got some syrup on my fingers and stuck them in my mouth to lick it off, only to look up and see that hungry look in Nick's eyes as he watched me. My blood heated up in response.

"So, uh, what are your plans today?" I asked, returning my attention to my faux food.

"Do you mean other than raising more money than you? Nothing until the anniversary party tonight."

The anniversary party. That we were going to together. Well, not *together*, but technically, we were going to the same place at the same time and arriving via the same car.

"What about you?" he asked.

"Beating you in the bet, and then Phyllis hosts her seniors' book club today."

"Do you think they have room for one more?"

"You're not going to want to join," I told him. "They read a lot of erotica. If you show up in the middle of that meeting, those ladies are going to objectify you so hard."

He laughed. "Nobody wants that."

I kind of did.

From there, we talked about more people in the town, which led to him telling me stories about the people he'd worked with on different sets, and I found myself fascinated by every new thing he revealed about himself.

Like the fact that he was scared of dogs due to an incident from his childhood, and his hatred of onions and celery. I shared some of my favorite things with him, including my love for chocolate chip cookies and young adult romance books, and some of the antics that Gretchen and I had gotten up to when we were younger.

Topics shifted and changed as we talked and talked. We traded stories about some of the hardest things we'd endured, like two warriors showing off their scars. He shared how difficult his parents' neglect had been on him growing up, how being a jinx had seriously screwed with his ability to see himself and his work clearly.

I told him about my relationship with Teddy, how that had messed me up for a long time. How one of the hardest parts of it for me was the way he'd just disappeared without taking any ownership of what he'd done. How coming back home had brought back some of those painful memories. Nick asked what it was like when my dad got sick, and I found myself telling him things I hadn't really shared with anyone else.

How terrified I'd been, how I'd blamed myself. That maybe if I'd visited more or paid closer attention I might have seen that he wasn't doing well.

"You couldn't have known," he told me. "There wasn't anything you should have done."

"No, but you're not always rational when someone you love is in danger." I could feel tears forming in my eyes. "I remember being so afraid that I would never see my father alive again. I packed up all of my stuff and moved back here that night."

"You're a good daughter."

That made the tears worse, and I shook my head like that could keep them from falling. "I didn't think I was."

"Honestly, you make me wish that I was a better son. That I had a better relationship with my parents."

"I'm not going to pretend to understand your whole dynamic with them, but they're still here. Which means you can try and get to a better place with them. I'm not saying it will work out the way that you want, but they'd be fools to not want to be closer to you."

"Do you want to be closer to me?" he asked in that tone of his that turned my knees to jelly.

My phone beeped, reminding me that I had to get ready for work. I did want to stay right where I was and continue our conversation about whether we should get closer. "You have a bet to try and win first," I reminded him as I got up from the table. "I'll see you when I get home from work tonight."

"Yes, dear," he said in a teasing voice. "And while you're gone I'm going to find out how to do dishes and I'll clean up."

That made me pause in the doorway. "I want to ask you if you're serious, but sadly enough, I know that you are."

"You shouldn't mock me for my lack of adult skills. That's not my fault. My parents didn't pay someone else to raise a fool, but the nannies forgot the part where I should learn basic life skills."

"I can show you later, if you'd like."

"I would like that. Very much." He was ten feet away, but when he said things like that, it was almost like he was standing right next to me, touching me.

"Okay. We will, uh, do that. I have to get ready." I hesitated in the doorway. I really did not want to go to the library and leave him. "You're going to lose, you know."

He was carrying the plates over to the sink. "I'm not."

"Your confidence is admirable, if mistaken. You really should quit while you're behind."

"I don't give up."

Again, I believed him. If he said he was going to win, well, who was I to argue with the very hot man currently rinsing dishes in my kitchen? Feeling a little light-headed, I left to go get ready. It really was going to be a slaughter. Everyone would sign up with me, and while I would enjoy seeing Nick in a tutu or whatever else Gretchen came up with, I was going to regret not being able to go on an official date with him.

Of course, I could always tell him I'd changed my mind. My fear was that he'd enjoy that too much and lord it over me for a long time.

How long? That was still debatable and I didn't have any answers. I didn't like the unknown. I liked things to be reliable and predictable. For one note to flow naturally into the next.

But Nick was like a bunch of discordant notes that shouldn't work but, when played together in the right pattern, ended up being the most beautiful thing you'd ever heard.

I couldn't do short-term. I wasn't a fling type of girl. I hoped he had understood that. I didn't know how to live in the moment.

Which was a bit ridiculous and unfair. It wasn't like we were going to fall in love and ride off into the Hollywood sunset together. But I did like being around him and I wanted to keep doing it.

I quickly got ready and yelled goodbye to him. He said it back from the kitchen. I grabbed my purse, then realized that I had forgotten the stack of potential sponsors in the music room. I ran in there and grabbed the stack, shoving it into my bag.

"Now I'm really leaving!" I said.

"Goodbye again!" he called back. I smiled. It was nice having someone there when I left in the morning.

Who was looking forward to me returning in the evening.

I could get used to that feeling.

And I lived in that happy moment for the exact amount of time it took me to reach the end of my long driveway.

Standing next to my mailbox were several photographers, all grabbing photos of me.

There was also a group of teenage girls holding up their phones and some signs for Nick. A girl ran over to my car and knocked on the window.

I rolled it down cautiously. "Can I help you?"

"Is this where Nick Haddon is staying?"

It was then that I realized what I had done. When we had announced to the entire world that Nick Haddon was here in Patience, why hadn't I believed his publicist when she'd warned me that it meant the world would come here looking for him?

Inside my house, I'd been in a little magical bubble with him, but now reality had shown up.

And I was worried what that would mean for me and Nick.

CHAPTER FIFTEEN

When I got to the library, I texted Nick to let him know about the paparazzi and fans outside the house and warned him to be careful. He sent back the thumbs-up emoji with a text that said:

Don't worry about it. I've got it handled.

I found myself scoping out the area around me as I walked inside the library, half expecting more photographers or teenage girls. There weren't any, but I wondered if that was about to become a huge problem for the town. Nick was probably used to it, but he was here without security. Maybe I should call Shanice to let her know, or the sheriff to see if we could get Nick like, a personal escort or something.

Reminding myself that Nick had said he had it, I opted not to do either. He was an adult. He could take care of himself.

It was just that . . . weirdly enough, I wanted to take care of him, too.

Gretchen was waiting for me inside. "Well?" she asked. "How did your breakfast go? Did Nick cook up a storm?"

I dropped my bag on the circulation desk. "What?"

"You know, a storm? Because Zeus is the god of lightning?"

"Isn't that Thor?"

"He's the god of thunder." But then she made an impatient noise and waved both her hands. "That's not the point. Don't try and sidetrack me. What did he say?"

I filled her in on my conversation with Nick and how things had gone, what we had said, about our bet. When I finished she gave me a smug smile and said, "I knew this wasn't a setup. I hate to say I told you so, but who are we kidding? We both know how much I love to say it. I told you so. What is it about people with Wagner DNA and refusing to recognize that I'm always right?"

I put a hand up to my chest. "Wow, Gretchen. You've really shown me the error of my—just kidding."

She shot me a sour look and then asked, "You're going to throw this bet, aren't you?"

"No! I've never intentionally lost anything in my entire life."

"Come on, make like laundry. Like a bad hand in poker. Origami."

I shot her a questioning look and she added, "Just fold already! This man is living rent-free in your head. He is painting walls and hanging up pictures and arranging his furniture. Why don't you just go out with him? Why are you so afraid of letting good things happen to you?"

Her words provoked an unexpected reaction. My eyes stung, like I was about to cry. I blinked away the wateriness. I didn't think I was afraid of letting good things happen to me.

It just seemed that all I'd had lately were a bunch of bad things that kept happening, one right after another.

Except Nick, that voice inside me whispered. I let out a shaky breath, trying to get a hold of myself.

Gretchen instinctively understood what I needed in that moment—a change of subject. "Do you know what your brother did?"

"Normally, I'd say something stupid, but since you're the one telling me, something impossibly romantic and perfect?"

"No. Heath needs your thoughts and prayers because he very tragically informed me this morning that he didn't buy me a present for our anniversary because the party, which he is not throwing, is my present.

He also pointed out that I had told him that I didn't need for him to get me a present this year."

"Which he obviously should have ignored and gotten you a present anyways." Why were men so dense? Didn't he know Gretchen better than that? And shouldn't he be actively trying not to piss her off right now?

"Yes, he should have. And that's when I remind myself that this all might have been so much worse because he had initially wanted us to get married on February fifteenth so that all the Valentine's stuff would be fifty percent off and he could buy it for our anniversary."

I laughed. I had totally forgotten about that fight. "Good luck with that. And please know that I can't help you bury any bodies because I hurt my back last week."

"Noted. I'm going to take off. My mom wants me to come by to talk about some last-minute details for the party. If anything else happens with Nick, text me immediately. Also, ignore your potential sponsors list. Let the man win." She waved and left.

I sat down at my desk and reached for my purse. I pulled out the stack of papers and flipped through the pages. About halfway through I found Nick's dollar bill paper-clipped to the page.

It made me smile. I enjoyed playing this game with him and was looking forward to returning the dollar bill to him soon. As I held up the bill, I wondered if I should take Gretchen's advice.

Even if I wanted to, I couldn't. We had to raise the money one way or the other. And it would go faster if two of us were working on it. Decision made, I put the dollar in my jeans pocket, then turned my attention to the list. Should I start from the beginning? Or was Nick already doing that? Maybe I should head to the last page. That seemed like the safer bet.

It was possible he hadn't even started calling people yet, but he seemed highly motivated.

Which sent a little zing of excitement through me. It was nice to be chased, to be somebody who a guy like him would go to this kind of effort for.

I dialed the number for Mrs. Zalinski. She had been my fourth-grade teacher and retired a few years ago to start her quilting shop. She answered right away.

"Zalinski's Quilting Supplies. This is Bea Zalinski. How may I help you?"

"Mrs. Zalinski, this is Jane Wagner. How are you doing today?"

"Jane! How lovely to hear from you. I am just fine, dear. How is your father?"

"He's doing so much better," I reassured her. "The doctor cleared him to return to work months ago, but you know how my mother is."

"I do, the poor thing. Send them both my love, will you?"

"I will. But the reason I'm calling is that the festival is trying to raise funds from local businesses, and we were hoping—"

She cut me off. "No need to give me the pitch again. I already told that nice young man I would contribute. Are you just confirming?"

This threw me off for a second. So Nick had started at the bottom of the list. I should have suspected he might. Sneaky. "Yes, I'm just confirming. I wanted to make sure Nick explained everything to you."

"Oh yes, he was quite helpful. And very charming."

He had said that was an advantage he had over me and it turned out he was right. I knew how hard it was to think rationally when he was beaming that charm on me, so I couldn't blame Mrs. Zalinski. I thanked her, told her to call me if she had any questions, and hung up.

I had hoped that would go better for me. Mrs. Zalinski clung to her way of doing things, and she'd never participated in the festival before this. She had told me once she thought that it was a bit too frivolous for her tastes, which were very old-school. She was the type of person who still considered Pluto a planet. I had thought that would work in my favor. How had Nick won her over so quickly?

I flipped back to the first page, but I was worried that Nick might be messing with me and had called the first few names at the beginning and the end of the list so that I wouldn't know where to start. There was only one way to find out. I called Allen's Hardware.

When a gruff-sounding man answered, I said, "Hi, this is Jane Wagner and I'm calling about your business possibly sponsoring the fall festival—"

"The movie star already called and we said yes." Then he hung up.

What if there was no order here? Was Nick just scattershotting the list, randomly hitting targets so that I would always be one step behind him?

It hadn't taken me that long to drive to the library and chat with Gretchen. How many people on the list had he already contacted?

My phone rang and for a moment, I wondered if it was him, calling to gloat. I glanced at the screen and saw a number I didn't recognize.

When I answered, it turned out to be a vendor who was having some issues with their permits for the festival. That call was followed by one from the place where we were renting tents; they didn't have the right size in stock. And about an hour after that, there was a phone call from the petting zoo people because there had been a mix-up with the bunnies. An assistant had put the male and female bunnies into the same pen and now they had a bunch of pregnant rabbits, and they wanted to talk substitutions.

In between all this, Mr. Mortenson accidentally knocked over the flimsy shelves that housed our nonfiction section with his oxygen tank, and as I was cleaning that up, I made the mistake of wondering aloud, "What else can go wrong today?"

My phone rang again and I was a little afraid to answer it. I let out a sigh of relief when I saw it was Nick.

When I picked up I immediately said, "Have you already called everyone on this list?"

"Not everyone. Not yet."

He sounded so smug. "Has anyone ever told you that you're very annoying?"

"Yes. Women, mostly."

I laughed. "So are you calling me to concede?" I knew there wasn't much of a chance of that being true, given his apparent success so far.

"I'm calling because the waterbed has sprung some kind of slow leak. I've got towels down, but there's a definite situation going on here." He sounded very apologetic.

Groaning, I leaned forward and put my face in my free hand. I did not need this today. "Don't leave me a bad review online."

"I wasn't planning on it," he said with a bit of laughter in his voice.

"That's good. Don't worry about it. I have a guy."

"You have a waterbed guy?"

"You kind of have to have a guy when you own a waterbed. This isn't the first time that it's happened. I'll give him a call."

"It sounds like you're dealing with a lot," he said.

"You should just call me FEMA with the way I'm handling emergencies today."

"I'm sorry." He paused. "But not sorry enough to not take advantage of this situation. Call your waterbed guy and then text me and let me know what I should do next. You won't be able to call me, because I plan on being on the phone."

He hung up before I could respond.

I was torn—I wanted to jump back into the competition with him, but I had to get the bed repaired as quickly as possible before the first floor of the house was flooded.

And all of that was being overwhelmed by the part of me that urged me to take Gretchen's advice and just let Nick win.

～

Eventually, I found names on the list that Nick hadn't called, but only by randomly picking a company and hoping for the best. The businesses in Patience almost always said yes, while the ones farther away from town were hit or miss.

Well, they were hit or miss for me. I had no idea how Nick was doing.

Plus, word had spread, and there were a few local businesses that told me they'd rather talk to Nick about the festival and that they were waiting for his phone call.

So much for my home-court advantage.

Franklin, the waterbed guy, was scheduled to meet me at my house after work. Nick could have let him in, but true to his word, he was not answering his phone. I tried texting, but there was no reply.

I let Franklin in and we walked to Nick's room together. Not that Franklin needed me to guide him there—he was well acquainted with the bed of a thousand leaks. I knocked on Nick's door. The door swung open to reveal Nick wearing only a towel around his waist.

All the blood drained from my head and my lungs stopped working.

"Hey, come on in!" he said, not seeming the least bit embarrassed. "I was just about to get in the shower."

I tried to say something, but words did not come out of my mouth. Instead, I made some kind of humiliating choking-on-my-own-tongue kind of sound.

My reaction made no sense. I'd seen him shirtless on more than one occasion. But this was more than just another run-of-the-mill shirtless situation.

This was Nearly Naked Nick.

I wanted to quickly escort Franklin from the house and come back to this room and rip the towel off Nick and have my way with him.

Was it always this hot in the house? Or was it just hot in here? I should really check the thermostat. I tried fanning my warm face, but it wasn't helping.

Unaware of my internal meltdown, Nick brought Franklin into the room and showed him where he thought the water was coming from. Franklin got his tools out. "I've dealt with this before," he said.

"Then it sounds like we're in good hands," Nick said, smiling at me like I wasn't having not-safe-for-work thoughts about him. "I'm going to jump in the shower, if you need me," he said, and then he went into his bathroom and shut the door.

I heard the shower start up and my mind started racing. What emergency could I need him for that would necessitate me interrupting him in the shower?

Argh. My brain went completely blank. I had nothing! Nothing!

I mean, I wasn't going to actually do anything, because there was the whole "completely inappropriate" aspect of it, but I did stand there and consider it.

Yep, I really was ready to be origami or clean laundry. I wanted to fold.

Franklin examined the leak and then stood up. "I don't currently have the materials I need to fix this properly. I can do a temporary patch job, but we're having supply chain issues and it might be a while before I get exactly what I need."

"Okay." I knew that Franklin was talking to me and I should pay attention, but I was too busy imagining what Nick looked like in the shower—all the water raining down on him, traveling over his broad shoulders and then circling around the muscles on his chest, making his skin glistening and shiny and . . . Oh. I realized that Franklin was trying to communicate with me. I forced myself to pay attention. "What does it mean if you can only do a temporary patch?"

"It means that for the time being, no one should be sleeping on this bed. I told you we had to replace the entire mattress."

"I've been conditioning the water!" I told him. I had been begging my parents to let me get rid of it. We definitely needed to get an actual bed in here, and despite what my mom kept saying, it was not going to be some kitschy thing we could advertise on an Airbnb type of site that would make hipsters want to stay here. Waterbeds were not a draw for anyone.

"No one caused this," Franklin said. "It's being taken care of properly; the vinyl is just getting old."

"I get it," I said. "It's okay. We'll figure something out. Just let me know when your stuff arrives and we can do a real fix on it."

Franklin nodded and said, "I'm going to go grab some things I need out of the truck. I'll be right back."

Nick wasn't going to be able to stay in this room. That meant he had to move upstairs. The problem was, the only finished guest room upstairs was currently unfurnished and had a temporary futon stored in there. The other rooms were in various states of disarray—they needed Sheetrock and had exposed wires and a bare subfloor.

There was only one other bed in the house that Nick could use.

Mine.

CHAPTER SIXTEEN

As I got ready for the anniversary party, I tried to tell myself to stop being so ridiculous. I was completely overreacting to Nick whenever I was around him. He was just a handsome man who was kind and thoughtful and funny and sweet and ambitious and . . . I shook my head. I was not going to list all the good things about him. That was just going to make me even more of a fangirl when I saw him.

Wells notwithstanding, it had been too long since I'd been out on a real date with a man I liked and was attracted to. In fact, I hadn't seriously dated anyone since my relationship with Teddy Newcastle had ended.

That made me set my mascara down on the counter and study my own reflection. Had it really been that long? No wonder I was ready to faint whenever I saw Nick Haddon's bare chest.

I needed to get back out there and live again. I had really shut down a lot of important parts of my life after Teddy, and then again after my dad's heart attack.

If nothing else, Nick coming here had shown me that. He wanted me to live in the moment—and maybe I couldn't do that exactly, but I could start going out again.

I glanced at my phone. We should have left already. I let out a little groan. If Gretchen was a stickler for not being late, her mother was the Supreme Commander of Being There on Time No Matter What.

"Nick!" I yelled down the stairs. "We need to go! We can't be late!"

"I need a few minutes!" he yelled back.

Why? He had started getting ready long before I did. I hadn't been able to get into the shower until after Franklin left. "Hurry up!"

My makeup was done, my hair up in a messy chignon, and I had on a sparkly dark pink cocktail dress that I'd picked up as an impulse buy while I was shopping in Cincinnati with Gretchen a few months ago. We'd gone there for baby things, and I'd come back with this dress.

Which had been totally impractical, as I couldn't imagine where I would wear it, but I bought it anyway. It was the most feminine thing I'd ever owned. It had a halter top and a belted waist, and thanks to the tulle crinoline Gretchen had insisted I get to go with it, the skirt flared out in a circle when I spun around.

The entire dress was covered in a layer of tiny sparkly crystals that caught the light when I moved, and it made me feel like a princess.

I was glad I finally had a reason to wear it.

Another part of me was more glad that I had someone to wear it for.

Even though this was not a date.

I got the clutch that my mom had lent me to go with my dress and slid on my silver heels, then messed with the straps. I had forgotten how fickle those shoes were. I hadn't worn them in a long time—my last boyfriend was slightly shorter than me, and I hadn't been allowed to wear high heels or else he would sulk in a corner all night because I'd embarrassed him.

There were a lot of ways that I'd let Teddy limit me because I'd thought I was in love with him. I didn't want to have those kinds of restrictions on me anymore. I wanted to be with someone who accepted and appreciated all of me.

I let out a long breath, as if I could exhale that memory. I didn't want to start my evening off in a bad mood. I went into the kitchen to make sure Patches was all taken care of and then headed to the front door to grab my coat.

"Nick!" I tried again. "Gretchen's mom is going to murder me if I'm not on time."

Glancing at my phone, I realized that it was too late. We were definitely going to be making a grand entrance where everyone would be looking at us.

I would be showing up with Nick Haddon, which meant that was sort of inevitable either way, but I was hoping to fly a bit under the radar and not make everyone turn when we walked in.

"I'm coming!" he said, but still no Nick.

Patches meowed at me from the other room, like she wanted to be part of the conversation, too. I grabbed my jacket and put it on, making sure the dollar bill was in my pocket. I wiggled my toes; I'd forgotten how tight these shoes were.

That made me realize that the strap of my right shoe felt loose, and I lifted my foot to try to adjust it. I perched precariously on my left leg while doing it. I probably should have just sat down to fix the strap properly, but we were in a hurry.

"On a scale of nine to ten, how do I look?" Nick asked, coming into the front hallway.

I gasped and fell sideways, shoulder first, into the wall when I saw him. I dropped my right foot and made myself stand upright again.

How did he look? He looked like he should be riding a horse out of the ocean in a cologne commercial. Space and time no longer had meaning. I couldn't feel my toes, although that might have been due to my shoes and not his *I just fell out of a book about Greek mythology* thing he had going on.

His suit was perfectly fitted to him, emphasizing the broadness of his shoulders, and he looked like, well, somebody out of the movies. What was it about a man in a tailored suit that made them look so yummy? His hair was artfully ruffled, pushed up from his face, his eyes twinkling at me.

But the thing I noticed most? He'd shaved. Part of me felt a bit sad—I had come to really enjoy the stubble. I had wanted to feel it against my face, turning my skin red and sensitized. Then I remembered I had told him that I preferred clean-shaven men, and here we were.

I put my hand over my stomach, trying to still the chaos happening there. He had shaved for me.

Plus, now I got to imagine what it would be like to kiss his smooth cheeks, trailing my lips along that jawline of his, and wow. That worked, too.

He looked a little off and I'd become so accustomed to the stubble that, for a split second, he seemed like a different person. But then he smiled at me and there he was.

My Nick.

Where did that come from? an internal voice demanded. Right. I shouldn't think those things. He wasn't my anything.

And despite liking him, I reminded myself that there wasn't a future here.

"Who . . . what . . . ," I said, and I didn't know what I was trying to communicate. It wasn't coherent—I knew that—but I couldn't have explained myself to him if I'd tried.

"It's Gucci," he said. Like we were on a red carpet and I was a reporter asking him who he was wearing.

"You brought a designer suit with you?"

"No, I had my assistant overnight it to me when Gretchen invited me to the party."

"Right, as one does."

"Do you like it?" There was a tone in his voice I didn't recognize immediately, and then I realized that my opinion mattered to him.

That just like he'd shaved for me, this suit had been chosen with me in mind.

The thought was overwhelming.

My instinct was to protect myself, to not be too vulnerable with him. It was too scary. "I suppose you'll do," I said.

"Do?" he echoed innocently. "Who?"

My ovaries immediately volunteered the rest of my body as tribute.

"That wasn't what . . . never mind." I tucked my clutch under my arm. Nick turned toward the mirror hanging in the front hall and messed a little with his hair.

"You can stop," I told him. "You're the fairest of them all."

"Do you think so?" he said, looking at me in the mirror.

Did I think so? This was my brother and best friend's anniversary party, but right now I was kind of willing to risk my relationships with them to blow the whole thing off so that I could stay right where I was and have a private party with Nick.

"Yes, your huntsman and I agree. Definitely the fairest. We have to go because we're going to be late."

He glanced at an expensive watch on his left wrist. "We're only going to be like fifteen minutes late. That's California early."

"Ha ha," I said. "This isn't Los Angeles. Let's go."

Nick ran over to open the door for me, an unnecessary but sweet gesture. Then he kind of killed that vibe when he jokingly said, "I'm glad we're going to be at a party. I think it might be a waste for you to be the only person to see me looking like this."

"That's one of the things I like best about you, Nick. The way you're always thinking of others." I walked past him onto the porch, and he pulled the door shut behind him as he followed me.

I noticed two things—the first was that Nick was still taller than me, even with my heels on, and I knew that even if he hadn't been, he wouldn't have cared.

The second was how strong that urge to stay home with him was. I didn't want to go anywhere and I didn't want to see other people. I didn't want anyone staring at us and making comments. I'd been the center of negative gossip before, and that run-in with the fans at my mailbox earlier made me think of something Nick had said.

"What's up?" he asked.

"I'm not sure I want to go," I confessed.

"It's one night."

"So is *The Purge*."

He laughed. "It won't be as bad as that."

No, it probably wouldn't be. "Everybody's going to be talking about us. Staring at us."

"How could they not? I look amazing."

Now it was my turn to laugh. "You really are fishing for that compliment, aren't you?"

"Maybe you could let me land one."

I smiled and turned to face him. I straightened the lapels on his suit jacket, running my fingers down the front. "You look like a movie star," I told him, and with him being fully distracted by my nearness, I took the dollar bill out of my pocket and slid it into his.

His hands were at my side again, like he wanted to touch me but didn't follow through. "I suppose I'll have to take what I can get." He took a step back and offered me his arm. "We have a date to get to. Shall we?"

I took his arm and we walked to my car, but I had to set the record straight. I tried not to think about how much I enjoyed holding on to him. "This is not a date. You don't get to piggyback off of someone else's hard work. You'll have to come up with your own date. One that you plan and execute. But that's only if you win the bet."

"That's not going to be a problem," he said with a little smile. "How did your fundraising go?"

While we drove to Gretchen's mom and dad's house, I told him about the businesses I'd spoken to, but I didn't give him any exact numbers of what I'd actually raised. I had come up with a spreadsheet to figure out how many of the remaining businesses needed to commit and the dollar amount necessary from each one. I probably shouldn't have been sharing my entire battle strategy with him, but it was hard to not talk when someone looked at you like you were the most interesting person in the whole world. I noticed him smiling at me.

I had just pulled into a parking spot and turned the car off. "What?" I asked him.

"Nothing. I just love it when you talk data to me."

I laughed, and that had clearly been his intent. We got out of the car and walked around to the backyard.

Keeping all of our arms to ourselves.

It had been transformed into a fairyland. A large tent had been put up and there were Christmas lights and potted trees and white linen tablecloths. A large dance floor had been set up, but everyone was busy getting food from the buffet and talking.

A woman I didn't recognize stopped me. She was holding a clipboard. "Name?" she asked.

"Jane Wagner."

She scanned down the list and then put a checkmark next to my name. "And this is your plus-one?"

"He's not—"

Nick interrupted me. "I'm not her plus-one, because this is most definitely not a date. I don't think I'm even her minus-one."

The woman finally glanced up from her clipboard and stared at him. She gasped, dropping her clipboard. Her mouth gaped slightly and she froze, her hands clutched to her chest.

Nick leaned in to whisper in my ear, "We might have to reboot her."

I reached down and got her clipboard and tried to hand it to her, but she didn't seem able to take it back. After a few seconds of standing there, a woman with a headset approached. "I'm Evelyn, the party planner. Is everything okay?"

How was I supposed to explain that the sight of Nick Haddon had rendered her assistant speechless?

Especially since I was particularly prone to the same phenomenon?

"It's fine," I said, trying again to hand the clipboard back.

Nick very smoothly took it out of my hands. "Yes, I was just going to sign this for . . . What was your name again?"

"Jennifer," she finally whispered.

"'To Jennifer, with love, Nick Haddon,'" he said, signing his name with a flourish on her clipboard and handing it back to her.

There were tears in her eyes when she took it back. "Thank you. You're my favorite person. I love you."

Nick smiled at her. "You're very kind. Thanks for doing such a great job here."

Evelyn the party planner looked as if she wasn't sure what to do, and it dawned on me that she had no idea who Nick was. "Let me grab your jacket," she said. "The tent is heated. Dinner has been put out, so go ahead and seat yourselves wherever you'd like and grab something to eat."

I started to shrug off my jacket and felt Nick's fingers brush against the top of my shoulders, and all the nerve endings in that area lit up in response, making me suck in a deep breath.

He finished taking it off for me, which was a good thing because my entire upper body had stopped working and was waiting for his touch again. He handed it to Evelyn, who told us to have a good night.

"Let's go in," Nick said, apparently oblivious to the fact that Jennifer was still staring at him, holding her clipboard against her chest.

"Okay."

He put his hand on my lower back to guide me into the tent. My bare lower back.

When I'd bought this dress, not once did I consider the fact that someday, Nick Haddon would put his large, strong hand against the small of my back to guide me into an event. It felt like his handprint was searing itself into my skin. As if I were going to have a permanent mark there.

My skin was not the only place he was leaving his mark, though.

"Does that happen a lot?" I asked as we walked in. People were looking at us, but no one was staring like I'd thought they would. I pointed at a nearby table so that we could sit down, not wanting to draw any more attention to us than was strictly necessary.

Plus, I needed him to move his hand so that tongues didn't start wagging.

Including my own.

"Pretty often," he admitted as he sat next to me. "It's a strange thing to go through the world and have that be people's reaction to you—crying, screaming, freezing."

I nodded. "It would be a hard thing to get accustomed to. I can't take you anywhere, can I?"

"No, you can't," he agreed. "It's pretty rare that I don't get recognized. That is one of the things I've enjoyed about Patience. Nobody here seems to care who I am."

"They care, but we have a lot going on. And at this point you're basically an honorary citizen with all that you're doing for the town. We protect our own."

"I know. I like it."

"Although that might change," I told him. "Like with that group of fans outside of my house this morning? I'm worried about what might happen."

"Most people are respectful. Yes, they'll ask for selfies if you're at a restaurant or in an airport, but I've never had someone show up and knock on my front door. I think most people understand what's appropriate."

What if someone came up and knocked on my door? Or worse? It made me worry about him in a way I hadn't before. "But what about the ones who don't?"

"It does happen. It has happened to me in the past, but you get a restraining order and move on." My concerned expression finally seemed to register with him. "Are you worried?"

"Should I be? Do you currently have a stalker?"

"Not as far as I know. Don't worry, I'd protect you." He put his hand over mine, holding it gently. It caused a warmth to start up inside my chest that spread through the rest of me until I felt like I was glowing.

We were both looking at our hands and I thought he expected me to take mine away, but I didn't. He flexed his hand slightly, which made me think that maybe he'd retreat, but he didn't, either.

"I'm assuming your parents are at this party?" he asked, his tone light.

"They are. They're over there." They were talking to their neighbors, the Silversteins.

He smiled in a way that was concerning.

"What's that look for?" I asked.

"I'm just trying to figure out in what order I should ask them questions about you. Am I going for a chronological timeline or asking them to share your childhood stories based on how humiliating they are?" he said thoughtfully, like he was really going to do it.

When I'd thought about this evening, it had never once occurred to me that Nick would meet my parents.

Who would find the best ways possible to embarrass me. I put my free hand on top of his. "You're not going to go over there."

"Oh, I'm afraid I very much am," he said and stood up. I could only watch in horror as he walked over to where my parents were chatting with their friends and introduced himself.

I didn't know what to do. It was like watching a car wreck happening in slow motion in front of me. Who knew what inappropriate things my mother would say? How overprotective my dad would get? Would Heath join in and turn this into a free-for-all?

Here I'd been worried about having to protect him from possible stalkers, but I hadn't thought about protecting him from my mother, the Grand Inquisitor. Oh, she was going to ask him so many personal and invasive questions.

I knew I should run over there and intervene, but I couldn't move.

And speaking of stalkers, that birch Brenda Schumacher walked into the tent, wearing a dress that probably violated several state laws.

Her mother and Gretchen's mom were friends, so it made sense that she would come. I didn't like it, though.

Then I heard glasses crashing, and I turned in the opposite direction to see Wells standing by the buffet table.

Fantastic. Just two more Horsemen, and we'd have ourselves an apocalypse.

This evening was not going to end well.

CHAPTER SEVENTEEN

Wells interpreted me looking at him as some kind of cue to come over. He waved at me, but I did not wave back.

Unfortunately, this did not deter him.

He took Nick's seat. "Jane! How are you?"

I didn't want to be rude, but I didn't want to encourage him, either. "I'm good. How are you?"

"Good. I tried texting you today and you didn't respond."

I glanced over at Nick, who was deep in conversation with my parents. They seemed to be hanging on his every word. "I'm sorry. I was really busy today."

"Drinks?" he asked, and I forced myself to pay attention.

"In general or with you?" I responded.

"With me. If you'd like to get out of here."

I'd never had an issue with conflict, and it would probably make my life easier if I told him straight out that I wasn't interested, but my midwestern upbringing was still there, urging me to be polite. "No, thank you."

"Really?"

Why did he sound so surprised? Did he really not know that last night had not gone well? "Yes, really."

"Why?" He sounded annoyed. Surprised, like women didn't turn him down. It struck me as arrogant and made me dislike him even more. He followed my gaze and then nodded in Nick's direction. "I thought you said you weren't interested in him."

I'd been so busy telling everyone that tonight wasn't a date that of course it would come back to bite me in the butt. "I'm sorry, Wells, but I think we're better off as friends."

After blinking at me for a moment, he said, "Your loss. I can do so much better than you."

He got up and walked away, and I wasn't sure how to feel. I had thought he was a nice guy, if a little misguided, but it turned out that he was kind of a jerk. I was allowed to not want to date him; he didn't have to be mean about it.

I heard Nick laughing, and my attention was quickly turned back to the unholy trinity and their apparent bonding session. While I was stressing over Nick talking to my parents, freaking out over what story my mom was telling him, Gretchen came over to hug me hello. I hugged her back and wished her a happy anniversary, and she sat down next to me, letting out a relieved sigh.

"Why is Wells here?" I asked her, totally annoyed.

She rested her hands on her stomach. "I invited several people from my doctor's office, but he's the only one who came." Had he done it just to see me? I hoped he would leave.

That feeling intensified when Gretchen added, "I'm honestly surprised he showed up. I texted Meagan, that really chatty nurse, to ask about him, and I found out the other nurses think he's really self-centered and egotistical."

"You don't think that would have been helpful information to uncover before you encouraged me to go out with him?"

"Sorry?" she offered weakly and then attempted to change the subject. "You know, when you and Nick walked in, you looked like a matched set," she said. "Like candlesticks."

"We look like candlesticks?" I glanced down at my dress, willing to let the Wells thing completely drop. I guessed my outfit was a little shiny.

"No, you two just look like you belong together."

"You had a guest list at the door," I observed, wanting to change the topic. "Fancy."

"My mom was worried when I told her Nick was coming. She thought random people might try to sneak in, so she talked to Evelyn and suggested we have a list. Nick's name isn't on it because I knew he was coming with you and this way no one could tip off the paparazzi."

"Smart." I was grateful for the assist in keeping him safe. Watching over Nick could seriously be a full-time job.

"When are you going to end all of our misery and just get together with this guy? I mean, obviously you should play hard to get by showing up for your first date with all of your clothes on, but after that? Like I said earlier, fold already!"

So much for changing the subject. It was like all roads led to him. "Obviously, I would be fully dressed if I went on a date with Nick."

"Good! I'm glad we're on the same page."

"We're not even in the same book," I told her with a sigh. "Do you remember when we talked and you said you weren't going to push me to go out with Nick anymore because you were afraid it would backfire?"

She made a face. "No, because that doesn't sound at all like something I'd say. But I thought we were past all your excuses and rationalizations. You can admit that you like him now, right?"

No, I hadn't been able to admit it. Because once I said those words out loud, it would be over. I wouldn't be able to keep my heart safe any longer.

"I feel like I'm fighting above my weight class," I confessed to her. "He's so out of my league. He's an Olympic gold medalist and I'm the person who watches the Olympics on her couch. He's Gucci and Prada, and I'm . . . *The Devil Wears Target*."

"You don't get to put yourself down," she said fiercely, more intense than I'd seen her in a long time. "That is my best friend and sister you're talking about, and she's amazing. Got that?"

I nodded, swallowing down a knot in my throat.

"Good." She nodded. "Even if it was true, which it's not, everyone roots for the underdog. They want the maid to end up with the prince. The innkeeper lands the movie star and the audience cheers."

I wasn't going to be his innkeeper for long. "He's probably going to have to move out."

"What? Why?"

"The waterbed is leaking again."

"He can take your room."

Which meant I was going to have to be on the couch, and the couch was terrible to sleep on. "He could."

"Or you could share your bed with him." She laughed as she realized that I had considered it. "Okay, Miss I Won't Admit I Like Nick Haddon, tell me, what exactly were you two doing when you broke the waterbed?"

"That's not what happened."

She flashed me an evil grin. "It will be when I retell this story." She got up so quickly that it surprised me.

"Gretchen, do not tell people—" I stopped talking when Nick approached, carrying drinks. He and Gretchen exchanged greetings, and he wished her a happy anniversary.

"Thank you, Nick. I hope you have the best night ever," she said in an exaggerated tone. "I have to make the rounds." She waggled her fingers at me and I was torn between following after her to beg her to keep quiet and finding out what Nick had said to my parents.

Sexy Nick in a suit won.

He offered me one of the glasses and I took a sip—plain fruit punch. "You didn't spike it?"

"I'm not drinking right now and I didn't think about it." Right. I'd forgotten. It was part of his big life change. "Do you want me to go back and get you something with a little more bite?"

"That's probably not a good idea." I needed my wits about me.

"I saw you talking to that oak-hole earlier. What's his name again? Spring?"

"Oak-hole?" I repeated.

"Did I do that right? Brenda's a birch, so Spring is an oak-hole."

I shook my head, smiling. "His name is Wells."

"Ah. I knew it was something to do with water."

That Nick seemed a bit jealous gave me a tiny thrill. I liked him being a little territorial and deliberately misremembering Wells's name. But it seemed mean to let him possibly stress about it, especially when I had it in my power to reassure him. He did not have anything to worry about. "It went fine. He's not a bad guy, but he's not right for me."

That made Nick lean forward so that his knees were touching my leg. "Oh? Who is right for you?"

You.

I paused, terrified that I'd said the word out loud. When he didn't react I allowed myself a tiny sigh of relief.

To cover up my momentary lapse, I said, "What did you talk about with my parents?"

He gave me a secretive smile. "That's for me to know."

"And for me to find out?"

"I'm very good at keeping secrets. All you need to know is that I'm excellent with parents that are not mine. I think I'm their new favorite person."

Normally, I wouldn't have believed him, but I'd seen their enthusiastic response to him, the way they laughed and looked so engaged. Why wasn't he telling me what they'd discussed?

As if she'd been summoned by our discussion of birches and oak trees, Brenda walked by, talking loudly into her phone, preventing me from grilling Nick further. "I miss you, too, lover. I'll be home soon. This party's a definite dud. Bye-bye."

She hung up and I hoped she'd keep walking, because the one thing I was not going to do at this event was make a scene by throat punching Brenda.

But she did not keep going. She stood directly behind Nick and me and announced, "That was my boyfriend. We have a rule that we always say how much we love each other every day because you never know—" Someone said hello to Brenda, and she stopped midsentence to respond and wave.

Nick leaned over to me and whispered, "Because you never know when he's going to die?"

"Because you never know when she'll find someone better."

We smiled at each other. I loved that Nick got my sense of humor and seemed to share it.

Brenda interrupted my giddy little moment. "Look at you all dressed up, Janie. Did they not have a dress that actually fit you?"

I found myself doing Nick's breathing exercise. When I finished I said, "I'm not going to stoop to your level, because I would have to stoop down really low and I'm wearing heels."

"I didn't realize they made those in clown sizes."

Breathing exercises again. I was not going to impale Brenda Schumacher with my shoe here at Gretchen's anniversary party.

Then there was this Zen-like moment, like the clouds parting so that the sun could shine through, where I took a step back and saw this interaction between us. Saw how Brenda could so easily provoke me. How much power I had given her. How much time and energy I had wasted on her. I'd let her become this massive villain in my life, and even now, while I was enjoying my time with Nick, I was allowing her to ruin it.

No more, I silently whispered to myself. I was done giving Brenda so much real estate in my brain. I had other, more important people in my life and it was time to let this rivalry with her end.

I could be the bigger person.

There was relief in that realization. Freedom that came from making this choice.

"Brenda, I hope you and Wilfred are really, really happy." *For whatever time he has left,* I mentally added, proud of myself for not saying it out loud. There might have been some Zen-like reflection going on, but I was still me.

My unsarcastic wish stunned her into silence, and she walked away with a very confused look on her face.

"Look at that," Nick said. "You handled Brenda so nicely. You didn't get down in the muck with her."

Part of me had wanted to tell her to muck off, but he was right. "I did. That's probably your influence."

"So what you're saying is, I make you a better person."

It was true. But if I told him that, he'd just gloat. "That's not—"

"The time has come to get this party started!" the DJ announced, interrupting me. "Will Mr. and Mrs. Wagner please report to the dance floor?"

We applauded along with the rest of the partygoers as Heath and Gretchen walked out onto the dance floor. The song they'd played for their first dance at their wedding started up, and Heath swirled her around once before pulling her in tightly.

They looked so blissful together. So in love. They danced together slowly, Gretchen's baby bump making it almost impossible for Heath to reach his arms around her.

The sight of them made me sigh happily.

"How long have they been married?" Nick asked.

"Two years."

"They got married young."

"Yep. But Gretchen says when you know it's right, what's the point in waiting? The pregnancy was unplanned, but they're thrilled. And her parents have come around."

"What happened?" he asked.

"Her parents were furious that she got married at twenty, and her mom said they wouldn't last longer than three months. Things between Gretchen and her parents are great now. They all constantly joke about it, and to make up for being so negative, Gretchen's mom threw them a big blowout party for their first anniversary. She got pretty drunk and promised them she'd throw a massive party for them every year that they were married. An annual party to celebrate how wrong she was. And now she and my mom spend their time arguing over who will get to see the grandbaby the most."

"It all worked out," Nick said and I nodded.

Other couples joined them on the dance floor, dancing alongside them. "Much as I give Gretchen and Heath a hard time, I'm really glad that they found each other."

Nick studied me for a moment and then said, "We didn't have dinner yet. Do you want to grab something to eat, or do you want to dance?"

"With you?" I clarified. It was a stupid thing to ask. Obviously he meant with him.

He grinned. "Yes, with me."

I quickly weighed my options and said, "I'm not hungry." At least not for food, anyway.

Because the idea of swaying with him while he held me tightly? Uh, yes please.

I craved it.

"Dancing it is, then." He stood and offered me his hand. I took it and forced myself to ignore the electrical shocks that shot up and down my arm. We walked together and for a moment it felt like everyone was staring at us, but then Nick turned me and took me in his arms, and the rest of the world disappeared. I put my arms around his neck, and it was almost a relief to get to touch him like this.

His hands were at my waist and moved around to my back, pulling me in tightly so that we were pressed against each other. He made a sound at the back of his throat when we made contact.

Perfection. This was sheer, utter perfection. Like the chords of a harmony blending together seamlessly.

I felt light-headed and grounded at the same time. Then Nick started trailing the fingers of his right hand slowly up and down my spine.

It turned out that apparently I had very weak knees as, for the second time that evening, they nearly buckled. (Technically, the first time they had buckled and I ran into a wall, but since I hadn't fallen to the floor, I was counting it as an almost-buckled.)

"I know what you're doing," I told him.

"Yes, but it's still working," he murmured close to my ear, sending warm shivers of delight dancing across my exposed skin.

He was right. It was totally working.

Then he added, "You know, I never pegged you as a player."

"A player? Me?"

"A date with the oak-hole last night, one with me tonight."

"Tonight is not a date," I reminded him. Or maybe I was trying to remind myself.

"You say potato, I say this is definitely a date."

He was exasperating. "I'm not a player, either. This is the most I've gone out in like a year."

"Me too."

Ha. As if. "What are you talking about? I've seen the photos. You're always going out."

"That's work stuff. That's not me going on a real date with someone I like."

"When was the last time that happened?"

He paused, considering my question. "Two, maybe three years?"

I stopped dancing. "Why? Have you seen you?"

Nick tugged me slightly so that I'd start moving with him again. "I've been too busy. I haven't been in a place in my life where a relationship mattered to me. Or was something I even wanted. But now . . ."

His voice trailed off and I fought off the urge to kick him in the shin. Why did he flirt with me like that? *Oh, I don't go on dates, but you're special and I want to date you.*

Yeah, okay. That was totally how the universe worked.

"You like me, don't you, Jane?" His lips were now officially touching my ear, and I had to suck in a deep breath. Which was hard because my lungs were no longer functioning properly.

This was the problem. He oozed charisma, and physically I was totally defenseless against him. I wanted to do what he'd urged me to do—take things one day at a time, see where they went, date him—but it still felt scary and overwhelming.

I had never considered myself a flaky person. Usually, I made a decision quickly and stuck to it. Which I'd done here, telling him we couldn't date, but he was persuading me word by word, touch by touch, bet by bet to change my mind.

And that fear of letting go, of getting my heart broken all over again—I just couldn't shake it. As I'd thought earlier, admitting that I was interested would make me lose what little control I had left.

"Like's a strong word," I said, trying to maintain some of my dignity. If he was going to shatter all of my defenses, I at least wanted it to be a hard fight. What I really wanted was to roll over and offer myself up to him, like some virgin sacrifice presented to Zeus, but I found myself still resisting. "Indifferent, maybe."

Every female hormone inside me violently disagreed with that assessment.

He smiled against my ear and those shivers intensified. "Yes, I can feel the indifference rolling off of you."

I leaned my head slightly to the right so that he would stop using my sensitive ear to affect me. He pulled back to look me in the eyes, and he was doing that amused thing again.

"I didn't get to tell you earlier, but you're a ten," he said.

"What?" Was this some Hollywood thing I was unfamiliar with? Then I remembered what he'd said when he'd come downstairs earlier.

"On your scale of nine to ten? You do understand that that's not a big compliment?"

"No, I realized that I didn't tell you how beautiful you looked tonight. That was because I was so blown away when I first saw you that I couldn't say anything, and now I'm playfully rectifying the situation."

His words were every bit as thrilling as his touch. Another man might have sounded practiced, but Nick was totally sincere. "You got away with a lot of things growing up, didn't you?"

"What makes you say that?"

"I've never met anyone as smooth as you are."

"I did shave," he agreed, deliberately misunderstanding me. "And it wasn't a line. It was just how I feel. You take my breath away."

Something inside my stomach turned somersaults at his words, twisting and warming me. I cleared my throat and said, "At least I'm moving up."

"What do you mean?" he asked, looking adorably confused.

"First I was pretty, then cute, now beautiful."

His smile spread slowly until it lit up his whole face. "Jane Wagner, are you keeping track of the compliments I give you?"

Obviously, but there was no way I could admit to that because that would tell him things I wasn't ready to say. "I think you're just complimenting me to make me like you."

His right hand pressed into my back. "I know you like me. You flirt with me all the time."

I absolutely did not. "I'm not sure you're clear on our dynamic, but thank you for playing. We have some lovely parting gifts for you."

He slid his right hand up to rest on the back of my neck and squeezed gently. "Not with your words. Don't get me wrong—words are important. Very important." The way he said it, dropping his voice lower, made me literally quiver in his arms.

Nick was so right. Words were Very Important.

Especially the ones he said to me.

"But there are more than just words not being spoken here. I've seen the way you look at me. At my arms, like you wonder what it would feel like if I held you, just like this. My hands, because you want to slide your fingers through mine. My stubble, because you want to know what it would feel like against your soft skin." He moved closer so that our breaths intermingled. "My lips, because more than anything else, you want to know what it would be like if they pressed against yours."

What little space existed between our bodies was charged with so much electricity I was surprised we didn't burn down the entire venue around us.

He feinted forward slightly, as if he intended to kiss me, but then stopped. Letting his mouth hover over mine. "Am I wrong?" he whispered.

No, he was not. "I don't answer questions that prove someone else's point."

At that, he smiled and he was so tantalizingly close that the only thing I wanted to do was prove his point.

"There's something we should discuss," he said.

"Is it about how your air purifier is just a fan? Or why you need more skin-care products than I do?"

"No, but maybe it should be about how you're snooping in my room."

My spine went rigid. "I wasn't snooping. I was just being . . . aggressively curious. Besides, you told me I could go in there whenever I wanted, and it would be rude to refuse that kind of invitation."

He laughed while stroking my spine with his thumb to get me to relax. It totally worked, as my bones turned to Jell-O and I leaned into him. "You're right. I did invite you. And now with the waterbed leak . . . you can't make plans to accept my invitation later this evening."

That relaxed feeling immediately went away. "What would you be inviting me to do?"

"I don't know. We could . . . play Crazy Eights."

Now it was my turn to smile. "That's not really my game."

"It isn't?"

"No, I'm more of an Old Maid girl." At least, my mother certainly thought so.

"I thought you were going to say Go Fish was more your speed."

At that, I threw my head back and laughed. He joined me, turning us around quickly before coming to a stop. We stared at each other and I watched as the laughter in his eyes went away, replaced by a hunger and intensity that I recognized all too well.

Nick smoldered at me. I'd never met someone who actually smoldered.

He breathed deeply. "You smell like sugar."

"You're anti-sugar," I reminded him.

"I'm not against sugar. I happen to adore sugar. All that sticky, tasty sweetness that makes your pulse race—I just know what it does to my body."

"I know what I'd like to do to your body."

My eyes widened at his expression. Oh no, that one had escaped; I'd actually said it. He looked so delighted. I had to stop it. "Unhear that."

"Too late. It's in the vault permanently now. I'll never forget you said it and I plan on teasing you about it for a long time."

That was what I wanted. I wanted a long time with him. Not the week and a half I had left.

I opened my mouth, wanting to tell him that, but his hungry gaze had fallen to my lips and I lost my ability to speak.

"Jane, can I kiss you?" he asked softly.

CHAPTER EIGHTEEN

Yes. Yes, yes, yes, yes, yes. Yes.

Yes.

I yearned for him. My entire body burned and ached with want, had a desperate need to know how Nick felt, how he tasted.

Nothing else existed beyond him and me. I didn't care that everyone I knew and loved was here and would witness our kiss and live off that gossip for at least a month.

I didn't care about anything but his mouth on mine.

So much for taking things slow. So much for protecting my heart.

My scaredy-cat heart was on its own.

"Okay," I whispered.

He reached around to gently brush his fingertips against my face, and the burning only intensified, leaving trails of fire everywhere he touched. There was no way he wasn't doing permanent damage to my skin. I'd never had this kind of physical reaction to someone before.

He cupped the right side of my face, and I leaned into his palm.

I waited. And waited.

And waited.

He didn't kiss me.

Instead, Nick put his hand down and twirled me away from him before pulling me back. We weren't as close as before, and my body was demanding I move closer.

I was totally confused.

"There's something you should know," he said.

My body tensed with fearful anticipation. He was married.

Or something equally bad.

"I won the bet."

"Our bet?" Which was not a good question because obviously *our* bet. What other bet was there?

He nodded.

I stood still, dumbfounded. "How did you raise that much money in a single day?"

"I was just . . . persuasive."

Boy, did I believe that. "I'm sure it didn't hurt that you're Nick Haddon."

"It did not," he agreed.

"I'm still stuck on the 'how did you do this' part of it. It was so much money."

"Now you don't have to worry about the festival. Everything has been taken care of."

I did feel lighter. Like the worry over raising the funds had been pressing down hard on me and I hadn't realized I was carrying around that weight until Nick removed it.

"Thank you. That's incredible."

"You're welcome. Here." Then he slipped something into my right hand. I lifted it away from his neck and it was our dollar bill.

How had he found it so quickly? When had he found it? I'd just put it in his pocket. But he wasn't playing by our unspoken rules. "It's supposed to be a surprise when you give it back to me. You can't just hand it to me."

"Read it."

I let go of him to unfurl the dollar. "I've already read it. *Payment in full.*"

"Look at the opposite corner."

There he had written the words WILL YOU GO ON A DATE WITH ME?

How could one man be this cute? "This was unnecessary. No romantic gesture needed. I made my bet and now I have to lie in it."

"Promises, promises," he teased.

"Is tonight our date?" I asked him, teasing in return. "Because I only said one date."

"As you keep reminding me, tonight is not a date. But don't worry. It will happen soon."

"Am I going to get a heads-up before it happens?"

"I like surprises," he said.

Okay. I was going on a date with Nick Haddon.

And the thought didn't fill me with fear or concern or a desire to protect myself.

I was . . . excited.

It was also a bit of a relief that the decision was out of my hands. No more internal struggling over this big problem—I had to keep my word.

But even as I thought it, I knew it wasn't true. If I told Nick I didn't want to go out with him, I knew he would respect that, no questions asked.

Because he was a good man.

"So what now?" I asked.

"Now we dance and have fun together, and you introduce me to everyone who knows you so that I can gather up more stories to tease you about, and then we go home."

Home.

I liked the way that sounded.

~

We did exactly what he suggested. We had a blast together. Everyone wanted to talk to him or to me about him, but we had so much fun. We danced and ate and talked and danced some more.

Besides me, the only other people he danced with were Gretchen and his number one teenage fan, Connie. Connie looked like she was about to burst and I completely understood. He was impossibly sweet and thoughtful for asking her.

While they danced, my mother came up to berate me. "Why didn't you tell me how wonderful Nick Haddon is?"

"The man you were disparaging for being an actor?" I reminded her.

She waved my words away with her hand. "You should have told me how delightful he is. So charming. Your dad and I want you two to come over to dinner. I'll call and we'll set something up."

A voice inside me said, *They never liked Teddy.*

It was true. From our first date until our last, my parents had been against me dating Teddy. They'd never said anything bad about him, but I couldn't recall them ever saying a nice thing about him, either.

They'd certainly never gushed over him the way my mom just had with Nick.

I couldn't believe I was actually going to go on a date with Nick Haddon. That this was all happening despite my best efforts to stop it or convince myself that I didn't feel the things that I did.

As much as I wanted to let go, to leave everything up to fate and just have a good time, instead I felt a little like the *Titanic*, and Nick Haddon was the impossibly sexy iceberg in my path.

Only I could see him coming, but no matter what I did, I couldn't get myself onto another course.

I seemed destined to run straight into him.

We were quiet on our way home. I didn't know what he was thinking about, but I found myself obsessing ever so slightly over why he had asked to kiss me and hadn't actually done it.

Had he changed his mind? I hoped that wasn't it.

I guessed that he might not be too eager for our first kiss to be in front of other people. That made sense, given that so much of his life was not private. He could have wanted it to be for just the two of us.

Maybe he'd been caught up in the moment and then immediately regretted the impulse. Although that didn't make any sense, because he was the one pursuing me and soliciting a ton of money from businesses just to be able to take me on a date.

He had told me with his words that he wanted me.

I needed him to show it, too.

We got home and headed inside together, still silent. We were in the front hallway and I turned the light on, and hung up my jacket. There was this sense of anticipation that made my hands jittery. His eyes were on me, but he didn't say anything. I wasn't sure what to do.

Was he waiting for me to make the first move?

It seemed like I was going to have to be the first one to speak, at the very least. "We haven't really discussed where you're going to sleep now."

And it was in that exact moment that I realized how that sounded.

"I mean, you can't sleep on the waterbed. Obviously. The patch is temporary. So it can't take any weight. Or movement." I was going to start babbling in a second. "There are four bedrooms upstairs. Mine, two that are still under construction, and a fourth that's finished but only has an old futon in it."

Here it was. I had to say the thing I'd been dreading ever since Franklin gave me the news. "You don't have to stay here. There are other places in town that you could go. Like Brenda's inn."

Ugh, it physically pained me to say that. I might have been ready to be the bigger person, but I did not want Nick sleeping under her roof.

"Do you want me to stay somewhere else?"

"No." My answer was immediate, without me overanalyzing my response. "Do you want to stay somewhere else?"

"No." His response was just as quick as mine.

"Okay. Good." I didn't want to make him sleep on that futon, though. It was Heath's from college and Nick might catch a disease or some kind of parasite from it. "You can take my room and I'll sleep on the couch."

Again, his response was quick. "I'm not taking your room." He paused. "Unless . . ."

There were entire volumes contained in that pause. "Unless?" I asked pretty desperately.

He shook his head, as if he'd changed his mind about something. But he didn't complete his sentence.

"My parents have an air mattress. I could have them bring it over tomorrow." I was feeling so guilty about him not having a comfortable place to sleep that I was searching for a way to make it okay.

Or I was saying random things so that I didn't obsess over his "unless."

"Don't worry about it," he said. "I can sleep on the futon. It'll be like camping."

"I can tell you've never actually been camping."

That earned me a hint of his smile. "I haven't."

It was getting weird and awkward standing with him in the hallway, not knowing what to do with myself. "It's late. Do you need me to help move your stuff upstairs?"

"I'll get changed and move everything in the morning."

That made more sense. "I'm going to go to bed, then."

Stop me. Kiss me. Do something.

But Nick couldn't read my mind. "Good night."

I walked past him, my skirt brushing his leg as I went by, but he didn't say anything. He didn't stop me. Or kiss me. Or do anything besides watch me go.

Where had it gone wrong? Why was he being so standoffish now? Had I done or said something awful?

I had just reached the second-floor landing when he came bounding up the stairs behind me. "Jane?"

My heart was pounding hard in my chest as I gripped the banister and turned to look at him, hopeful. "Yes?"

He walked up the last couple of steps until we were both on the landing. He put his hands on my shoulders, and there was a lot of internal rejoicing that this was finally happening. An angelic chorus sang exultant hymns.

But Nick leaned forward and missed the target.

He kissed me on my forehead softly, sweetly, tenderly.

"I'll see you in the morning," he said against my skin before he released me and went downstairs.

I stood on the landing and watched him go, not sure of what had just happened. I went into my bathroom and washed my face. I'd always found scrubbing off my makeup to be soothing. Therapeutic, even.

There was an impulse to leave my forehead alone, to not wipe away the one kiss he'd given me, but that was silly.

When my face was clean, I decided to go get changed before I brushed my hair and my teeth. Nick was moving around downstairs. I stopped to listen for a second, then headed into my bedroom and shut the door. I sat down on my bed and Patches rolled over to have her belly rubbed.

Flopping backward, I lay next to my cat and petted her. Part of me wanted to go downstairs and demand that he tell me what was happening, but most of me was too embarrassed. How could I go from saying I wasn't interested and didn't want to date him to now demanding implied-but-not-yet-delivered kisses?

I blinked slowly, overcome with exhaustion. We'd had such a good time tonight. Why was he friend zoning me now?

Maybe things would be clearer in the morning.

～

I woke up still in my dress and high heels, my cat sprawled across my legs. There was a disgusting taste in my mouth. I had to stop falling asleep without at least brushing my teeth first.

My room was dark and I didn't know why I was suddenly wide awake. Then I heard what had woken me up—a knock at my door.

Nick.

What if something was wrong? I jumped out of my bed and rushed over to throw the door open.

The upstairs-hallway light was on and it took my eyes a second to adjust. Nick looked clean and fresh, and I tried to make out the time on the grandfather clock off to his right. "Good morning, Jane. Do you know what time it is?"

"It's stupid o'clock in the morning."

"No, it's time for our date. You should go get dressed."

At his mention of the word *dressed*, I remembered that my face was bare and my hair probably bore more than a passing resemblance to a rat's nest. I closed my eyes, like I was a little kid and if I couldn't see him, he couldn't see me.

It didn't make sense, but it was really early in the morning.

"You can't see me like this!"

"Like what?" He sounded genuinely puzzled. "Like yourself?"

"Like I need to put on makeup first and be a better version of me."

He put his hands on either side of my face and my eyelids flew up. "Not possible. You are always your best self and you are always beautiful."

It wasn't a line. He meant it. This man spent his life being surrounded by the most glamorous and gorgeous people in the world, and he thought I was beautiful this early in the morning?

I did not know what to do with this. I chased away the emotions he was causing, because they were overwhelming and I didn't feel ready for them. "Do you know the sun's not out yet?"

He dropped his hands. "That's the point."

"The point is to fumble around in the dark?" I mean, the idea of fumbling around with him in the dark definitely had some merit, but it was so early.

"We're going on a hike."

"I can't. I have a conflict."

He frowned. "You told me last night you don't have to be at the library until eleven today."

"Going on a hike conflicts with my enjoyment of life. I feel about hiking the way I do about paragliding or fried Twinkies. You have your fun, but none for me, thanks."

Nick grinned at me. "You can go on a hike. It's easy. Left foot, right foot, repeat. Trust me."

"Two words that get people into a lot of trouble. Or stranded while hiking."

"Neither one will happen. This is a *get to*, not a *have to*. Let's go binge some fresh air, smell the roses, and I can have the vague pleasure of your company."

Yeah, okay, I was being grumpy. While I technically hadn't promised to be in a good mood on our date, it seemed like the least I could do after he'd raised so much money. I smiled. "Let me get changed."

"I think you should definitely go in what you're wearing now." He was not as funny as he thought he was. "But please hurry. We have to get there before sunrise. This is our first date and you don't want to be late."

It was too early for rhyming. "Okay, Dr. Zeus. Just give me a few minutes. The sun rises for a long time."

I closed the door on his smiley face and undid my high heels.

Being willing to go hiking was a testament that I must have really liked him. Thanks to the everchanging weather, I wasn't sure what to wear. I'd never been much of an outdoors type of person, but I was going to do what he'd advised and think of this as a *get to*, not a *have to*.

I put on a pair of leggings, a tank top, and a hoodie with a zipper. I figured that should cover all of my bases. I left my room in order to use the bathroom and brush my teeth.

When I grabbed for my toothbrush, it felt off. I realized it was because it was actually Nick's toothbrush.

Oh. We were sharing a bathroom.

That made sense—if all his stuff was upstairs, he was going to use this bathroom instead of running up and down the stairs to get ready. I opened the medicine cabinet and his things were in there, too. I liked how it looked, all of my stuff and his stuff together, and decided this was due to my lack of sleep as I could barely admit to even liking him and here I was waxing poetic over our personal-hygiene products comingling.

One bottle caught my eye. His cologne. I took off the lid and sniffed it. Smelled just like him; I caught myself smiling at the scent.

Okay, this was really bad. I put the bottle back and focused on finishing getting ready. After I brushed my teeth and put my hair up in a ponytail, I returned to my room to put on my tennis shoes.

The dollar bill was on my nightstand, and feeling inspired, I grabbed it and took it into the bathroom. I wrapped it around the handle of his toothbrush, securing it in place with a tiny see-through rubber band.

When I returned to my room, I thought of him urging me to hurry and considered whether I had time to put on makeup. It was something I had always done. Teddy had let me know repeatedly that he preferred me to wear it.

Nick doesn't care.

Maybe that was another thing I needed to let go of.

The front doorbell rang and I blinked in surprise. Who would be here at this hour?

I grabbed my phone, but there weren't any texts. What if Gretchen had gone into labor early? I ran downstairs to answer it, wondering why Nick hadn't, since he was already up and dressed.

But when I opened the door, it was Nick standing there, with a paper bag in one hand and a bunch of wildflowers in the other.

"What are you doing?" I asked.

He handed me the flowers. "Picking you up for our date."

I held the bouquet in my hand, unsure of what to do next. "No one has ever brought me flowers before."

"And I've never given a woman flowers before. It just seemed right." He held up the paper bag. "And there are homemade Nutella scones in here. I hear they're your favorite."

"Did Heath make these?" I asked in surprise.

Nick nodded.

Heath only made these scones on special occasions. So had Nick managed to charm my brother? Or had this been Gretchen's doing? Either way, it was very thoughtful.

I took the bag. "I don't know if I should accept this. You know what they say—beware of Greeks bearing gifts."

"Then it's a good thing I only played a Greek god on TV."

"Let me go put these in water." I gestured toward the kitchen because I expected him to follow me.

He stayed put on the porch. "I'll be here waiting."

As I went into the kitchen to find a vase, I realized that he was going out of his way to make our official date special. I had thought we'd do like a typical dinner-and-movie kind of thing.

Instead, he was doing something unique and making it feel as date-like as possible.

I'd never gone on a predawn hike as a date before, and I couldn't remember the last time I had been this excited to go out with someone.

And a huge part of me hoped that maybe this date would end with a kiss.

CHAPTER NINETEEN

We were walking up a sloping trail and I was dying. I was more sweat than human at this point. I took off my hoodie and tied it around my waist. It was still cold and dark out, but all the exertion was making me hot. I forgot all about my resolution to be in a good mood. "So for our date you chose to torture me?"

Nick still looked just as bright eyed and bushy tailed as he had when he first knocked on my bedroom door. He turned around so that we were facing each other and walked backward on the trail. "It's not torture! This is supposed to be fun."

I made a dismissive gesture with my hand. "Yes, yes. Nature is awesome, relaxing; I'm seizing the day or whatever. I just wish relaxing involved a little less, you know, exercise."

He smiled at me and then faced forward again, leading the way. He turned slightly to offer me a water bottle, and I gratefully took a big swig. I'd been so excited earlier and now I was ready to melt into a Jane puddle and have him leave me on the side of the trail.

"This wasn't quite what I pictured," I told him. "It's been so long since either one of us has been on a date that maybe we're doing it wrong."

"Dating's just like riding a bike."

"If the bike is rusty and missing the pedals and the wheels." I tried to pull the tank top away from my body to let the morning air cool down my skin. "Can you get appendicitis in your legs from walking? Because if you can, I think I have that. Like something's going to cramp up and then explode."

"Your legs aren't going to explode," he said. "No hiking. I'll keep that in mind for our next date."

I would *not* turn silly over his declaration that we had more dates in our future. "Who says I'm going out with you again? I only agreed to one date. Let's see how this goes and then we can talk about another."

"So I'm being graded?"

"And things are not off to a great start. But if we do go out again, you should probably know that under no circumstances can we go to the Historical Society Museum, because I've been banned for life and it was warranted and before you ask, yes, Gretchen was involved."

"Not that I'd want to go to the Historical Society Museum, but what did you two do?"

"That's more of a sixth-date confession."

"Five more to go." He grinned and then took off his backpack to put it on the ground. "Let's rest for a minute."

I nodded, taking another drink from my water bottle. Why didn't Nick look sweaty or exhausted? Annoying.

"Look," he said, pointing to a nearby bush. "So cool. It's a praying mantis."

Did they not have bugs in California? We had so very many of them here. The little green insect was waving her long arms around. She was probably excited to be meeting her first movie star. "You might want to watch out. It's mating season."

He nodded. "She was giving me that seductive bug-eyed look."

"That's how they lure you in, and next thing you know, you're headless."

Nick grinned at me while I wiped sweat from my forehead with the back of my forearm. He took his phone out and checked the screen.

"Are we almost there?" I asked. I was kind of over nature.

"Pretty close. Didn't anyone ever tell you not to focus on the destination and try to enjoy the journey? Getting there is the fun part."

"I'm more of a 'let's get to the good stuff at the end' kind of person. Which means . . . what? That we're basically incompatible?"

He seemed to seriously consider my question. "I think it means that we'll get to appreciate things more together because we'll see the world from each other's perspective. You'll remind me to get to my end goal, and I'll remind you to slow down and enjoy where you are in the moment."

That was cheeringly optimistic of him. Maybe our two styles would mesh well. I again noted that he talked about us like we had this big future, but we hadn't even kissed yet.

Given that I was already hot and bothered and sweaty, maybe this was the time. I edged over to him, directing my gaze toward his lips.

It didn't take him long to register what I was doing. That heated look was there in his eyes, but he grabbed his backpack and then said, "Let's go."

The disappointment I felt was massive. Despite what he'd said earlier, maybe he didn't like me being all disheveled. It would be understandable if he didn't want to hold me, given how sweaty I was.

I hated how insecure this was all making me feel. He wanted a date so badly—but why didn't he seem to want me?

When Nick had said a sunrise hike, I hadn't realized that there would so much uphill to it. The sky turned lighter and lighter as we walked. I did exactly what he'd suggested—left foot, right foot, repeat. I kept an eye on the trail in front of me, not wanting to risk tripping and adding a possible injury to the insult of him apparently not being interested in me.

He came to a sudden stop and I nearly smacked into him.

"We're here," he announced.

I walked around him to see what he was staring at. *Here* was a lake, surrounded by trees with red, orange, and gold leaves that fluttered in a slight breeze. It was beautiful and serene.

Just up ahead of us there was a little dock and a small fishing boat tied up at the end of it.

"Come on," he said.

I was going to ask him if he knew what he was doing, but he untied the boat confidently and offered me his hand. "Climb in."

Hesitating for just a moment, I put my hand in his and got into the boat cautiously. It wobbled a bit, but it didn't tip over. He got in after me and there was more wobbling, but we stayed upright.

Nick started the engine easily.

"How did you find this place?" What if Brenda had taken him out here on her quest to steal him from me? Maybe he was wrong about which lake she'd brought him to. That would taint everything.

I reminded myself that Brenda didn't matter and I needed to let it go.

"Tony told me about it. He comes fishing up here sometimes."

"Maybe we should introduce him to Wells."

"Why would you do that to poor Tony?" he asked, and I laughed.

We went to the center of the lake and Nick turned off the engine. We sat there for a moment until I asked, "Now what?"

"Now we wait. You could have had your scones out here if you hadn't demolished them in the car."

I was still hungry. It was probably all that walking. My body needed calories to regenerate itself after what I had just put it through.

Taking in my surroundings, I wondered if this had been Nick's plan. Gorgeous scenery, a sunrise, the quiet and stillness of this moment. Maybe he was trying to orchestrate a perfect, movie-worthy kiss.

"I did what you suggested," he said. "I spoke with Shanice and she looked at the script."

"And?"

"And she thought it was well done and she urged me to audition."

"So your intuition was right," I said. "And I was right to encourage you. Basically, now I'm the one helping you to be a better person."

"You are," he agreed and I wondered why words carried so much weight with me. "I'm just going to have to have a very unpleasant conversation with my agent."

That confused me. "Doesn't he work for you?"

"Yes, but I've never been very good with confrontation. My family is much more into the whole 'take off and avoid' method of dealing with problems."

"Give me his number. I'll call him. I'm excellent at conflict."

"You would, wouldn't you?"

"Absolutely."

At that, he reached over to rest his hand on my knee for a brief moment before letting go.

Again, it was very sad how excited I was from such a small touch.

Then I had to wonder if my knees were sweaty, and there was no way to verify that without him noticing.

"When you're having your conflicts, do you always think you're right?" he asked, sounding amused.

I thought about it and, yeah, usually. I wouldn't be having the conflict otherwise. "Sometimes I'm just aggressively sure of myself."

"Have you noticed how all of your descriptions of yourself include the word *aggressively*? It's interesting because you don't really seem to go after the things you truly want."

That was not at all what I'd expected him to say and my heart raced in response. What was he getting at? "What is that supposed to mean?"

"I'm sorry. I don't want to overstep my bounds here."

"No. Say what you're thinking."

"Do you ever feel like you're letting life happen to you?" he asked.

Was he asking it because it was how he felt about his own life? Or was his question directed solely toward me? "I'm doing things. I came home to help out. I'm running the biggest festival in the entire county. I convinced a movie star to help me promote it. Life is not just happening to me."

"But what about stuff that is just for you? Why aren't you in Los Angeles, pursuing your dreams?"

I sputtered several times, not able to respond right away. I was upset that he was asking, but part of me suspected that I was more upset about how close he was to the truth. "My parents needed me. They still do."

"That's not what I heard." He said it so kindly and tenderly that I couldn't be mad.

Not true. I was a little mad, but it was directed mostly at my parents for telling him. My mother was the one who hadn't come back to her job, which I was still covering.

When I didn't answer he added, "They both worry a lot about you. They hate the idea that you've given up your dreams for them."

"I deferred. Deferred isn't giving up. I still have time." I felt like I said that a lot.

"It's been almost a year. Your deferment is going to be over and then you're going to miss out on a once-in-a-lifetime opportunity."

What was there to say to that? This had my parents' fingerprints all over it. They'd certainly brought it up with me a lot over the last couple of months. He wasn't just speaking for them, though—he sounded like he cared, too.

This time he took my hand, covering it with both his. "It's okay to go after the things you want. Aggressively, even."

"I'm scared." I hadn't ever said that to anyone else, and I felt my eyes well up with unshed tears. I pulled my hand out of his. "Yes, I got this mentorship, but what if I get out there and I'm terrible? What if I've been fooling myself all along and I'm not actually going to be able to score movies? That everyone will find out I'm a fraud?"

"My opinion probably doesn't mean a whole lot here, but I've heard you play. Your music is incredible. Don't sell yourself short. You don't even know what you're capable of yet."

"You're very sweet," I told him. "But I've watched you stress about finding the right parts, looking for success—and I'm here on a different path, where I'm not getting rejected and I don't have to worry about whether or not I'm going to fail."

He considered what I said. "You're right. And as someone who has failed a lot in his life, I get it. But when you succeed? There's nothing else like that feeling. The greater the risk, the greater the reward."

I needed something to do with my hands, so I reached up and pulled my hair tie out to readjust my ponytail. "The last time I took a big risk, it blew up in my face."

At Nick's questioning glance, I said, "Teddy. I was worried about us continuing to date while being at different colleges, but I stupidly trusted his word that we'd be together forever and shut myself out of having a social life while I was at school." I gathered my hair back and tightened the hair tie around it. "Funny how it only takes one guy's betrayal to wreck your ability to trust. In other people and yourself."

"If that's true, then maybe it would only take one to help fix things."

I found myself wanting to believe him.

"Are you still hung up on him?" Nick asked, his tone strange.

I let out a little laugh. "Do I still have feelings for him? No. I got over Teddy a long time ago. And to be honest I don't think I actually loved him the way I imagined that I did. It was more like puppy love. I think I sometimes conflate my relationship with him with my dad getting sick. That if we'd moved back here together, I would have been here in Patience and . . ."

"Somehow prevented your dad's heart attack?" He asked it gently, but it still made me feel ridiculous.

"I know. It's weird how situations and events can get twisted together in your mind so that you don't know where one begins and one ends, where the specific pain comes from." My fear didn't come from some great love story. I'd never been head over heels for Teddy. "I don't want to be hurt."

Nobody liked to get hurt. Nobody liked losing people they had once cared about. And Nick was scary in that sense. I just knew that if I loved and lost him, it would be a million times worse than my last so-called relationship. So how was I supposed to forget myself and have a good time with Nick, taking one day at a time, when some part of me was afraid of what would happen when he left?

He said, "Then we have to go back to those two words. Trust me."

Despite me telling him earlier those were the words that got me into trouble more times than I could count, I needed them to be true. I wanted to trust him. To be able to offer him my heart and not have him stomp all over it. For him to not run away and ghost me when things got hard.

But if that was what I hoped for, then I had to follow his advice. Aggressively go after things that I wanted.

I leaned over and wrapped my arms around his neck and hugged him tightly. "I will."

There was a moment of surprise, and then he was putting his arms around me and pulling me in close. "Thank you."

The boat started to wobble again, as we were off-balance, and Nick said, "Come over here and sit next to me so that we don't capsize."

I did as he suggested, moving carefully. We sat between two of the benches so that our heads were resting against one and our legs up on the other. The sun began to come up over the horizon and he pointed at the sky. "The show is starting."

The clouds were orange and pink and yellow, and the lake reflected the colors back. As sunlight hit the trees around us, they looked, as Nick had observed on our first day together, like they were on fire.

I turned to study his profile. Early on I'd hoped that prolonged exposure would make him less attractive to me. Like I'd get accustomed to his face and not react every time I so much as glanced at him, but that wasn't happening.

If anything, as I got to know him, the opposite was true. He had become even more attractive to me. The sun lovingly bathed his skin and highlighted the sharp angles of his face. That same light touched his hair and made it look like he had on one of those golden crowns Zeus would wear—he seemed otherworldly.

He turned to smile at me, and it took my breath away for the millionth time.

"What do you think?" he asked. His face was so close to mine.

"Beautiful," I finally managed.

The smile faded, his gaze intent on me. "I was just thinking the same thing."

CHAPTER TWENTY

He did not kiss me.

Again.

It felt like a perfect moment—our faces close together; sharing our deepest, darkest fears and hopes—but it didn't happen. Instead, we stayed on the lake for a couple of hours, lying in the boat, continuing to talk and share. It was so easy for us to talk. The only awkwardness that existed between us was the physicality.

Or more specifically, the lack thereof.

If Nick had been waiting for the opportune moment, he'd had an overabundance of it.

I supposed I could have kissed him, but that was a step too far for me. I needed some reassurance from him before I could move on to that next step. That there was more than just words here.

He didn't give me that.

The walk back to the car was much quicker than the walk up. We chatted the entire way home, where the crowd of fans and paparazzi had increased exponentially.

"There he is!" someone screamed, and then everyone around her started screaming, too.

Nick was a good sport, waving and smiling as we went up the driveway.

"I don't know if I could ever get used to that," I told him as I drove a bit more quickly so that we could get clear of them.

"You can get used to just about anything," he said in a tone that made my heart break for him.

Obviously, he wasn't going to kiss me on the porch like it was the ending of a real date with a bunch of long-range cameras behind us. But he didn't kiss me inside the house, either.

I locked the front door, just in case. So that we would definitely have privacy.

But nothing.

He didn't do it when we got to the landing upstairs. Instead, he said, "Would you mind if I get in the shower first?"

I just nodded and waited for a second longer just in case, but he went into his room and closed the door.

This was supremely frustrating. I figured I should probably take a cold shower when it was my turn.

For the second time that morning, the doorbell rang. I went to answer it, wondering if maybe one of his fans had been emboldened enough to do it.

I unlocked and slowly opened the door, and Gretchen stood there, holding my clutch from last night. "You forgot this in all the excitement. Do you know you have a horde of teenage girls by your mailbox?"

"I'm aware."

"Why was the door locked?" she asked as she came inside.

"The horde of teenage girls."

"Smart," she said, shrugging off her coat and throwing it over the back of my couch. She settled in and sighed. Then she waved in my general direction. "What's happening here?"

"I went hiking this morning."

"On purpose?"

She didn't know about it. Which meant Nick had somehow convinced Heath all on his own to make his scones. I sat down on the couch next to her. "Nick won the bet and we had our first official date."

She hit my leg with excitement and said, "So that was a pig I saw flying past my car this morning! How was it?"

"I realized that I'm very out of shape and Nick is basically a robot under all that muscle. But it was pretty great. We were out smelling the roses, seizing the day kind of a thing."

"Did you carpe his diem?" she asked, waggling her eyebrows at me.

"I did not. Not even close."

"Wait. I'm confused. I saw you together last night. There were so many sparks between you that if someone could have bottled it, the two of you could have powered Patience's power grid by yourselves."

I glanced at the stairs, paranoid that Nick might come down and hear us talking about him. "I think we're just friends."

She let out a sigh of disgust. "Why would you think that? Oh, right. I forgot you're 'just friends' despite how you feel about each other and look at each other and the way you go on official dates."

"I don't know what to tell you."

"At the very least, you can tell me how the kiss was."

"I wouldn't know," I said. "I wasn't a part of it."

"He kissed someone else?" she asked indignantly.

"As far as I know, he's not kissing anyone. Especially me."

"Okay, I'm obviously missing something here. You need to catch me up. Start with last night and tell me everything."

So I told her everything, this time including my own feelings about him. If I was going to get her expert opinion, she needed to have all the facts. Her eyes got larger and rounder as my story went on.

"And then he asked if he could kiss me and I said he could."

She clasped her hands against her chest. "Oh, that is so romantic. The only thing better would have been if he'd grabbed you and kissed you."

"I guess he was trying to see if I wanted him to."

"He knows you do. That's why he asked."

I wasn't exactly following her logic, but before we could discuss it further, she went back to solving the case.

"So he asked, but then he didn't kiss you," she verified. When I nodded she said, "What was your exact answer?"

"I think I said 'okay.'"

"Maybe that's the problem. Consent is supposed to be enthusiastic. Not 'okay.'"

Huh. What if that was the issue? I considered it until I noticed the smug look on her face. "What?"

"You've spent all this time pushing him away when you've always liked him, and now that you're finally admitting it, he won't kiss you even though you really want him to. Do you know what that is? It's spelled K-A-R-M-A, and it's pronounced ha ha ha."

"Pregnancy has made you exceptionally snarky," I told her. "That's supposed to be my domain."

"I'll go back to being sunshine and light when this adorable little kicking watermelon is out of my body," she said. "So he asked to kiss you and you want him to but he won't, and now you don't know what to do?"

"Yes."

"Kiss him first."

"Uh, no," I said.

"Why not?"

"Because . . ." Because I'd been dealing with crushing insecurity since I was sixteen years old. First from Brenda's bullying and then from Teddy's cheating. "I'm already doubting myself and whether or not he likes me. This whole situation makes me think he's changed his mind."

"He literally told you he wants you."

Even the memory of those words made my blood heat up. "Yeah, he said it and then nothing. I do have some pride, you know."

"Pride is *not* worth not kissing Nick Haddon."

Maybe she had a point.

"If he doesn't want to kiss me, I'm not going to throw myself at him."

"Your stubbornness is going to be the death of me," she said.

I understood how she felt because it was going to be the death of somebody. "Do you think it's possible to explode from unresolved sexual tension?"

"I think you're about to be the first person who finds out."

At that, I let out a groan of annoyance and leaned back against the couch. "When you ask someone if you can kiss them, that's like an implied social contract that you should follow through on. You don't ask someone, 'Can I sit here?' and then not sit down. It's like he's revving the engine and not putting the car into gear."

"Sometimes revving the engine can be fun."

I glared at her. "Driving is better."

"My guess is you're not missing out on anything. He's probably not any good at it. The kind of guy who sits back and expects the woman to do all the work."

"Do you really think that's true?"

"Sweetie, no. I was just trying to make you feel better."

She had meant to make me laugh, but this was bothering me too much.

"You didn't ask him any follow-up questions last night or this morning?" she asked.

"I didn't want to be pathetic."

"Yes, staying in the dark and not knowing what is going on was clearly the better choice," she said sarcastically. "I should text the festival committee and get their opinions."

I served her snark back to her. "Right. We should absolutely bring more people in to participate in my humiliation."

Ignoring me, Gretchen got on her phone and typed something. I had thought she'd been kidding about asking other people. Her phone buzzed. "Dee-Dee says maybe he's trying to take things slow. Didn't he say that to you?"

If I'd had *embarrass myself completely* on a to-do list, I could have officially checked it off. "I didn't know he meant like the tortoise from *The Tortoise and the Hare* slow."

"The tortoise won that race in the end," she reminded me.

"You're not helping."

"Phyllis said maybe he's leaving it up to your imagination so that you'll cave. She says not to, and to not give away any free milk."

"Am I the cow in that scenario?"

She shrugged. "Connie says just kiss him. I second that."

"This isn't a committee meeting. You guys don't get a vote."

"Answer me this—honestly, this time. Do you like him?"

I pressed my hands together and put them on my lap. "I feel like he gets me. That he likes me for who I am and not who I pretend to be."

"He's certainly seen you at your worst and you haven't scared him off yet."

I scowled slightly at her. "Being with him, it's kind of like hanging out with you, only . . ."

"You want to climb him like a tree?" she offered. "Do you know who I felt that way about? Your brother. When you have someone you like so much as a person and a friend that you're seriously attracted to? That's some fairy-tale magic right there."

I didn't know what to say to that.

"It's going to be a short hop, skip, and a jump until you're completely in love with him."

"Don't go there," I said. That was too far. I was barely at the *I'm close to admitting I like him* stage.

"The committee and I decided in our group text that we all officially live in the city of Jane Is Going to Fall in Love with Nick Haddon. It's a quick commute. You should join us."

"Wait. You have a group committee text that I'm not a part of? Why?"

"Duh, so we can talk about you and Nick and how much he likes you but you refuse to see it."

There was a crushing feeling on my chest, like it physically hurt to say this out loud. "I don't think he likes me. I think he changed his mind. That's why he hasn't tried to kiss me."

"O she of little faith, you are going to be so surprised. Personally, I'm ready to drive south across the river into Kentucky so that I can buy a cowgirl hat and boots to officially get on this wagon. But there's only one way to resolve this. You're going to have to ovary up and have a conversation with him."

That was the last thing I wanted to do. Because as long as we didn't talk about it, I could live in a state of denial. If I asked him and he had to let me down gently, I wasn't sure I would get over it.

Wells's face flashed in my mind and I thought that maybe Gretchen was right. This was karma. I hadn't liked Wells and maybe hadn't handled it well, and now I was going to be on the receiving end of it.

The grandfather clock upstairs bonged, letting me know that it was getting late. "I have to get ready for work," I told her.

"Okay. Can I get that *Duel of the Fae* book I lent you?"

"Sure. It's up in my room."

Gretchen scooted to the end of the couch and then struggled to stand.

"Stay here," I said. "I'll go grab it for you."

"No, the doctor says I should be walking, that it will help induce labor, and I am all for anything that does that. What did you think of the book?"

"I really liked it. It made me want to watch the movies again."

"Yes. Malec Shadowfire is totally my book boyfriend." She waved away my hands as I tried to help her up, and she managed it on her own. "I've got this. So did Nick move upstairs? Did he elect to sleep on the futon?"

"He did."

"I don't know how you can wonder whether or not he likes you. That proves it right there. That thing is so uncomfortable."

"Right? He should stay somewhere else."

"Gee, I wonder why he doesn't." She moved slowly up the stairs with me, and when we got to the landing, she heard the shower going. "You're sharing a bathroom too?"

"We are. I guess one of us could use the downstairs one, but this is easier."

"That's so domestic of you. You're using this to your advantage, aren't you? Accidentally walking in while he's in the shower?"

"No." I knew she was joking, but there was a tiny part of me that thought her idea had some merit. I put it aside.

Then everything seemed to be happening at once. Gretchen playfully put her hand on the doorknob, like she was going to barge in. I grabbed her wrist to stop her, and that was the moment Nick opened the door, with a towel around his waist and using another to dry his hair.

He was glorious. Still damp, his hair wet and dark, that towel slung low on his hips, all of his fabulous chest and arm muscles out on display, still shiny from his shower.

It was enough to make a girl feel faint.

I actually did feel faint.

If he was surprised to see us standing outside the bathroom door, he didn't show it. He smiled and nodded politely. "Jane, Gretchen."

My sister-in-law's voice was strangled. "Nick."

"Pardon me, excuse me," he said as he scooted past us. Then he turned and faced me. "Sorry about that. I hope I'm not too much of a distraction."

That cocky little smile of his said he knew exactly what he was doing to me, and I was still falling for it.

"I'm a married woman, I'm a married woman," Gretchen muttered to herself as he went into his bedroom and shut the door.

I got the impulse. Seeing him like that was a little like getting crushed by a boulder falling off a sixty-foot cliff. I'd been totally flattened by lust.

We just stood there, staring at his closed door. I put both my hands on my cheeks and could feel the heat I was emanating.

"I guess as far as roommate situations go, this is a pretty ideal one," she said.

"It's like he's torturing me. Showing me what I can't have. I feel like I'm going to die if I can't kiss him. And he is triggering my lizard brain, and I want to do unspeakable things to his abs," I admitted.

"I don't blame you." She turned around. "Oh, your mom is going to be so embarrassed when the paramedics inform her how you died. Because, Jane Wagner, you are, to use a technical term, so screwed."

CHAPTER TWENTY-ONE

I didn't get much done at the library that day. Not only because I had all these wonderful mental images of him half-naked to flip through in my brain like a catalog, but also because I didn't know what to do about my situation and couldn't come up with a solution.

Gretchen was no help. She—and by extension, the rest of the festival committee—urged me to talk to him. Connie had oh-so-helpfully suggested that I take him back to the lake and pretend to drown so that he'd be forced to do mouth-to-mouth and then I could kiss him.

I texted Gretchen back and said I didn't want to come across like a flake, having told him I wasn't interested one minute and then the next being so desperate for him that I was considering taking Connie's deranged advice and putting myself in mortal danger.

She lovingly told me all of my fears were stupid and again told me to ask him because he was the only person who had the answers.

Logically, it seemed like the best course of action. I was the one who had bragged to him about not being afraid of conflict. And normally, I wasn't, but I was scared of being told that he wasn't interested in me.

That was a rejection I didn't think I could take.

When I got home that night, I felt completely sore and wiped out. I thought maybe I should just go to bed and avoid Nick entirely, but he was in the living room and came out into the hallway when he heard me come in.

His whole face lit up when he saw me, and that delighted smile of his made it hard to breathe. He said, "Hey, you're home. Are you hungry? Tony sent a pizza over and it's in the fridge."

"Tony doesn't do delivery."

He shrugged. "He does now, I guess. It was really nice of him." Tony had never done takeout or delivery of any kind, ever. What was Nick doing to the people in this town?

Including me?

"How was your day?" he asked.

All he needed to do was add a *dear* onto the end of his question and we really would be the cute little domestic couple Gretchen accused us of being. I pushed it out of my mind. "It was fine. Kind of stressful."

"Do you know what's good for that?"

Making out? I wanted to ask. "What?"

"There's a couple of low-intensity stretches I could show you."

Yoga. Of course. Then I immediately brightened, as he would have to help me do the different poses correctly. "Okay."

But saying that made me flash back to my answer when he'd asked if he could kiss me, and I glanced at him, wanting him to remember, too. He had permission. He just needed to work on his follow-through.

He didn't, though. He just led me over to his yoga mat and guided me through a series of poses that he named off for me—standing forward bend, cat-cow pose, head-to-knee forward bend. They were harder than I'd expected, and I wondered how he could do them so effortlessly. It was like I was missing vital muscles.

I particularly enjoyed the corpse pose, which was basically me lying on the floor, breathing deeply while I thought about the different parts of my body under his direction.

That time was spent thinking about the parts of his body instead, but I didn't mention that to him. He talked me through each stance and told me how it should feel.

We finished up with the easy pose, which was sitting on the floor with my legs crossed, hands on my knees and trying to align my spine and lift my chest. He sat across from me, doing the same thing, like a mirror image. His eyes were closed, and I took advantage of the opportunity to study his face.

Why was I sweating again? It wasn't even hard.

It had to be him.

I was wearing a tank top under my long-sleeve shirt, so I reached for the bottom hem and tried to pull it up, but my arms weren't cooperating. My shoulders were killing me. My shirt got stuck halfway up. I made a sound and saw one of his eyelids pop open and then the other.

"Are you okay?"

"If I tell you what's happening, you're going to think I'm weird."

"I think you're kind of running that risk either way."

"I'm trying to raise my arms and it's not working. I thought you said this was low impact."

He grinned at me and leaned forward. "Let me help you." He grabbed the shirt and gently tugged it over my head.

Nick Haddon is undressing us! my hormones rejoiced, and I didn't even have it in me to tell them to stop. Because that was the thought going through my brain as well as he pulled the sleeves down my arms until I was free.

That heated gaze of his was on me again, but it quickly went away.

Before I could wonder why his moods seemed to shift so quickly, he said, "You are burned."

"What?"

"Your shoulders."

I got up and went over to the hallway mirror to look. My shoulders were a bright red. I'd gotten sunburned this morning on the boat. No wonder I couldn't lift my shirt off. "We were out so early that it didn't even occur to me to put on sunscreen," I said. That was very unlike me. I usually slathered it on before I so much as peeked outside, but in my defense, an extremely hot movie star had been distracting me a lot lately.

"I'm so sorry. If I'd known that you were going to fry like an egg on a sidewalk in Vegas, I would have reminded you. You are so sunburned."

"Nothing good can come from hiking!" I said.

He tried not to smile and then looked to his right. "I saw some aloe in the bathroom under the sink. Go sit on the mat. I'll be right back."

I inspected my shoulders. I pressed a fingertip into the right one, leaving a white mark that hurt. They'd actually been hurting all day, but I'd blamed it on the physical activity from the hike.

Sighing, I went and sat on the mat, feeling sorry for myself. It was going to be hard to sleep tonight because I was a side sleeper and this would make me miserable.

Nick came right back with the aloe vera bottle. I reached for it, but he sat down behind me, his folded legs pressing against my back.

"I can do it," I tried to protest.

"I know you can. I just want to help."

"You don't get to do nice things for me after you're the one responsible for burning me." I knew I was being irrational.

He seemed to understand that and his voice was reassuring. "The sun's responsible for burning you. And I like being nice to you."

That set off tingles of excitement along my veins. I heard him squeeze the bottle, and the next thing I felt was the cold gel against my skin and him rubbing it in. I sucked in an audible breath.

"Cold?" he asked.

That wasn't why I was reacting. It was because of his clever fingertips, which were making small circles on my shoulders. I didn't understand how this was happening—my skin was screaming for attention, literally burning itself off my body, and I was still giving all of my focus to him and his touch.

His hypnotic movements were careful as he smoothed the aloe in, like he was trying not to press down too hard. Everywhere he touched sent little icy pinpricks of awareness and want across my skin. How could he make me burn and shiver all at the same time?

Maybe I had sun poisoning.

Nick spread the gel over my shoulders, front and back. Then he headed to the back of my neck and now I was pretty sure he was messing with me, because he was actually massaging the aloe in, creating little patterns against my skin. I felt his mouth hovering above my neck, the heat he created even more intense because of the burn.

I still wanted him to press a kiss there. I didn't care how much it might hurt. It would be worth it. I held my breath in anticipation, my heart thudding low and hard, but he didn't do it.

An aching longing for him made my stomach feel light and heavy all at the same time, and I tried to swallow back the desire that was roaring to life inside me.

Closing my eyes, I attempted to regulate my desperate little breaths and think of something, anything else. "What did you do today?"

His mouth was still close to the back of my neck, and I could feel his words. "I talked to my agent, and he's not happy that I'm passing on the reboot, but he's going to set up the audition for the rom-com."

"Wow! You must be excited," I said a bit too brightly, as if my bones weren't about to dissolve inside me.

"I am," he agreed. "I also did more filming with the documentary crew today. Shanice is going to start releasing that footage soon, so I think we should draw even more of a crowd."

I bit back a moan as he lightened the pressure of his fingertips, skimming along the surface of my back. "That's good." Not what he was saying but what he was doing.

His fingers stilled and his voice went low and seductive. "What is?"

Not able to lie to him, or calm my raging heartbeat, I said, "The way that you're touching me. That's good."

His hand was still on my neck and he pushed slightly against my skin. I wished I could see his face as he said, "Good is good."

The words reverberated deeply in his chest, which was just behind my back, and I wanted to lean against him, even if it would make my shoulders ache. That would be an acceptable sacrifice in order to be held.

Because good was very, very good.

My lungs refused to cooperate with me, but I did manage to draw in a shaky breath. I suddenly felt scared. Here I was telling myself that I wanted him to be closer to me, and the second things turned that direction, I was ready to make jokes. "I heard that the girls you date get burned. I just didn't know they meant literally."

"I'd like to say I won't do anything else that will turn you bright red, but we both know that would be a lie." His breath stirred the little hairs along my nape, making my shivers multiply in intensity. "It's so easy to make you blush."

There were definitely quite a few ways Nick could make me blush. So many times, he already had. That made the fear melt away. Why did I keep fighting this? Why did I, like Gretchen had said, run away from things that might make me happy?

Gathering up my courage, I turned my head over my shoulder to look at him. "Why haven't you kissed me?"

He froze, his expression unreadable, and then he picked up my defensive playbook and made his own joke. "Why would I do that? You don't even like me."

Now I turned around completely so that I was facing him. My knees were on top of his, like I was trapping him there and making him have this conversation with me. It had been really hard to ask him that question, and he wasn't going to get away that easily. "I don't like you? Says who?"

"You, repeatedly," he said. "I had to convince you into begrudgingly going out with me."

Oh, that. Right. "You know that I like you."

"It's the first that I'm hearing about it."

He had a really good point. "I'm not good at saying things like that." I looked down at our legs, and he put his fingers underneath my chin to lift my face up so that our gazes met.

"What are you afraid of?" he asked softly.

Time to be really honest. With him and with myself. "That if I told you about my feelings, then this becomes real and I could get hurt."

"I have that fear, too." He cupped the side of my face with his hand. "I promise to be careful with your heart." His thumb brushed my cheek as he studied me; then he released me.

Nick leaned back, putting both his hands on the floor to support his weight. Like he was trying to move his torso and face as far away from me as he could, but he left his folded legs where they were, underneath mine.

"You should stay away from me," he said as he lifted one of his hands to rub at his chest. "You deserve better than me."

Better than Nick? "I'm pretty sure they don't make better than you. You broke the mold."

Now he was the one looking down at the space between us. "I ruin everything I touch. Like some kind of reverse Midas."

I didn't even know how to answer that. People adored Nick. Everyone here in town, his fans . . .

Me.

"How can you think you ruin things? You make them better just by being here."

"That jinx thing finds a way to destroy everything I care about."

It probably wouldn't be appropriate to tell him that his superstition was not real and was, in fact, silly.

"I reject that as an excuse," I told him. "What else do you have?"

"There's what you pointed out earlier. If we kiss, then it might change everything. If I kissed you, it might mean that nothing would ever be the same."

"Maybe that wouldn't be a bad thing. And maybe I shouldn't have jumped to that conclusion." I couldn't believe I was the one saying this. I was basically admitting that I'd been wrong. "But as for that jinx thing . . . do you think I could convince you to forget about that?"

"You probably could," he said with a wicked little grin that made my heart flip over. "And if you did persuade me to put that superstition aside, there's something else I've been thinking about a lot lately. Do you remember when I told you about how people don't tell me no? That I had a habit of indulging in whatever's offered to me?"

Jealous, jealous, jealous . . . Okay. All better. "Yes."

"I've been thinking about how it would be nice to wait. To want something but to delay gratification. Wondering how that would feel."

"Frustrating?" I said.

He sat back up and offered me his hand. After a moment I gave him mine, and he laced our fingers together, holding our hands up. Joyful shocks of electricity sparked inside me. "People hurry through these steps, and I want to savor each one with you. It means something to brush my fingers against yours. You make me feel things I'd forgotten about in my rush to get to the finish line. There are so many moments along the way that I've been taking for granted. Holding your hand is significant, and I get to appreciate this small moment with you."

He pulled my hand up to his mouth and kissed the back, and I gasped and shuddered slightly.

"That sound. That reaction. I want that," he said. "I want to hold you on the couch while we watch a movie together and be aware of your breathing, of every time you shift beside me, how soft your hair is, how good you feel in my arms. When I touch you and when I do eventually kiss you, I want it to mean something."

Wow. How was I supposed to respond to that? I'd never had anyone say something like that to me before.

"So . . . you want to wait to kiss me?" I clarified.

"I do."

"Then why did you ask me if you could?"

"To make sure you wanted to. For when it does happen."

He was still holding my hand, rubbing my palm with his thumb, and had it not been for that, I might have stormed off. He was being incredibly sweet and romantic, but the frustration was real. "For future reference, if you ask a woman if you can kiss her, do it right after. Don't make it the Kiss That Was Promised."

Nick grinned at me and then said, "Do you have any idea how hard you are to resist?"

His words thrilled me and I felt desire spearing me low in my gut. I was grateful that I was sitting down, because I was pretty sure my knees would have given way again. "And yet you're able to do just that."

"Barely. I didn't realize I had any self-control. It's enlightening. I guess it's like any other muscle. The more you exercise it, the stronger it gets."

At the mention of the word *muscle*, I glanced at his shoulders. His very strong shoulders.

Part of me wondered whether I could entice him to change his mind but quickly realized that it would be a crappy thing to do. He was trying to prove something to himself in his quest to become a better person, and I wouldn't have cared very much about him if I pushed him to forget about it.

"You're being quiet," he commented. "Do you want to give me a dirty look so that I know things are still okay between us?"

"What I want to do is convince you to change your mind, but I think that would be a bad thing to do and not very respectful to you."

I saw his Adam's apple bob, his jaw clench. "Thank you. And on that note, maybe we should go to bed." He paused. "I mean, you go to your bed and I go sleep on that thing you call a futon but what was clearly a torture device in a previous life."

He stood up and then helped me to my feet. I swayed toward him, wanting to stay close. "I told you, you can have my room. Or go stay somewhere else."

Nick caressed the side of my face, tucking a strand of hair behind my ear. "There is nowhere else I'd rather be than right here with you."

I decided to forget all of my noble ideals about respecting him. I was going to devour his face.

"Come on," he said, most likely reading my unspoken thoughts, and led me upstairs. I wasn't tired yet, but he was correct—it was probably a good idea for us to have some walls between us right now.

We stopped outside my bedroom door and he was still holding my hand, a fact I was keenly aware of every moment that it was happening. I felt stupid for not asking him about this earlier. Gretchen and the committee were right—talking to him had been the right thing to do.

After all, he was the one who'd said I should be more aggressive about going after the things I wanted.

In the spirit of that epiphany, I wanted to know where the lines were. I asked, "What about touching? Are we allowed to touch each other?"

He made a strangled noise at the back of his throat and then said, "You already are."

I was? I looked down, and sure enough, I'd somehow managed to let go of his hand without realizing it and now both my hands were on his stomach. "Will you look at that? I *am* touching you." He felt so strong and capable, like he could fight off that invading horde at the end of my driveway, keeping me safe. I liked that feeling.

I really, really liked how his muscles felt beneath my fingertips, the way they twitched in response to the slightest pressure. They were so hard and firm. I wanted to make a more thorough examination, but he grabbed my hands and held them aloft.

"You could touch me, too. If you wanted," I offered, trying to make amends for my fingers having a mind of their own.

"That's the problem, Jane. I do want to. All the time." He brought my arms up around his neck, and I ignored how much it hurt my shoulders when he pressed the side of his face against mine. His hands went to my waist and he pulled me flush against him. I sighed with happiness and felt a bit delirious at the same time. He was so strong. Solid.

Then his lips were next to my overly sensitive ear, and he said, "What I really want is to pick you up, kick in your bedroom door, throw you on your bed, and make sure you don't want to get up for at least a week."

Breathing became impossible. His words slammed into me like bolts of lightning, crackling and sparking as they lit up every cell in my body.

"Nick . . ." I didn't know why I was saying his name. What I hoped to accomplish. I just clung to him, relying on his strength and wishing he would do what he'd just said. My heart hammered with anticipation and want.

His lips brushed my ear. Not a kiss but definite contact. "I have to be careful how much I touch you. And hold you."

That was probably a good idea, given that this hug was probably starting to border on harassment. But it was also making me feel connected to him. Close. Intimate.

"You're humming," he said with a smile against my cheek.

Again, I'd been unaware. But if I was going to be totally honest with him, I might as well go for broke. "It's because you make me happy. You bring out the music in me."

His body stiffened underneath mine for a moment before he relaxed again. "I have to go. Good night."

Then he was gone and I was left alone, wondering what had just happened as his door closed behind him. What was going to happen in the future. Where this was all headed. I went into my room and sat on the edge of my bed.

I knew it was going to be hard to sleep, and it wouldn't be because of the sunburn.

CHAPTER TWENTY-TWO

I caught up Gretchen and the rest of the festival committee the next morning at the library, and I couldn't remember the last time I'd seen my best friend so giddy. She said a lot of smug *I knew it!*s and *I told you so!*s, but that was to be expected.

Then I explained how Nick wanted us to wait before we kissed.

There was dead silence, and then Gretchen said, "I guess slow and steady wins the girl."

Michelle grimaced. "Or he'll end up losing her over it because he takes too long."

"That won't happen," Phyllis said. "Jane is not going to lose her interest."

True.

"I think it's romantic," Dee-Dee said with a sigh. "That he likes her so much he wants to wait so that they don't rush and ruin things. They'll get to really know each other."

Connie totally disregarded what I said and informed us that she had been thinking about other ways to trick him into it. "If you're not willing to go the CPR route, then maybe you could do like, a Sleeping Beauty thing?"

I blinked and waited for her to explain, but she didn't. "You want me to pretend to be in a coma and hope he thinks the only way that I'll wake up is for him to kiss me?"

She nodded enthusiastically, and I just smiled back at her. She didn't understand that I wasn't going to do anything that Nick didn't want to do. I might have been in a hurry, but I was willing to wait and see how things went.

Maybe I could focus on the anticipation rather than the frustration.

Easier said than done, though.

For the next five days, he and I spent all our free time together. I confessed to Gretchen that I was worried Nick and I were playing house and that made it easier to buy into the fantasy. He asked me to go on a date every day. Somehow he managed to always come up with something unexpected and unique.

Including tonight, when he started off the evening by asking me, "Do you want to accompany me to toilet paper the Historical Society Museum?"

"That would be illegal and disrespectful, and my mom would kill us if she found out."

"So you're in?" he asked with a captivating grin.

"Did I not make that clear? What's a little vandalism between friends?"

We dressed in all black, parked a block away, and sneaked around the various buildings in the town square. The whole thing struck me as hysterically funny and I couldn't stop laughing as we completely covered the front of the museum with toilet paper. "This is why they were right to ban me," I said.

He grabbed me into a big hug and whirled me around. "Now they'll have to ban me, too."

There was a heart-stopping moment when I thought that he might kiss me. Declare the wait over.

But as he studied my lips, I was the one who stepped back. I knew that even if he was caught up in this moment, he didn't want this. Not yet, anyway. I could wait.

Waiting sucked, but I could do it.

Anticipation and not frustration, I reminded myself, and I almost believed it.

After we finished with our mayhem, we went back to the house and he suggested we watch *Raiders of the Lost Ark.* I cuddled up against him and we held hands as the movie started. He asked me to explain why I loved the soundtrack and the score.

I enthusiastically did just that. "For the first ten minutes, with those sinister-sounding brass chords, you don't even know if Indiana Jones is the good guy or the bad guy. All the apprehension in that opening sequence—the music does that." I explained the various instruments used to evoke tension, and that led to me talking about why I loved this movie so much—it was Williams's score that led us from adventure to comedy to knuckle-gripping tension to love to one of the most recognizable themes in movie history, "Raiders March," and one of the most romantic, "Marion's Theme."

"Nobody does themes like John Williams. The way he made it fit each character while being catchy and engaging your emotions, bringing you into this adventure and romance, it's just sheer perfection." I sighed happily. "Sorry for going on like that."

"I'm the one who asked," he reminded me. "You could talk about fishing and I'd still be entertained."

The same was true in reverse—everything Nick said, I found utterly fascinating and I wanted to know more.

I was also fascinated by the ways he touched me. Like now. He was pressing tiny kisses against the length of my inner arm, from my palm to the crook of my elbow, and I had no idea I was so sensitive there.

"I love how soft your skin is," he murmured, and my stomach quivered from the feel of his mouth, his words, and the intoxicating warmth that filled me.

While I understood what he was trying to accomplish, and I loved snuggling with him and holding his hand, I was craving more. I thought about it constantly. Which probably was not a good thing, given our current situation, but I couldn't help it. He was so attentive, so careful, so thorough in the things that he allowed himself to do. I knew how amazing the next step would be—and the next step, and the next one after that—given the chemistry and feelings between us, and I let myself look forward to it while still enjoying everything between us for the moment.

He was right, though, about being able to savor each part. The first time he ran his fingers through my hair while he held me close, when he had his hand on my bare back while we watched a movie together, when he laid his head in my lap during a nighttime picnic and I traced the outline of his handsome face—we both got to experience those feelings like we were giddy teenagers, doing it for the first time.

While I went about the daily activities of my life—work, friends, the festival—my thoughts were always turned toward him. I found myself wanting to know what he would think about what I was doing, to get his opinion and hear his insights. I wanted to know everything about his life, which was so very different from mine, and all the things we had in common.

It was bonkers how seamlessly Nick fit into my life, how domestic and easy everything was between us. How much this felt like it could be so much more.

And then, with the festival getting closer and closer, everything almost fell apart.

The crowds of fans had intensified. I routinely had to honk my horn to get through the people gathered at the end of my driveway. When Nick went out during the day, Barney the Uber driver would come over and pick him up. Nick would climb into the back seat and get on the floor, covering up with a blanket. The image of this tall, broad man trying to fit on the floor of a Kia made me laugh, but it also made me sad that it was how he had to live his life.

The town did a really good job of managing the fans. Tony didn't let anyone in the diner who didn't already live in Patience. I tried explaining to him that he was missing the entire point of tourism—we wanted them to patronize the businesses—but he insisted that Nick have a place where he could come and eat and not be hassled. He also taped butcher paper to the windows so that no one could see in.

Everyone was that way—super protective of Nick. Me, most of all. I got stopped on the street and approached in the library because of the photos that were out there of Nick and me together. None of them were necessarily romantic—it could all be easily explained that he was staying at the B and B and we were working together on the festival.

Gretchen wouldn't let me read the comments made on the photos, and I was happy to take her advice. I didn't want to know. I wasn't interested in a random person's opinion of me or of what was / was not going on with Nick. I did my best to put off the people who talked to me in real life, not giving them anything. I got very good at brushing people off in a nice way.

I did a lot of Nick's calming breathing exercises, too.

As the festival was approaching quickly, the committee had gathered at the library. We were going to follow up with the donor pledges and get them to officially send their money in.

As the women congregated around the circulation desk, saying their good mornings and sharing the doughnuts I had brought, I got a text from Nick.

Guess what?

I sent him back a question mark.

I GOT THE AUDITION!

That's amazing! I responded.

But the producers want me to come to LA tomorrow and I have to be out there for a few days

I wasn't sure what to say to that. I didn't want him to go, but I knew he had to. I tried to ignore the sinking feeling in my stomach.

There was a point coming very soon that he would be leaving permanently, and even if we decided to do the long-distance thing, this would be my life. Texts, messages, phone calls.

The thought made me unbelievably sad and I decided not to dwell on it. To be present for what I had now.

Good luck! Whoops, that was the wrong thing to say to an actor. I mean, break a leg!

The library doors swung open and I was not embarrassed to admit that part of me hoped it was Nick coming to surprise me and share his news with me in person.

Instead, it was a man in coveralls who I didn't recognize. "Hi, I'm Tad. I'm from Myriad Fiber. I just finished up with the fiber-connection point outside, and now I need to install your new modem."

I had no idea what he was talking about. "You're what?"

He repeated himself, but I didn't know how this could be happening. There wasn't anyone in a position of authority to set this up other than me, and I knew I hadn't told him to do it.

I didn't have the money to pay the fee to finish the installation.

"What's happening?" I asked.

Poor Tad looked very confused. "I'm installing the fiber-optic cable from Myriad Fiber. My coworkers and I have been doing this all over town. Didn't you know that we were coming?"

We all just sat there in silence, not knowing what to say, until Connie got up and volunteered to show the man where the current modem and router were located.

"Nick did this," Gretchen said. "Who else could have done it?"

That made no sense. Nick was broke. But she was right. Who else could it be? "Maybe it was Wilfred Newcastle because he's going to run for mayor again after we get the government back up and running."

We discussed some other possibilities—like maybe there was a secretly wealthy Patience resident who had arranged it—but all we had was a bunch of guesses. It was amazing news, though. This was going to make life a lot easier for everyone here in town.

Dee-Dee hung up her phone and looked at us. "Has anyone ever heard of Lexicon Heating and Air-Conditioning? It's listed here as one of the sponsors, but the phone number doesn't work and I can't look them up."

"No." It didn't sound familiar to me. That must have been one of the businesses on Nick's list.

Connie rejoined us and said, "Lexicon? That's the name of the spy organization that Nick Haddon's character Dax Jupiter was trying to bring down in that terrible *James Bond* rip-off movie."

My heart thumped hard. "Dee-Dee, who is the contact?"

"Dax," she confirmed.

This couldn't be happening. I grabbed the list and looked for another business I didn't recognize. "What about Argos Financial?"

"Argos? Is the contact name Jason?" Connie asked. "Like on *Olympus High*?"

Dee-Dee confirmed that it was and I felt so foolish. How could I have not noticed that?

I had a sick, hollowed-out feeling in my gut. Why had Nick done this?

I did a quick internet search and found that most of the names on the list were fictional, and they all had a tie to one of Nick's projects. I grabbed my bag, ignoring Gretchen calling my name. I drove straight home. I knew Nick might not be there, but that was a risk I had to take. I had to know what was going on. My chest ached with confusion and fear.

"Nick?" I called out when I got inside.

That lying redwood came out of the kitchen. "It's nice to see you this time of the day." He walked over like he was going to hug me, but I put my hand up and he stopped. "What's wrong?"

"The sponsors. The donations. They're all fake. You lied." I went into the living room and threw my bag on the couch.

He followed after me and stopped in the doorway. He put his hands in his pockets, his body tense. "The money's all there. I didn't lie about that."

"Tell me what's going on."

Nick sighed, rubbing the back of his neck. "It's my money. I did get a bunch of local businesses to agree to donate, and then I personally made up the difference."

There were so many questions demanding to be asked inside my head, but I settled on, "Then why did you give us the list? Didn't you know that I'd figure it out eventually?"

"Maybe that was the point? A subconscious way to tell you something that I wanted you to be aware of? I knew you believed something about me that wasn't true, but I liked that you believed it."

"Which was?"

"That you think I don't have money."

"You told me you were poor," I said. I remembered that part very clearly.

"No, you said I was broke and I agreed that it was true, relatively speaking. You know, from a certain point of view."

Who did he think he was? Obi-Wan Kenobi? *A certain point of view?* "Relative to what?"

He went over and sat down on the couch, rubbing his hands together. Like he was anxious. I'd never seen him this way. "The first season of *Olympus High,* my costar, Felicia Garcia—the actress who played Hera?" The pairing I'd shipped all through high school? I was aware. "She had started a charitable organization to help kids in the area she grew up in. She was the one who made me aware of how privileged my life had been. Every paycheck I've ever made goes into Felicia's nonprofit. It's one of the things that makes me want to be successful—the bigger the paycheck, the more kids get to eat and have opportunities they might not have otherwise."

Any anger I'd been feeling up to that point immediately fled. I collapsed on the chair across from him. I shouldn't have jumped to conclusions. I should have asked him first. It was all so admirable and I felt like an idiot for judging him without having all the facts. "Why didn't you tell me?"

At that, he looked up, his aquamarine eyes intense. "I will admit that it was selfish of me. When someone new comes into my life, I have to wonder how much of their interest is due to my fame or the way I look or my wealth, and you let me remove one of those things from the equation. So that you could know me without the money."

"I don't care about any of those things," I told him. If anything, they'd been a hindrance to me letting myself care about him.

He smiled ruefully. "I know that. And the money that I have is from my parents. That's how I pay the bills. I don't really consider it to be mine, though. Which is where the *relatively speaking* thing came from."

"But why go through all this effort?" I asked. "To fabricate all those names?"

I understood that he wanted to protect himself, but my mind immediately went someplace dark. Was this a manipulation? He'd gotten me on a date under false pretenses. "Did you do this to win the bet?"

He gave me a pointed look. "We both know I didn't need to win that bet."

I bristled at his suggestion but relaxed when I realized that he was right. I would have caved. He'd just given me a way to do it that let me keep my pride. Even if I'd known that it absolutely was going to lead to heartache, I still would have wanted this time with him.

Wanted him.

"You cheated," I said.

"Technically, I didn't. We agreed the sponsor had to be within a twenty-mile radius and I am in that twenty-mile radius."

I shook my head. So sneaky. I almost had to admire him for it. "I'm still going to claim the moral victory, then."

"It's yours. I'm sorry that I misled you," he said.

I got up and went over to sit next to him. "I understand why you did." Then I hugged him, and his arms immediately went around me, holding me close. He even pulled me onto his lap, something he'd never done before.

"This is new," I said as I curled up on his chest. He kissed the top of my forehead, and it made shivery sparkles radiate across my scalp. I looked up at him; our lips were so tantalizingly close.

"Jane," he said, his voice throaty and desperate as his fingers dug into the exposed skin of my back just above my jeans.

There was this pull in my belly, a heated awareness and longing, and I didn't help the situation by reaching up to stroke his face, running my fingertips along his cheekbones, and then lightly tracing the outline of his lips.

He made a sound deep in his chest that thrilled me. His lips were so soft and firm at the same time. His chest was a solid wall underneath me and I felt his breath quicken, his heart beating as hard as my own.

Nick bobbed forward slightly like he was about to kiss me, but he changed his mind at the last possible second.

He stood up so quickly I nearly fell off his lap. He grabbed me and kept me upright.

"Don't you have to get back to work?" he asked me.

I felt off-kilter, dazed, and it took me a moment for blood to return to my brain. Work. Yes. I had just taken off to come here to confront him. "Right. I should go back. Speaking of, are you responsible for the town getting high-speed internet, too?"

He had an *aw, shucks* expression on his face. "I just made a few phone calls and got the process started. It was easy enough."

That made me remember our conversation about how he'd have to cure cancer, end hunger, and stop wars before I'd date him. How he'd just revealed that he dedicated all his salary to helping kids and kept trying to make things better for the people I loved. "You took that whole 'fixing the world' thing seriously, didn't you?"

"I don't know about fixing the world, but I can at least fix some problems Patience is having."

"You must really like the people here."

His voice went into that lower octave that did unmentionable things to me. "I didn't do it for them. I did it for you."

While I rationally knew that I should keep being respectful to him, in that moment I did not care due to the surge of emotions he'd just caused. I stepped forward, intent on throwing myself at him.

Apparently perceiving my intent, he moved back too fast and tripped backward over the ottoman.

I peered down at him sprawled on the floor, reminding myself to not feel too disappointed. I'd agreed to this. "This might start getting a little insulting," I told him lightheartedly.

"You should take it as a huge compliment," he said with a grin. "You make it so hard to remember to keep my hands to myself."

"You don't have to," I told him.

"I know. Soon."

I hoped his *soon* and my *soon* meant the same thing, because I wasn't sure how much more of this *anticipation* I could take.

CHAPTER TWENTY-THREE

"What have you and Nick *not* been up to?" Gretchen asked from my phone's screen. Heath had a dermatologist appointment in the city first thing in the morning, so he was staying there overnight with an old friend. My sister-in-law hated being alone at night, so when situations like this came up, we would do a video call.

Heath would always go to bed early, especially while he was on the road, so she called me after he ended their call to go to bed. Gretchen and I had fallen asleep chatting before and she claimed that I snored like my brother, but I didn't believe her. She told me she found it comforting.

"Ha ha," I said to her dig. She was far too delighted at the fact that Nick didn't want us to kiss yet, and she teased me about it constantly. "It would be especially hard for us to kiss when he is in a different state." Nick had gone out to audition for his rom-com and the house felt empty without him. "Speaking of missing love interests, when is Heath going to be back?"

"He's driving straight home after his appointment. I did tell him that the dermatologist wanted him to shave his leg and arm hair. The dermatologist did not say that, by the way, and I didn't think Heath would believe me. Before I could tell him, he'd already done it! He looks a little like a dolphin." She started giggling and I joined in. "He's going to be so mad when he finds out."

. I had just finished applying the last coat of nail polish to my toes and capped the lid. "He'll get over it. He adores you."

"Speaking of people who adore other people, how's your boyfriend, Saint Nick?"

"Saint Nick?" I repeated. He was Santa Claus now?

"He's doing such a good job of not kissing you that I figure he's either a saint or a martyr."

A little bit of both, probably. "He's not my boyfriend. Personally, I don't think I can call someone my boyfriend if I haven't ever kissed him."

"Good things come to those who wait. I'm guessing that means you haven't had the talk."

"We have not," I said. "We've been talking and texting while he's been gone, but nothing relationship related. It's too soon for that. We're going slow."

"You're a better person than me," she said. "I'd spend all my waking moments figuring out ways to seduce him."

That had obviously crossed my mind repeatedly and it was getting harder and harder to fight off that urge. To tempt him, just a little. "It's not easy, but I'm being respectful."

"Good for you but boo for me for not getting the play-by-play afterwards. When does he get back?"

"Tomorrow," I said, putting the nail polish on the nightstand. It surprised me how much I'd missed him. It was like there was a Nick-shaped hole in my heart that felt empty without him.

It had gotten so bad that I'd gone into the bathroom and put some of his cologne on a cotton ball. Gretchen would mock me relentlessly over it, so I didn't mention it.

"Are you still in that 'he's perfect' stage, or does he have actual flaws?" she asked.

It was a fair question. Nick did seem pretty perfect. "He's late to everything and he's kind of a slob. And sometimes, there's this stubbornness, where he thinks he's right about things, but at least he's willing to admit when he is mistaken. I'm sure there are other things wrong with him but—"

"But you have your blinders on and everything is basically rose colored right now."

"Pretty much." I unintentionally let out a wistful sigh.

"You should have gone with him to California," she said, shaking her head.

"He'd probably have to invite me first."

"No, you should have gone with him and talked to Maxine Portman about ending your deferment and starting your mentorship program." She said it gently and carefully, like I was fragile and needed to be handled with care. "I think it's time. Don't you?"

"I want to be here when the baby is born," I told her. "I want to see him grow up."

"They have these newfangled things called airplanes where you can fly back and visit us, and we can video chat. I've loved having you here in Patience, but you have a life you want to live. Not to mention that it means you and Nick would keep being in the same city at the same time."

That thought had crossed my mind, as I'd let myself imagine a future with Nick. One where we were both in Los Angeles. There was also the obvious long-distance possibility, but if I was missing him this much over a few days, I couldn't imagine what it would be like to be apart for months at a time.

I also wanted that mentorship. I had been hiding out here in Ohio because I was afraid to fail. But like Nick had pointed out—what if I didn't fail? What if my dreams could come true and I might earn the chance to score movies?

I didn't want to spend my whole life wondering what if, whether I might have been good enough. I knew it would be a huge regret if

I blew the mentorship off. The things that had brought me back to Patience had been fixed, and now I had an additional reason to go.

Not that I was ready to discuss that with anyone yet.

"If I do go, it will have nothing to do with Nick. It's too soon to even be talking about something like that." I couldn't admit the truth.

And I probably wouldn't be picturing a future for us if he didn't bring it up all the time. He always spoke like there was going to be something more here, something that would last. Like it was an objective fact.

I shifted our conversational gears and asked Gretchen about her latest checkup, and the last thing I remembered was listening to her talking about an argument her mom was having with her hairstylist.

The next thing I heard was a crashing sound coming from the kitchen. I woke up with my heart pounding hard in my chest, a sickly, silvery fear congesting my lungs as I dragged in some panicked breaths.

For a moment I told myself it was Patches, but then I realized my cat was lying next to me in my bed.

I glanced at my phone's screen and Gretchen was still wide awake, her hand on her stomach while she watched TV.

"Did you hear that?" I asked her.

She startled and then paused her TV. "Hear what?"

Another crashing sound. My heavy heartbeat felt like it was echoing in my chest.

One of Nick's fans had broken into the house. I was about to be killed by one of his stalkers.

"Somebody's in the kitchen," I told her.

"Do you want me to call the sheriff?"

"I don't know. Maybe it's nothing. Maybe I'm hearing things," I said. I unplugged my phone and started creeping down the stairs. It was like I was in a horror movie, only instead of running away like I was always yelling at those sorority girls to do, I was moving directly toward the source.

"Maybe it's raccoons," Gretchen said.

"In my kitchen? That's a huge problem if they're inside my house instead of the trash cans," I whispered to her. I wasn't going to have a way to defend myself. "That's where all my weapons are."

"In the trash can?"

"No! In the kitchen."

"Turn the phone around so that I can see what you see."

I did as she requested and when I went into the kitchen, the only light was coming from the fridge. "I'm on the phone with the police!" I yelled as I flipped the light switch.

"Jane?"

Oh, it was Nick. Nick was back. Relief engulfed me.

I went over to him and collapsed into his arms. "You scared me to death."

He hugged me, apparently every bit as happy to see me as I was to see him. "I was trying not to wake you up."

"You are really bad at it!" I lifted my phone up to see Gretchen, who was grinning at the screen. I clicked the red button to hang up the call. I'd call her back later.

Maybe.

"Your heart is beating really hard and you're shivering. You don't seem like the kind of person who gets scared easily."

At this point it was part scared, part excited at Nick being home. "I get scared of so many things. Zombies. The apocalypse. Alien invasions from outer space." One of his fans breaking into my house.

"Those are very specific and irrational fears," he said, his lips brushing against my forehead.

"Yeah, well, I don't get to control what my anxiety decides to give me insomnia over."

He held on to me, doing that amazing thing with his hand where he stroked my spine so that I wanted to arch against him. I sighed instead. It was probably supposed to relax me, but it had the opposite effect.

"Better?" he asked.

"Uh-huh," I said, choking the words out. But better in the it-felt-amazing way, not better in that it was calming down my heart rate. That was still pounding pretty heavily.

This was giving me so much serotonin. Or was it dopamine? I couldn't remember which was which.

It was the one that made me feel hazy and drowsy and good, and I wanted nothing more than for this feeling to continue for forever.

"Did you miss me?" he asked.

"Parts of me did."

"Which parts?" He sounded very interested.

"I would show you, but you won't let me."

His lips brushed my forehead again. "I am a stupid, stupid man."

"You are," I agreed.

"It doesn't help that you're wearing this." I felt him fingering the fabric of the satiny tank top and matching shorts I had on.

"It's what I sleep in."

He swallowed hard and then took a step back. Again putting that boundary between us.

I'm respecting him, I reminded my overactive hormones. I needed sugar, as there was no way I was going to be able to return to my room and go back to sleep. I felt too wired and needed to be soothed. "I'm going to make chocolate chip cookies," I announced.

"Now? Isn't it a little late?"

"There's no bad time to have chocolate chip cookies."

"Two o'clock in the morning might be it," he disagreed with me. "I thought you didn't bake."

I turned the oven on to 375 degrees and went over to the fridge. "I have refrigerated dough. It won't take long, and it's not technically baking. Just heating something up." I got the dough and a cookie sheet and started spacing the squares on the tray.

"There's kale in the fridge, if you're hungry," I told him. "I saw this really cool recipe online where you sauté the kale and then add coconut oil, and it makes it much easier to scrape the whole thing into the trash."

He was grinning at me as he folded his arms and leaned against the counter. "I caught an earlier flight home because I really, really missed you, Jane."

There was so much raw emotion in his voice that it made me freeze for a moment, like I couldn't quite process it. So I made light of it instead. "Which parts of you missed me?"

He didn't play along. "Every part of me."

That sent a charge of emotion through me. Adrenaline and something else I couldn't quite identify.

Or, more accurately, feelings I didn't want to name.

Too soon, I reminded myself. I put the cookies into the oven and set the timer. "How did your audition go?"

He hesitated a moment, and I wondered whether he would let me change the subject or if he wanted to talk more about our feelings, but then he told me how well the audition had gone, how excited he was to hopefully get the part.

A part that would take him far away from me.

Unless you go to California, too, a voice inside reminded me.

I wiped down countertops while I listened to him, needing something to do with my hands.

The timer buzzed and I turned it off. I put on an oven mitt and pulled out the cookies. There were few things I loved more than warm chocolate chip cookies. I used a spatula to pick one up, and it was melty and perfect. I blew on it and then popped the whole thing into my mouth.

I let out a groan of appreciation.

"That good, huh?" he asked.

I picked up another cookie with the spatula, just as warm. "Do you want one?"

"You know I can't."

"You could." I dipped my finger into a chocolate chip on top of the cookie. "If you won't eat the whole cookie, what about just one chocolate chip?"

His eyes had darkened. "Are you trying to tempt me?"

"Little bit."

"What if I told you it was working?"

His words gave me a delicious thrill and I came closer to him, the chocolate still on my fingertip. "Then I would say, you should try it. Let the chocolate melt on your tongue, the sweetness exploding across your taste buds. Sink into the rich, decadent flavor. And when the sugar hits your bloodstream? There's nothing like it."

His hands went to my waist as I pressed myself against him. "Are we still talking about chocolate chips?"

"That depends. Did I sufficiently tempt you?"

"I'm always tempted by you."

Maybe it was the words that made me feel empowered or the discussion I'd had earlier with Gretchen—whatever it was, I wanted more from him. Just even a tiny bit.

The smallest morsel.

I held my fingertip up, close to his mouth. "It's just one little chocolate chip. Barely any calories. It doesn't even count. It's harmless. Innocent."

"Said no innocent person ever." He let out a quaking breath, and the magnetism in this moment was hard to deny. "It's really hard to say no to you when you look at me like that."

"It's why I look at you like that," I whispered. But I wasn't the only one with an intense gaze. His was heavy, warm. Heady. I wanted him so much I felt like I was going to burst. "Taste it."

I hadn't imagined he would actually take the bait. But then his warm tongue was on my finger, licking the chocolate clean, and the shock of it made my bones give way. It was a good thing he had his arm around me. My entire body was shaking from that brief contact, the blood racing around hotly in my veins.

His pulse beat erratically at the base of his throat and I wanted to press a kiss there.

"Delicious," he murmured.

Not able to help myself, I reached down to get more melted chocolate on my finger and reached up to put it on his lips. "Whoops," I said, my voice trembling. "I better clean that up."

"Jane." His voice was pleading, like he was begging me to retreat, but I couldn't stop. I knew that I should, had so many times before, but I didn't want to.

"Just one small, little kiss," I said. "A soft, sweet peck isn't even a kiss. It hardly counts. People kiss each other that way to say hello."

His breath quickened, but he didn't say anything. There was a low hum of the current building between us, and it turned my whole body into one desperate rhythmic ache.

"One small kiss," I repeated, moving my lips closer to his until they were tingling with anticipation. "If you don't want me to kiss you, just say the word."

"The word," he breathed, but that glint in his eye, the way he was watching my lips so carefully, how he moved even closer toward me, led me to believe that he was teasing, not refusing.

"The word is 'no.' Or 'stop.' Or 'I don't want you to do that.'" Technically, the last one was seven words, but if he gave me a negative response, I would leave him alone. Even if it killed me. "Weren't you the one telling me I had to take risks to get rewards? I'm taking a risk."

I saw the moment when I'd won.

He murmured, "Hello."

I couldn't help but smile. I reached up and, with the tip of my tongue, carefully licked some of the chocolate off his lips, the warm, rich flavor making him taste even sweeter.

He made a groaning noise, his body shuddering against me, and then said, "That's not a peck."

"Not yet. I'm working up to it."

"You are soul-shatteringly intoxicating," he said, his voice hoarse and straining. Like he was struggling to keep himself in check.

I wanted nothing more than to lean in and finish what I'd started, but I reminded myself of how unfair I was being to him. Even though every cell in my body rebelled against the thought of slowing down, I decided to stop tormenting the poor man.

And myself.

I gently pressed my lips to his. Our mouths fit perfectly, like they'd been designed for this very moment. A key fitting into a lock. It was supposed to be innocent and sweet, but it was like somebody had dropped a match into a vat of gasoline-soaked fireworks. Synapses and nerve endings I didn't even know I had lit up from the brief, warm contact. His arms tightened around me; it felt like he might crush me, and I welcomed it.

Then, as quickly as it had started, it was over. He was breathing hard and I could feel the tension in his body, the way he was restraining himself, as if he could barely keep it together. "Not yet."

"Okay." I nodded, trying to remember myself. "Do you have an estimation of when, though?"

"I need to know that I can wait. I have to know that I can be different from how I used to be."

My mind was too muddled and hazy to make him clarify. It seemed so simple to my libido—we didn't have to stop. These were arbitrary rules he'd made up and he could change them anytime he wanted to.

Because I was certainly more than willing.

But if he needed to prove something to himself, who was I to interfere with that?

"I didn't know you before, but you're a good man," I said with a deep sigh. Obviously, I had a dog in this particular fight, but he should know that somebody recognized his attempts to change.

He reached up between us to run his fingers across my cheeks, leaving trails of fire everywhere he touched me. I closed my eyes against the sensation.

"Thank you for that. Well, I'm off to bed," he said. I opened my eyes in surprise. He smiled at me with a mixture of charm and mischief, and I found myself both enchanted and aggravated.

"Stay with me," I invited, the words falling out of my mouth before I could stop them.

"Not tonight. We have all the time in the world."

That was the thing. I didn't feel like we had time, and I didn't know why. It felt a little like things were slipping through my fingers, and I was desperate to hold on to him.

It made no sense to feel that way, because Nick had been nothing but encouraging.

He murmured, "Just think about how good it will be when it does happen."

Then he was gone, leaving an empty vacuum in his wake.

I rubbed my fingers across my lips, still able to feel the phantom imprint of his mouth on mine.

When I pulled my hand back, I realized that there was chocolate on my lips, transferred there by him. I licked my lips, tasting it, and wondered if I'd ever be able to have another chocolate chip cookie again without thinking of him and this moment.

And now that I'd been overwhelmed by the smallest of tastes from him, what was I going to do with a full meal?

CHAPTER TWENTY-FOUR

The opening of the festival was just two days away. We'd had several things pop up, but with the help of my committee and Nick's superfast internet, we were able to successfully solve each problem as it arose.

Nick had asked to see the fairgrounds, and on our way there, I explained that we had two major areas—that the food sellers and other vendors would be in the town square, situated around the gazebo. "My parents got married in that gazebo," I told him. "They danced there together on their first date. It has always been the most romantic place in the world to me." Maybe we'd head over there next and we could have our own dance.

He was twirling his fingers through the ends of my hair while I drove and said, as if reading my mind, "You'll have to show it to me."

"I will. After you see where all the rides are going to be and the corn maze." That part of the festival was being set up at the old Robinson farm. Nobody actually lived on the property anymore, since the Robinsons had retired, but their son, who had moved to New York, rented it to us at a steep discount.

I pulled up to the fairgrounds, and there was a line of semitrucks with a bunch of disassembled rides that they were going to start setting up first thing in the morning. As we got out of the car, I took in a deep breath of the night air. It was the perfect temperature, and the stars were peeking out at us in between the clouds. A chorus of noisy cicadas making their high-pitched whine greeted us, accompanied by chirping crickets. I wished it were still lightning bug season, as that would have made this moment feel even more summery and perfect. A breeze stirred my hair slightly, and I turned back to smile at Nick. As long as this weather held, the festival was sure to be a success.

I pointed out the rides that were about to be set up. "We'll have bouncy houses, inflatable slides, and there's also going to be a Ferris wheel, a merry-go-round, and a bunch of stuff that flings you around or swings you back and forth."

He took my hand and interlaced our fingers, and then, as was his habit, he kissed the back of my hand. I thought I'd be used to it by now, but I wasn't. That excited thrill was still there. Every single time.

"It sounds like a lot of fun," he said.

"It will be! And there's so many carnival games that you can play."

"Maybe I'll have to try those and win you a prize."

"I've got a dollar you can use to buy a ticket," I said, leaning against his arm.

Nick patted his jean pocket. I'd put it in with his spinach in the fridge, and he'd found it when he was making his morning smoothie. "I'll never spend that."

I was wondering how he was going to sneak it back to me when we hit the edge of the corn maze.

"What's your plan here in luring me to the spooky corn maze?" he asked as I tugged him toward an entrance. "Are you going to murder me, or are you trying to have your way with me?"

I smiled at him invitingly and said, "I'm not planning to kill you."

"How do you make that sound seductive?" he asked in a frustrated tone, and I laughed.

Then he pulled on my hand to get me into his arms. I sighed against his chest. I loved when he held me.

"Do you know you're my favorite person in the whole world?" he asked against the top of my head. "I feel like I've known you my entire life."

I knew exactly what he meant and said, "Same." It had been such a short amount of time, but he had become so important to me. "Do you think the festival is going to be a success?"

"All of your hard work is about to pay off," he said. "I'm really proud of you and what you've accomplished."

I felt like I was glowing inside. "Thank you."

He kissed the top of my head. He hadn't trusted himself to kiss me anyplace else since our chocolate chip cookie incident, and I was patiently waiting.

Well, not patiently, but waiting.

I'd been wondering lately if he needed something more to move things forward. Obviously, there was the component of him proving something to himself, but maybe I should let him know that I was on board.

That I also saw a future for us.

"And speaking of accomplishments," I said, suddenly feeling nervous and panicky because I didn't know how he'd react, "I got in touch with Maxine Portman's assistant, and we're going to set up a meeting to talk about starting my mentorship."

I waited, the blood thrumming in my ears.

His face stayed neutral. "So you're moving out to California?"

Was he not excited about this? "I should be. Soon."

"That's . . . great."

It sounded decidedly not great. I didn't understand his reaction, and I rushed to explain so that he wouldn't think I was trying to force him into something. "I know it might seem like a lot of pressure and I don't mean it to be. I don't want to be making assumptions, but I wanted to let you know what my plans are for the immediate future."

I had thought he wanted to be part of those plans, but now I was second-guessing myself. It was obvious that something was bothering him.

But I knew him well enough that I just had to be patient and eventually he would tell me. I took a few steps back, leading him into the maze. As soon as we stepped over the threshold, there was a sonic boom of thunder, so close that it reverberated through my body, rattling my teeth.

He looked at the sky. "We should go back to the car."

It definitely wasn't safe to stay out here in the open. I nodded, and there was another clap of thunder, shaking the ground beneath my feet. Lightning streaked across the sky, turning it a dark purple. I was about to tell Nick that the storm was right on top of us when the heavens opened and began pouring down rain.

I knew the Robinson barn was much closer than the car, so I began racing in that direction, pulling Nick with me. He helped me open the heavy door and get inside. We were both drenched. My hoodie was soaked through. I unzipped it and put it on a hook on a nearby post. He looked around at our surroundings and pushed his wet hair up off his face, and it was so unbelievably sexy.

He pulled off his jacket; the rain had soaked the front of his shirt to his body, outlining every muscle and making my mouth go dry.

"You're shivering," he said as he put his bomber jacket on me. The inside was warm and smelled just like him. I slid my arms into his sleeves. It was too big for me, but I liked that aspect, too. Then he searched around the barn, probably looking for something else to wrap me up in. I could have told him it was a waste of time—not only because I knew the Robinsons had cleared out the barn when they moved down to Florida, but also because I wasn't shivering due to the rain.

It was because of him.

I had a scrunchie on my wrist, and I used it to get my own hair off my face, putting it in a bun so that it would stop dripping water down my shirt.

The rain hit the tin roof of the barn hard, sounding like little incoming missiles, falling hard and fast like my pulse as I watched Nick search.

"There's nothing else here," he said apologetically.

"It's okay," I told him as I walked over, wrapping my arms around him. He hugged me close and I kept trembling, not able to stop.

"Jane?" He pulled his head back and waited until I met his eyes before he continued. "There's something I need you to know."

"What is it?"

He shook his head, giving me a sad little smile. "When you told me about California, I was really happy and excited, but there is a part of me that is scared at the same time."

"What are you scared of?" I asked, mesmerized by his mouth, loving the way it moved to form words.

"I want you to make the choices that are best for you and your life. The most important thing to me is that you're happy, and like I've told you, I'm jinxed. And I don't want to mess up anything for you."

"You think that if I come out to Los Angeles, you'll ruin my career somehow?"

He nodded. "And I couldn't handle it if that happened, because . . . I'm in love with you, Jane."

My heart jumped up into my throat, crowding out my ability to breathe.

A loud boom of thunder crashed just over the barn, but I didn't even notice.

Nick Haddon was in love with me?

"Before you made any decisions about going out west, I wanted you to know how I feel. It's important to me to always be honest with you."

I forgot about the thunderstorm, forgot about being soaking wet, forgot about everything except his words. The entire world went away and there was only Nick, telling me that he was in love with me.

Did I feel the same?

I'd thought about us being more serious and considered having a long-term relationship with him, but I'd never really examined my feelings for him. I'd been too busy taking his advice to live in the moment.

Maybe I'd been afraid to think about it. I couldn't even admit that I was attracted to the man and liked him because of my fear about the ramifications of what it might do to my heart, so whether I loved him hadn't even crossed my mind.

I opened my mouth, but no words came out.

His hands were on my face, cradling me close. "I don't need you to say it back. I just wanted you to know."

I might not have examined my own feelings closely, but that desire to be near him, to have everything else disappear, to have that connection—that, I understood. My breathing sped up and he noticed. The air between us was heated and electric, like the thunderstorm was inside the barn.

Inside me.

Standing with him like this made me feel like I was having a series of unfortunate mini-strokes, unable to control myself or my reactions to him. I should have been cold, but he was heating me up; I half expected to see steam rising between us.

"Have you proven your point?" I asked, the words breathy and soft. "You've resisted for a long, long time."

"I have." His lips came in so that our breath intermingled, and there was nothing I loved more than breathing him in.

"Did you figure out whatever you needed to figure out?"

"Yes."

"Does that mean we can—"

He reached up and ran the pad of his thumb over my sensitized lips, causing those tingling shocks inside me to increase exponentially. "You're so beautiful," he told me.

"Not as beautiful as you."

He grinned and then said, "Hello."

Understanding what that meant, my entire body tensed with anticipation. He was going to kiss me. Then, to my exuberant delight, he leaned forward, pressing his mouth to mine.

It was literally like being struck with a bolt of lightning. He wasn't fighting it, I wasn't tricking him into it—he wanted to kiss me and he did.

He pulled back slightly before pressing forward again for a few seconds, then retreated. It was like seeing lightning and waiting for the thunder, counting until he kissed me and made the lightning strike again.

His tender tentativeness was exploratory and sweet, a prelude to something bigger and better, waiting to see how I would respond.

It wasn't a question that needed answering, because I was a hundred percent in.

My veins were throbbing in time to my escalating heartbeat, and now I was the one holding back, waiting for him—letting him explore and test. He kissed me with a devastating slowness, a tenderness that made my tightened abdomen swirl with heat.

He continued to linger over my lips, like he wanted to commit them to memory, causing my nerve endings to explode. His fingers explored my throat, my scalp; he rubbed his thumb against my jawline as he tilted my head up so that he could have better access to my neck.

Then he started pressing hot, slightly damp kisses along my throat, and I couldn't help the moan that escaped.

"Tell me," he urged in a voice rough with desire, his words burning into my skin. "Tell me what you need. What you want."

I gripped his soft hair between my fingers and pulled so that he would look me in the eyes. "You," I said, completely out of breath. "I need and want you."

And finally, he let himself really kiss me—devouring kisses, frantic with need, desperate.

It was like waking up. Like I'd been sleepwalking through my life and now I got to feel truly alive.

I'd once thought that sometimes being with Nick was like a melody played with just one hand on a piano. Like important components were missing.

None of those things were missing now. Kissing him was a full-blown symphony played by the best orchestra with the most amazing conductor—his heartbeat keeping rapid time like the percussion, his hands moving and kneading and stroking and skimming and pressing and keeping me off-balance, his mouth expertly kissing mine like I was a violin and he was a virtuoso who knew just how to play me so that we could make the most beautiful music together.

Nick kissed unlike any other man I'd ever been with—he was so hard and hungry and consuming, possessing me completely without even realizing it. I was his. I belonged to him and always would. My nerves shredded to bits; I wanted him desperately, overwhelmed with the pleasure he was giving me.

I tried to make sure that he was getting as good as he was giving, and I was rewarded with a deep groan from his chest that sounded like thunder. The sound caused sparks to ignite in my cells, making me feel like I'd been living in the dark and he was the one who'd managed to plug me in and make me glow.

His kiss gentled then, retreating away from that all-consuming fire. That lasted for a bit until he was doing it again—his mouth eager on mine, savage, intense. He was, in turn, hard and soft, back and forth— like he'd forget himself and then remember, only to immediately forget again.

It was driving me insane.

"I'm sorry," he said, his fingers tangled in my wet hair, tugging at the scrunchie. He managed to get it loose, and the shock of the strands of my cold hair hitting my heated skin surprised me. "This isn't exactly taking things slow. Is this too much?"

"No such thing," I murmured against his lips. That briefly made me wonder if there were rules for this particular encounter, but I didn't bother asking because I didn't care. If things came to a stop, fine. I'd deal with it then. But until that happened, I was going to revel in the feel of his lips on mine.

Our mouths moved in harmonic frenzy, sensations whipping through me like electrical currents. He broke it off, both of us breathing hard.

"Nick . . ." Now I was the one pleading, clinging to him like my life depended on it.

"Shh," he said. "I've got you." He nuzzled my neck, pressing small kisses there, exploring me with his lips. He kissed my face, my cheeks, my eyelids while I tried to keep breathing. The skin on my chin and jaw ached, hypersensitive from where his stubble had rubbed against it. He teased me, never staying in one place for too long, and evaded my feeble attempts to get him to kiss me properly again.

It was like he was marking me with tiny invisible scars that I knew would never really go away.

And I didn't want them to. I wanted to always have the feel of him on my skin.

He moved to the side of my face and pressed one last kiss before murmuring, "I've wanted to do this for so long." He said the words against my earlobe, which felt like a live, exposed wire from the way he was breathing on it. My insides coiled tightly, waiting, and then he was doing just what I'd been dying for—nibbling my earlobe, drawing it gently into his mouth. I let out a breathy moan and collapsed against him, my pulse beating so quickly that it turned my entire body into a large drum. Pounding and pounding, blocking everything else out.

Electricity, fire, a thumping bass—all of it combined inside me, making me dizzy and devastated in the best possible way.

He finally returned his mouth to mine, after he had made sure to liquefy all of my bones so that I could no longer stand, and kissed me again. There was no more hesitation, no questioning, no back-and-forth. He kissed me with a single-minded intensity, as if he meant to shatter every cell in my body.

"How?" he asked, whispering the words against my lips, his voice sounding thick in his throat. "How is this possible?"

"What?" I asked, slightly annoyed at first. Why was he talking when there so many better uses for his mouth? My heart was at an allegro tempo—fast and bright. Too fast. It was going to beat its way out of my body pretty soon.

He cradled my face, looking deeply into my eyes. I couldn't help but gasp at his expression.

Nick had said he loved me, but now I could see it for myself.

"This is better than I ever imagined," he said, and the desire in his voice seared me. "And I have imagined."

"So have I," I said.

Shrugging, I let his jacket fall from my arms, faintly registering the moment when it hit the ground. My hands were on his shirt, tugging at it. Nick seemed as dazed as me, but he finally caught on and reached behind his head to take his shirt off completely.

My mouth went dry as I drew in a sharp breath. Beethoven's "Ode to Joy" started up in my head, and I wanted to compose my own masterpiece as an ode to his torso. Better than I remembered, and it was mine to explore. I ran my fingertips over the ridges and planes of the muscles on his chest, marveling at the way he shuddered at my touch.

I reached over to kiss at the pulse point in his throat, the one that was beating so erratically, so out of control. He made a strangled sound that was part growl and part groan, and I took that as my cue to suck lightly on his neck.

My heart seemed to be skipping actual beats, stopping and starting up again. He didn't let me explore for very long before he had me back in his arms, moving me over to the post where my hoodie hung. He pressed me up against the wood and shifted his body against mine.

He parted my lips with his, and all I could think about, taste, feel was Nick. I'd complained once about him revving my engine up without starting the car, but it was definitely in gear now. His fingers stroked the skin on my back, sending tiny bolts of lightning along my veins.

Heat pooled low in my gut and I made whimpering, begging sounds against his mouth.

Which is why I didn't hear the sound at first.

Blood thundered in my ears, along with Nick's harsh breathing, the music of his heartbeat, so that there wasn't room for anything else.

There. I heard it again.

My vision was blurry, but I tried to open my eyes and focus, as if that would help me listen better.

I shoved my hands against his bare shoulders. "Nick, wait."

He stopped immediately and lifted his head away from me. "What is it?"

"I think I hear sirens," I said.

He gave me his mischievous grin and said, "I thought I made you hear music."

"No. Actual sirens." There was no mistaking it now. Definitely multiple sirens. Something big was happening.

His face went slack when he heard it, and he grabbed his shirt, putting it on as I went over to the barn door. The rain had stopped—another thing I hadn't noticed. I stepped outside and turned my head toward the sound.

The sirens were coming from the center of town. Then I saw it—a faint plume of gray-and-white smoke and the smell of something burning.

A building was on fire.

CHAPTER TWENTY-FIVE

Nick and I pulled up on the street across from the town square. There were multiple fire trucks with flashing lights and the overwhelming smell of burning wood. Firefighters ran around, shouting things at each other; an ambulance waited nearby, and the townspeople were gathering in a big crowd.

I held on to Nick's hand as we made our way through the people hanging around behind police tape. There was a ton of smoke in the air. Somebody had to have answers.

"Do you think everyone is okay?" I asked Nick, but he knew only as much as I did.

Dee-Dee was there, looking as concerned as I felt. I let go of Nick's hand long enough to hug her. "What's happening?" I asked. "Was anyone hurt?"

"As far as I know, everyone is fine. They don't have all the details about the fire and how far it's spread, but I know they're worried because some of the food vendors had propane tanks. That's one of the reasons they're making us stay over here."

If fire hit those propane tanks . . . who knew how much damage that would cause? Were we even going to be able to have the festival?

My instinct was to rush across the street to help out in some way, but Nick grabbed my hand again. Like he knew exactly what I was planning. He wrapped his arms around my shoulders so that my back was pressed against his front. "There's nothing you can do," he told me.

"I don't know what I'm going to do if this is all ruined." How would Patience move on from this? What if the fire got out of control and started destroying more things? Tony's? The library? City hall?

Somebody mentioned that it must have been lightning hitting the gazebo that caused the fire; another person argued back that that didn't make sense, given there were taller buildings surrounding it.

The gazebo? My parents' gazebo? I felt like I was about to throw up. Nick's arms tightened around me.

The general consensus was that nobody seemed to know how it had started or whether it was completely out.

Nick kept saying sweet things to me about how it would all be okay, things were fine, we didn't even know where the fire was or how bad things were, that it might all work out.

I only half listened.

The one thing I did know was that no one had been hurt. The people around me seemed pretty sure about that, which was the biggest relief. Everyone had safely been evacuated from the town square.

After about twenty minutes of standing there, I saw the fire chief, Tom Hardison. He was friends with my dad. I flagged him down. His face was covered in soot and sweat.

"Jane?" he said. "It's a good thing you're here so that we can talk about the festival going forward. The gazebo's gone."

I stiffened against Nick, and I felt him squeeze a bit tighter in an attempt to soothe me. "Just breathe," he whispered.

"Gone?" My voice broke. Having him confirm the gazebo had been destroyed felt like too much to process.

"As far as we can tell, some of the camera equipment being stored there malfunctioned, and the gazebo went up like a roman candle. It's a good thing there was a quick rainstorm earlier; it stopped the fire from spreading too far and kept it pretty contained. The building is a total loss, and we're going to cordon off the entire area until we know more."

My heart sank so hard in my stomach that I physically flinched. "Does this mean the festival has to be canceled?"

"I don't know yet. I'll let you know when I have more information."

Someone called the chief, and he nodded at me and then ran over to the firefighter.

Dee-Dee said, "I'm going to call the rest of the committee members and have them meet here. We have to figure out our next steps."

I nodded. I couldn't believe that the gazebo, the centerpiece of our fair, was gone. Not just that, but it had meant so much to my family. When I was a little girl, I'd looked at pictures of my parents' wedding and imagined that someday I'd get married there, too. Now it was gone. I turned around to hug Nick, but his arms were at his side.

"Nick?"

His face was stricken. "Did you hear him? It was the camera equipment belonging to the documentary crew that started the fire."

I didn't understand why he was so upset. It was really sad that the gazebo was gone but good news that, as far as we knew, nothing else had been ruined. "So?"

He stepped away from me, and there was a coldness between us that I'd never experienced with him before. It sent icy spikes of unease through me.

"So I'm responsible for the fire," he said. "They're here to film me. I did this. I caused it."

He wasn't making any sense. I said, "You didn't do anything—"

"I knew this was going to happen." He put both his hands in his hair, a frustrated and frantic gesture I'd never seen from him before. "I knew it and I went ahead anyways. The festival is ruined. This is my fault. I . . . I have to go."

My ears rang and there was a metal taste in my mouth as terror gripped my spine. What was he saying? I tried to catch my breath to ask, but it was as if my lungs had frozen over and I couldn't speak. I tried to reach for him, but he moved away from my touch.

That scared me worse than anything else.

"Jane!" The fire chief gestured me over, past the police tape.

Nick walked away quickly without looking back. All I wanted to do was chase after him to talk to him. The things he was saying were totally illogical. He wasn't responsible for the fire. His jinx thing hadn't caused this. It was just an accident.

But there was something about his tone, about the way he was leaving right now, that felt so scarily final.

I shook my head, trying to swallow down the knot in my throat. I was overreacting. It couldn't be possible. Nick wouldn't tell me he loved me and then just walk out of my life. I convinced myself that I was overanalyzing.

Chief Hardison called my name again, and although I still felt torn, I had an obligation to the town and to the festival and needed to take care of my responsibilities.

I walked over to talk with Chief Hardison, keeping my eye on the crowd, wanting to see the moment that Nick reappeared.

That moment never happened.

Gretchen arrived with Heath, and I waved them over. The chief took us to the gazebo, and it was like something out of a movie—the roof completely gone; blackened, charred posts; a ton of ash; the stifling smell of burned wood. Chief Hardison reiterated that everyone had gotten away safely and there didn't seem to be damage to other structures.

"The fire didn't spread, like I mentioned earlier. We've soaked the remains and the ground around it. I'm not sure the debris-removal company will be able to get to it before the festival starts." Chief Hardison said it so apologetically, and I was worried about the next words to come out of his mouth.

Gretchen got an excited look on her face and took charge. "What if we erected some fencing around it and put up a sign saying something like *the god of lightning is starting this festival off in the right way*? I can overnight one of those life-sized pictures of Nick as Zeus and put it next to it. Trust me, people will want to take pictures here. It will be a big hit."

The chief seemed to consider her proposition. She went on, "We'll get volunteers to make sure that nobody climbs over the fence, and in a couple of days, when the festival actually begins, there shouldn't be any concerns over smoldering embers or anything like that."

"As long as the area is surrounded by a fence that's being monitored, I think that would be all right."

Gretchen looked visibly relieved and hugged Heath, but I didn't feel anything but that sickly, aching fear. Why hadn't Nick come back yet? Things weren't as dire as he'd initially thought. He hadn't ruined the festival. It was just like he'd told me earlier—it would all be okay and things were going to work out.

I texted him. Anytime I sent him a message, he always responded immediately.

But there was no reply from his end.

My heart felt like a terrified bird trapped in a cage, flapping hysterically to get free. I tried calling him, but I went straight to voice mail. That panicky dread started to get worse. I had to go find him.

The chief went off to talk to someone else, Heath excused himself to call and check on the store's employees, and Gretchen grabbed my arm. "Isn't that great news? I'm going to text the rest of the committee."

"Yeah, great news."

"What's going on with you?" she asked after she pushed the send button. There was no way to tell her that I was worried about Nick leaving suddenly without giving her the backstory. I told her about everything that had occurred, being caught in the rain, making out in the barn.

"You took a literal roll in the hay?" she squealed, apparently unaware of how upset I was.

"There was no hay."

"It was a barn. The imagery still stands. And then what?"

"Then he said he loved me."

"He what?" Gretchen let out a shriek. "I don't know if I'm having an actual contraction right now or if I'm just really, really excited. And what did he do when you told him you loved him, too?"

"I didn't."

"Why not? You do."

The truth of her words smacked into me with the force of a wrecking ball. Everything suddenly became so clear—like reaching the end of a complicated puzzle with only a few pieces left and there was no question how they fit together; it all fell into place. She was right, per usual. I put my hand on my chest. I was in love with Nick. I had been overwhelmed after he'd said it, but the truth was, of course I was in love with him. How could I not be? "It doesn't matter now. He's gone."

"What do you mean 'he's gone'?"

"When he found out that the documentary crew's equipment was responsible for the fire, he thought he'd ruined the festival, blamed his curse, and then left."

She blinked at me a few times, as if she didn't know what to make of that information. "He knows that jinx thing isn't real, right?"

"I don't think he does. He told me he was worried about messing up my life. That he held off on admitting his feelings for me and kissing me because he thought he'd wreck things somehow." I didn't point out the irony of his self-fulfilling prophecy. The only way he'd ruined things was by leaving. I rubbed my arms. I'd left my hoodie back at the barn, and it was so cold out there.

Or else the numbness inside me was spreading. "I'm glad I didn't say it. At least he doesn't get to have that part of me." I was trying to convince myself.

Gretchen's pointed look let me know that she wasn't falling for it. "You mean that part of you that you've already given him without realizing it? You just have to make him see reason, then. And don't jump to any conclusions about whether or not he took off. For all you know, he's back at the Pink House, waiting for you."

That made my heart lift with hope, but I squashed that feeling immediately. "What other conclusion can I jump to? He ran away."

At that, Gretchen folded her arms, pinning me down with her gaze. "So have you."

I jerked my head back in surprise. "I'm the one who's still here. I didn't run anywhere."

"Jane Wagner, you have been running away from that man and how you feel about him from the moment you met. He said he loves you and you couldn't say it back even though we both know that you do. You're still running."

Her words were a jolt to my entire system. I *had* been running. It was how I'd dealt with problems and hardships my entire life. Running away instead of facing them. I ran away from my future by coming home to Patience. Oh, I'd had a good reason, and I'd definitely helped as much as I could with my dad's recovery—but honestly? They would have gotten by without me. I'd been hiding out in my grandma's home, letting life happen to me instead of going after the things I wanted.

And Nick? I had definitely been running from him. I had longed for a connection with him but then fought it as hard as I could. He'd tried to develop that emotional intimacy between us, and I'd been too busy pushing for more of a physical relationship instead, to blanket over those feelings and pretend they weren't there.

I hadn't let him in. Even when he'd been so patient in waiting for me to wake up and realize how much I cared about him, I'd ignored it and focused on other stuff.

I had been such a fool.

"I'm so stupid," I said.

"If you're waiting for me to disagree with you, that's not going to happen. Come on."

Gretchen looped her arm through mine and walked me over to where Dee-Dee and Michelle were waiting. They were on their phones, and Connie ran over to join us, breathless, holding her phone up. "Phyllis is going to be the point of contact with the fire chief. The rest of us are following up with all the vendors, letting them know what's happened and that we're good to move forward."

"Do you see?" Gretchen asked. "We are going to be fine without you. We appreciate you and love you for everything that you've done, but we've got it from here. You don't have to stay. Go find Nick. Talk to him. Make him understand that everything will be okay."

That festival committee was another thing in my life that I'd thought couldn't function without me. Taking over my mom's job and the festival was just an extension of my running away that I hadn't recognized. I'd thrown myself into it as a way to justify my fearful choices. How could I go to California when I was so needed here? I had convinced myself that I had to stay in Patience to single-handedly make sure that the festival was a success.

Only my friends were showing me that wasn't the case. I hadn't relied on them like I should have. I hadn't let them completely in, either.

I could start doing that now. I hugged Gretchen and ran for my car. I turned the heater up full blast—my hair and my shirt were still damp. I wondered how Nick planned to get back to the house and kept an eye out for him along the road in case he was walking.

I didn't see him.

When I got home, the front door was unlocked. We'd gotten into the habit of locking it, mostly because of the fans who gathered outside daily. "Nick?" I called out.

Patches meowed back at me, but I brushed past her and ran up to his room, calling his name as I went.

The first thing I noticed was that his bags were gone. I opened the closet. Empty.

There, on the middle of the futon, was our dollar bill. I picked it up and saw the words I'm Sorry written along the top.

I sank down onto the futon.

I hadn't jumped to the wrong conclusion. Nick was gone. Gretchen would have urged me to find out where he had gone, as I wouldn't be too far behind, but I wasn't going to chase after him. If he was this willing to walk away from me the first time something got hard, maybe he wasn't the right guy for me.

I shook my head. Even I couldn't believe that lie. Nick had been up front about his feelings around that jinx thing, and I had dismissed them and hadn't really gotten how seriously he felt about it. That was my fault. I was to blame. I couldn't shift it over to him.

If I'd really cared about him, I should have listened more. I should have accepted what he was saying instead of thinking it was silly.

But it was too late now to do anything about it. I probably could have tried to track him down, but would that mean, once again, I wasn't respecting him and his wishes? His boundaries? I didn't know what to do here.

I told myself that there were other things in my life to concentrate on. Someday my heart would stop feeling this way, wouldn't it? Like it was being pierced by little daggers, one after another, all the time?

I'd thought once that Nick made me feel like I was made out of glass because of how easily he seemed to see through me.

But now I was made of glass in a different way—one strong blow from him, and I was shattering into a million pieces.

I didn't know if I'd ever feel whole again.

CHAPTER TWENTY-SIX

I didn't sleep well that night, restless and unable to stop myself from jumping at every sound the house made as it settled, convinced it was Nick coming back. The worst part was, every time I woke up, there was this half second where I forgot what had happened, and then it came rushing back and I had to feel the same pain all over again.

It was like he left a dozen more times, and I got to reexperience it repeatedly.

Gretchen came over early with a bag of goodies that Heath had made for me. "How are you doing?" she asked sympathetically. I'd been texting her through the night to let her know that he hadn't returned and how I'd discovered the note on the dollar bill. She'd responded and told me that she knew; she'd found out that Barney had driven him to the airport and that Barney was busy telling everyone who would listen how sad Nick had been.

When she asked me how I was doing, I promptly burst into tears. She walked me into the living room, making soothing sounds, and sat me down, putting her arms around me. I hugged her and cried on her shoulder. She held me, rubbing my back.

Part of me wanted to ignore my feelings and go through the motions of finishing up the festival, but living that way had landed me here. Maybe if I'd been more honest with Nick and with myself, if I'd told him how I felt, he wouldn't have left. This was my chance to start doing that—being honest about my feelings. Even the awful ones. I was going to feel the pain of this, and I would sob and be sad and write pathetic love songs that sounded more like funeral dirges.

I also promised myself that I'd never let myself be in this position again. If I had feelings for someone, I would tell them. I'd tried so hard to protect my heart, and all I'd managed to do was make my heartache a million times worse.

Regret was funny that way.

I poured my heart out to her, all of the things I wished I'd done differently, how much I did love Nick and missed him.

"I was so sure I was going to keep my heart safe this time," I said between sobs.

"Is this making you think of Teddy?" she asked.

"Teddy?" The shock of her question was enough to make me stop crying. He so didn't play any part of this. "I never loved Teddy the way I love Nick. It's like comparing apples to cheating, lying snakes. Teddy betrayed me and I was hurt over that. I was probably more upset about him choosing Brenda as one of the people he cheated with than any feelings I thought I had for him. This is so different. It's like a piece of me is missing and I'm afraid that I'm never going to feel like myself again."

She was arranging her face carefully, probably so that she didn't look smug while attempting to comfort me. "I wish I knew what to say. We're here for you. No matter what you need."

I nodded. I did know that.

"Are you going to try and find him?" she asked carefully. "Explain everything to him?"

"How could I do that?" I had no idea how to even look for him. I didn't have his address, and he hadn't answered any of my texts or phone calls. "I don't know where he is and I'm worried that if I do try to track him down, I'll be crossing some boundary with him." I didn't want to do that.

Gretchen took my hand in hers, her face serious. "Does this mean you're not going to do the mentorship?"

That was one of the things I had thought long and hard about all last night. "I am doing it. Los Angeles is a pretty big place. I doubt I'll ever run into him or anything. But I'm not going for Nick. I need to move forward and stop spinning my wheels, which is what I've been doing here. If nothing else, at least he taught me that." My voice broke, and she was rubbing my back again.

"I'm glad you're not using your parents as an excuse anymore," she said and I nodded, agreeing with her.

My mom had called me earlier that morning to talk about what had happened with Nick, and it was then that she told me she'd been ready to return to work months ago. I'd been laboring under the delusion that my mom was babying my dad, but instead they'd agreed that they would back off because I seemed like I needed all of this—the library, the committee, the festival.

I'd made her promise to never do something like that again. Nick had been right about that, too. We all needed to be more honest about what we needed in our relationships and how we were feeling.

The bottom line was that my mother was going to take over the library starting on Monday, had offered to do whatever she could to help with the festival, and I was going to move on with my life.

"What about the meet and greet?" I asked Gretchen.

"I planned for that," she said. "My fear was that he was going to get called away for another opportunity or something, not . . ." Her voice trailed off, but then she continued, "We're going to have to refund the money for the VIP interaction. There's nothing else we can do."

"When are you going to tell the fans that he's not coming?"

"I think we should wait. Who knows? He still might show up."

That seemed highly unlikely to me. "Are we going to have enough money regardless?"

"We will. Nick's sponsorship money hit the account almost a week ago. There might be some general festivalgoers who will want to cancel their tickets when they find out he's not going to be there, but we did say we couldn't guarantee his appearance. It's always good to have a contingency plan in place."

"I wish I'd had a contingency plan for falling in love with him and him leaving."

She looked so sad and held up the paper bag. "Here. I brought gifts." I'd assumed it was scones, and that memory had made my heart squeeze with pain, but it turned out to be so much worse.

She'd brought chocolate chip cookies.

At that, I started sobbing all over again.

"I'm sorry," she said, putting the cookies away. "I can get you something else."

"I don't want anything else. I want Nick. I should have told him."

She nodded sympathetically, and that made the floodgates open up again. The crying and talking continued for a couple more hours, until she convinced me that working might be the most helpful thing for me. Not that I had to, because they had it covered, but she was right. I needed the distraction. I could be sad and arranging for volunteers to watch the gate around the gazebo at the same time.

Time somehow managed to pass both quickly and slowly. I thought about texting Nick again, but there was no point. He wouldn't answer. Every time my phone buzzed, my heart would jump, thinking it was him.

It never was.

~

The morning of the festival, I walked into the kitchen to grab something to eat and nearly tripped over my own feet when I saw Nick sitting at my kitchen table.

I had thought about him so often over the last two days that my first thought was that I was full-on hallucinating. That my sleep-deprived state was causing me to imagine that he was here.

"Hello, Jane."

I dragged in a shaky breath as my heart started thundering in my chest. Not a hallucination. He stayed seated, holding something in his hands.

"I wanted to return this to you." My keys. He slid them across the table toward me.

He'd needed to come here in person to return keys? "You could have put them in the mail." Or kept them. If he was only here to bring the keys back, I didn't know what I was going to do.

Because him being here was making me hopeful and scared at the same time.

"I could have." He nodded. "But I owed you an explanation. And an apology." He gestured at the seat across from him, but I shook my head and crossed my arms across my chest. I stayed in the doorway. His body leaned forward like he was planning on standing, but he must have changed his mind, because he sat back. "You must hate me."

"I could never hate you," I said, my plan on being more honest with my feelings already tripping me up.

There was relief written all over his annoyingly perfect face. "I've been hating myself enough for the both of us. I shouldn't have left."

"But you did leave," I said, unable to keep the hurt out of my voice.

My words seemed to cause him pain. "I don't even know how it happened. It's all a blur. One minute, I was with you at the fire, and the next, I was on a plane to California."

Was that it? Was that going to be his whole explanation?

"I know running away wasn't the solution," he said. "I'm sorry I didn't answer your texts or calls. And the only defense I can offer is that I had really poor relationship models and some deeply ingrained stuff I was imitating that I didn't even realize was there."

I thought of his parents, how he'd told me that they left whenever things got hard.

He pressed his lips together before he continued. "There are so many things in my life that happened to me, that I didn't have any choice over. So many decisions that I made from a place of fear. Fear that I wasn't actually talented enough, that I had my spot solely due to nepotism, that I'd never be anything more than the kid of two famous people. I was desperate and made bad decisions, and I really did feel like I was cursed. I didn't want my decisions, my poor choices, to have a negative effect on you."

Then he stood up but stayed standing next to the table. "It felt like some kind of cosmic retribution, proof that everything I love gets ruined. I got close to you and then I burned down your festival. Like the universe had to show me that I'm as messed up as I thought I was. And it completely destroyed me that I had, even inadvertently, been responsible for destroying something you cared so much about."

I wanted to object, to say that none of that was true, to reassure him, but I needed to hear what he had to say first.

"I didn't come back sooner because I wanted to fix the things that I could fix. I fired my agent. I'm going to find someone who cares about me and my career and not the fame, who will help me be the artist and the actor I want to be. You made me understand the parts of my life that matter. Because I realized that all of this means nothing without you by my side. Maybe it isn't fair for me to ask you to be part of my life, because you didn't ask for any of this, either."

He started walking slowly toward me.

"I should have stayed with you. I should have fought. I'm so, so sorry that I didn't. That I was such a coward. I should have realized that I can't possibly be a jinx as long as I have you, because you make me feel like the luckiest man in the whole world."

How was I not supposed to melt? With every word he spoke, the anger and fear that I felt floated away until all that was left was how much I loved him.

My pulse fluttered with anticipation as he moved closer. He kept his hands in his pockets, not reaching for me. Worried that he might, I held up my right hand, saying, "Wait."

I wondered if he could see the way my fingers trembled, but he just looked concerned. Fearful of a rejection that was not coming.

Instead, I was finally going to be completely honest with him. He was so mature and sensitive and giving that the very least I could do was return the favor.

Even if it terrified me.

"While you were gone, I've had nothing to do but reflect and think about the mistakes I made with you. I needed to figure things out, and I realized that I should have been honest with you from the beginning. Instead, I fought the feelings I had for you, running away from you, too. I should have told you. I'm sorry that I did that. That I couldn't be honest with you or with myself."

"And what would you have told me?" he asked, his voice soft.

"I would have admitted that you make me better. As an artist and a woman. That you make me laugh and enjoy myself when I'm prone to being grumpy and taking things too seriously. That being with you is the best thing that has ever happened to me, and I'm so worried that being so fearful of my own feelings chased you away permanently."

"I'm here."

I swallowed the lump in my throat and nodded at him. He was there. He had come back. "I should have gone to California to find you so that I could tell you all of this instead of running away again. I should have told you that I love you, too."

At first he didn't respond, and I watched as a bunch of different emotions flitted across his face, so quickly that I couldn't name them. Then he said, "I'd happily make a thousand bad movies as long as you were with me."

"A thousand?" I repeated. Had he not heard me tell him that I loved him?

"Yes, a thousand. I hope it won't come to that, but I would do it. I want you to know how serious I am about us. I'm in love with you. I never thought love was an actual thing. I thought it was something they made up to sell movies and greeting cards. But you showed me how real it is, how it is the most important thing. And I love you. I love you so much that if you asked me to go, say the word and I'll never bother you again."

"The word," I said, not able to stop myself from teasing him. "But you know I don't want you to go. I love you." Just in case he hadn't heard me the first time.

His smile let me know he'd heard just fine. He came closer. "Now that we've both been honest and we have both *finally* acknowledged out loud that we love each other, maybe we should figure out our next steps. I don't want to make too many assumptions, but I will buy a house here in Patience. Maybe that cottage for sale next to Heath and Gretchen."

My eyebrows flew up my forehead in surprise. Nick had been looking at local real estate?

"I will make Patience my home base, and if you let me, I will date you and court you and win your trust so that you know I'll never walk away from you ever again. I would do anything for you. If you want me to quit Hollywood, I will. I'll move here and start a beet farm or whatever it is they grow out here."

Another step, so close that we were almost touching.

"You would really give up being an actor if I asked you to? Just to be with me?" I would never ask that of him, but knowing how important his career was to him, it meant the world to me that he was willing to do it.

"Yes."

I felt like we had both given each other what we needed to move forward. "I won't run away from you anymore, either." I put my hands on his shoulders, and I heard his surprised intake of breath. It took him a moment to respond, but then his arms were around me, hugging me to him.

"And what kind of girlfriend would I be if I asked you to give up your dreams?"

He grinned then. "Girlfriend? I don't remember asking."

I shrugged one shoulder. "It seems to me, if you're in love with me and I'm in love with you, that we should make it official."

His eyes danced, delighted with me. "You don't know what it means to me to hear you say that you love me. For the third time. I

280

was probably supposed to be surprised when you said it earlier, but I've suspected for a while now."

"You probably knew way before I did," I agreed with him. "I'm sorry that I was so closed off. My fear of being hurt is why I developed this prickly exterior. To protect myself."

"I love your prickles."

"There's no one better at smoothing them down than you," I said. "But I promise that I'll do better."

"There is no one better," he said as he landed a gentle kiss on the tip of my nose.

And I knew he believed that.

"I love you," I told him.

"I love you." He breathed me in, his chest settling against mine, rumbling as he exhaled. "You're my *have to* and my *get to*. I'm lucky enough to get to be with you, but I also have to be with you because I don't want a life without you in it."

"I hope you know that there are going to be some hard times ahead. And if you ever leave me again, your air purifier is toast," I warned him.

"Deal." His hands pressed me even closer, making it hard to tell where I began and he ended. "Hello."

"Ah, your oh-so-subtle way of saying that you're going to kiss me now," I said.

"It's that, but from now on, when I say hello, it's a promise that I'm making. To always be with you. To stay and work things out no matter how hard it might get. To choose you. And us. A promise to give you the life you've dreamed about. A way to express to you how much I love you."

"In that case, hello," I said, my love for him filling me up, demanding to be expressed.

He grinned and leaned in to kiss me. Just before he touched his lips to mine, he said, "Hello. Also, you're humming."

I smiled back. "That's because you make me really, really happy."

EPILOGUE

Two years later

"Are you ready?" Nick asked, squeezing my hand.

I nodded, but I still felt like I was going to vomit. This was a lot. Exciting, but a lot.

We stood, waiting to walk down the red carpet. There'd been something of a traffic jam, and Shanice had shooed us off to the side so that we could make a proper debut.

"Think of it as just another small town," he said. "Everyone is about to know our business and will have opinions about it. But only if you're sure you're ready to tell them."

"I'm sure."

This was our moment to let the world know what we had done.

That we were officially husband and wife, and had been for a little over a year.

Shanice had been beside herself that we wouldn't let her sell pictures of our wedding to an online magazine, but we'd both been adamant that our private life wasn't for sale or public consumption.

It had been easy enough to arrange—Nick had surprised me by having the gazebo rebuilt to the exact same specifications after it had been an ash pile for a long time. Gretchen had been right; everybody wanted to take a picture with the gazebo that Nick Haddon / Zeus had burned to a crisp, and it had been quite the tourist destination. Our wedding was in the town square, in the new gazebo, attended by everyone I loved. My nephew, Hayden, was the ring bearer even though he had just learned to walk.

Brenda had tried to upstage us by eloping with Wilfred the day before, but it didn't matter to me at all. Both Nick's parents had come to the wedding, and they were very welcoming to me. They still seemed like the perfect couple on the surface. But I saw the times his mom stepped away from his dad, when she dropped his hand when people weren't looking. I was a little unsettled by their secret dynamic, but I could nod and smile for Nick's sake. It was the happiest day of my life and I wasn't going to let anyone else ruin it.

Once again Patience gathered around us and kept us safe from prying eyes. Gretchen had made good on her earlier threat to use her matron of honor speech to take full responsibility for the two of us getting together and shared every embarrassing story she could about the lengths she'd gone to and how stubborn I was.

I think Nick laughed hardest of all.

He and I had honeymooned on a private island that his father owned, and the world had been blissfully unaware. No one suspected a thing.

But I was wearing my wedding ring tonight, and I twisted it around my finger. It was a large emerald, to symbolize our dollar bill. Nick had given the dollar to me a year and a half ago with the words WILL YOU MARRY ME? written on it, and the game had ended when I insisted that we frame it.

Even though we'd managed to keep the wedding a secret, we both knew it was a matter of time until the truth came out. Nick had an issue with being too chatty in interviews and letting things slip that he shouldn't. He'd done his best to be careful, but we decided that it was time to let the rest of the world know about our marriage.

And given his success, those interviews were happening almost constantly. He had won the part in the rom-com *Find Me Love*, which ended up being a massive hit and earned Nick a Golden Globe nomination, though the *Olympus High* reboot had lasted only three episodes before it got canceled. Nick landed a new agent and had finally started to build the career he wanted.

I felt so lucky that I got to be right next to him while he did it.

I'd been pretty busy too—I'd completed my mentorship with Maxine Portman and had been able to network and make new connections and relationships that allowed me to start finding work. It had been mostly small indie movies so far. Nick had offered to make some introductions, but I hadn't let him. I wanted to succeed or fail on my own merits.

My phone buzzed with a text from my mom. **Good luck from the First Lady of Patience!** I showed him my screen, and he smiled. The festival had been a massive success; we'd raised all the funds necessary to reopen the government. My dad had decided to run for mayor and had won. My mom enjoyed being the librarian and the mayor's wife. They had hired someone to finish the renovations on the Pink House and open it as an official B and B so that they could focus on their grandson and their new political positions.

"They're ready for you," Shanice said.

I nodded and Nick squeezed my hand again. "Here we go," he said.

We stepped out onto the carpet and had only a moment before people realized that Nick Haddon had arrived. Then the crowd went bananas, the lights of the paparazzi flashing all around us. Nick waved and smiled as the reporters called out his name.

Shanice directed us to a well-known entertainment reporter, who grinned at us and exclaimed, "Nick! Nick Haddon is here tonight! After your amazing turn in *Find Me Love*, what's up next for you? Can you tell your fans about your latest project?"

"Normally, I'd love to, but that's not why I'm here. This is Jane Wagner-Haddon, and she was the composer of the score for the movie premiering tonight. I'm here to support my beautiful wife, and I could not be prouder of her."

The way the reporter's face froze in shock and then morphed into a big fake smile was almost comical. "Jane! Tell us all about what it's like to be married to the Nick Haddon. How long have you been married? Where did it happen?"

All we were going to share was that we'd gotten married. I sidestepped her questions. "If it's okay, I'd love to talk about the movie."

She blinked in surprise but did as I directed. I talked about scoring the film, how amazing the producers had been to work with, what a thrill it was for me to be there. Nick stayed at my side and I could feel him beaming. He was so proud of me, and that was better than the spotlight I was currently standing in.

I finished up the interview and we walked away, and now the reporters were calling my name along with Nick's. The news had spread quickly. I knew they didn't want to talk to me about composing the movie—that they only wanted to grill me about being married to Nick.

And I'd happily talk about how happy I was to have him as my husband all day long, but as I said, we were keeping that between the two of us.

Along with the entire town of Patience, Ohio.

"Now that they know, you know what's going to happen next, don't you?" Nick said, having to speak a bit louder so that I could hear him over the noise of the crowd.

"What?"

"Baby-bump watch. Every burrito you eat is going to be analyzed forty different ways."

"Then we're going to have to figure something out."

He turned toward me. "What do you mean?"

I had intended to wait to tell him, to do some elaborate setup, but we had talked about it so many times and I knew just how much Nick wanted to be a dad, to make up for the sad childhood that he'd had, that it was like I couldn't keep it to myself for a second longer.

"I'm pregnant. Six weeks along. The doctor confirmed it today."

His entire body lit up at my announcement, and he picked me up and spun me around, laughing.

"Oh, sorry," he said, putting me down. "I don't want to hurt the baby."

"It's fine. But one of these outlets is going to hire a lip reader and figure out this whole conversation if we're not careful. We can keep this quiet, too."

"This is everything," he said excitedly. "I love you so much. I love our baby so much." Then he kissed me.

As I kissed him back, I thought of how much he'd fulfilled his promise to me. That he'd supported me in pursuing my dreams, giving me the kind of home I'd always wanted.

One filled with love, laughter, and music.

And now? A baby.

A baby who we were not going to be able to keep a secret because Nick was making a public spectacle of himself. My wonderful idiot of a husband was down on his knees, letting every cat out of the bag.

He pressed a kiss to my stomach and then said, "Hello, little one."

AUTHOR'S NOTE

Thank you for reading my story! If this is your first time reading one of my books, I happen to really love the celebrity/regular-person romance trope, and I hope you adore Nick and Jane's love story as much as I enjoyed writing it. If you'd like to find out when I've written something new, make sure you sign up for my newsletter at www.sariahwilson. com, where I most definitely will not spam you. (If I manage to send a newsletter out once a month, I feel very accomplished!)

And if you feel so inclined, I'd love for you to leave a review on Amazon, Goodreads, or any other place where you'd like to share your thoughts about this story. Usually I try to write something witty here, but it's the end of the year and my brain has completely shut down, so just know that I'd be so grateful if you did review the story anywhere you'd like to. (And I might possibly level up if I get enough reviews. Which is a video game joke, so have your gamer loved ones explain it to you if it doesn't make sense.)

ACKNOWLEDGMENTS

I always start out by thanking my readers. You are the reason I do this. I have author friends who would happily write forever even if they were the only ones who ever got to read it. I'm not like that. I'm not sure I'd keep writing if there weren't an audience who enjoyed it. So thank you for motivating me and letting me have this job. I'm so grateful to you.

Alison Dasho—after so many books, I'm not sure what else there is to say, other than that you have my profound gratitude for being such an incredible person and an amazing editor, for pushing so hard for me, and for still choosing to work with me. I can't believe my good luck every time I get the chance to write another book with you as my editor. A big thanks to everyone at Montlake who has worked hard to make this story a success (Anh Schluep, Tricia Callahan, Cheryl Weisman, Stef Sloma, Jillian Cline, Erin Calligan Mooney, Kris Beecroft). And to Charlotte Herscher—basically you're not allowed to ever quit or change jobs because there's not another dev editor I want to work with besides you. As always, your suggestions and compliment/critique sandwiches are perfectly motivating, and you find just the right way to help me get to the heart of the story and what I meant to say rather than what I actually put on the page.

Thank you to the copy editors and proofreaders who found all my mistakes and continuity errors and gently guided me in the right direction. Again my thanks to Philip Pascuzzo for the incredible cover for this book. I feel very privileged to have been able to work with you so many times for so many of my books.

For my agent, Sarah Younger—I hope you get the sleep and personal space you need this year, because you are so hardworking and always looking out for me and my best interests. When I've come to you with insurmountable problems and pie-in-the-sky dreams, you've never once told me it couldn't be done and instead have spent your time figuring out how to kick down every door to make those things possible. You are a warrior. Thank you.

Thanks to Dana, Julia, Jordan, and Hailey of Dana Kaye Publicity for everything you all do and the way that you keep me on track (especially the gentle nudging/reminding) and all of your hard work.

Thank you to Christy Carew for talking to me about composing music for movies and for being an awesome Reylo and an even better friend. Look her up on Spotify—she's an incredible composer, and everyone should be listening to her music!

Thanks to Chris Hemsworth and the Australian town of Cowra. Your viral campaign to get a movie star to visit your small town inspired this story.

To John Williams for being an absolute legend and composing some of the most beautiful music to have ever existed—your music has been the soundtrack of my life, so thank you.

Never forget—#BenSoloDeservedBetter #GiveReyHerSoulmate (I will shut up about this when they're reunited.)

For my children—the last year has been a tough one for all of us, but I have every hope that there is brightness and joy ahead and will do whatever I have to do to support and love you.

And Kevin, I couldn't ask for a better partner and father for our kids. Hello.

ABOUT THE AUTHOR

Photo © 2020 Jordan Batt

Sariah Wilson is the *USA Today* bestselling author of *The Chemistry of Love*, *The Paid Bridesmaid*, *The Seat Filler*, *Roommaid*, *Just a Boyfriend*, the Royals of Monterra series, and the #Lovestruck novels. She is madly, passionately in love with her soulmate and is a fervent believer in happily ever afters—which is why she writes romance. She grew up in Southern California, graduated from Brigham Young University (go, Cougars!) with a semi-useless degree in history, and is the oldest of nine (yes, nine). She currently lives with the aforementioned soulmate and their children in Utah, along with three cats named Pixel, Callie, and Belle, who do not get along (the cats, not the kids—although the kids sometimes have their issues, too). For more information, visit her website at www.sariahwilson.com.